Wilful Behaviour

Donna Leon

Wilful Behaviour

WILLIAM HEINEMANN : LONDON

First published in the United Kingdom in 2002 by
William Heinemann

1 3 5 7 9 10 8 6 4 2

Copyright © Donna Leon and Diogenes Verlag AG Zurich 2001

Donna Leon has asserted her right under the Copyright, Designs and
Patents Act, 1988 to be identified as the author of this work

William Heinemann
The Random House Group Limited
20 Vauxhall Bridge Road, London, SW1V 2SA

Random House Australia (Pty) Limited
20 Alfred Street, Milsons Point, Sydney, New South Wales 2061, Australia

Random House New Zealand Limited
18 Poland Road, Glenfield
Auckland 10, New Zealand

Random House (Pty) Limited
Endulini, 5a Jubilee Road, Parktown 2193, South Africa

The Random House Group Limited Reg. No. 954009

www.randomhouse.co.uk

A CIP catalogue record for this book is available from the British Library

Papers used by Random House are natural, recyclable products made from
wood grown in sustainable forests. The manufacturing processes conform
to the environmental regulations of the country of origin

Typeset by SX Composing DTP, Rayleigh, Essex
Printed and bound in the United Kingdom by
Clays Ltd, St Ives PLC

ISBN 0 434 00994 6

for Daniel Hungerbühler

I dubbi, i sospetti
Gelare me fan.

Doubts and suspicions
Turn me to ice.

Mozart

Le Nozze di Figaro

1

The explosion came at breakfast. Brunetti's position as a commissario of police, though it made the possibility of explosion more likely than it would be for the average citizen, did not make the setting any less strange. The location, however, was related to Brunetti's personal situation as the husband of a woman of incandescent, if inconsistent, views and politics, not to his profession.

'Why do we bother to read this disgusting piece of garbage?' Paola exploded, slamming a folded copy of the day's *Gazzettino* angrily on to the breakfast table, where it upset the sugar bowl.

Brunetti leaned forward, pushed the edge of the paper aside with his forefinger and righted the bowl. He picked up a second brioche and took a bite, knowing that clarification would follow.

'Listen to this,' Paola said, picking up the paper and reading from the headline of the leading article on the front page: ' "Fulvia Prato Recounts her Terrible Ordeal." ' Like all of Italy, Brunetti was familiar with Fulvia Prato, the wife of a wealthy Florentine industrialist, who had been kidnapped thirteen months before and kept in a cellar for that entire time by her kidnappers. Freed by the *Carabinieri* two weeks before, she had spoken to the press for the first time the previous day. He had no idea what Paola could find especially offensive in the headline.

'And this,' she said, turning the paper to the bottom of page five. ' "EU Minister Confesses to Sexual Harassment in Her Former Workplace." ' Brunetti was familiar with this case, as well: a female commissioner on the European Commission, he couldn't remember what her exact position was – one of those trivial ones they give to women – had yesterday said at a press conference that she had been the victim of sexual aggression twenty years ago when she worked in a firm of civil engineers.

A man who had learned patience in his more than twenty years of married life, Brunetti awaited Paola's explanation. 'Can you believe they'd use that word? Signora Prato did not have to *confess* to having been the victim of kidnapping, but this poor woman *confessed* to having been the victim of some sort of sexual attack. And how typical of these troglodytes,' she said with a vicious jab at the paper, 'not to explain what happened, only to say that it was sexual. God, I don't know why we bother to read it.'

'It is hard to believe, isn't it?' Brunetti agreed, himself genuinely shocked by the use of the word and more shocked that he had not registered its dissonance until Paola pointed it out to him.

Years ago, he had begun to make gentle fun of what he then dubbed her 'coffee sermons', the fulminations with which she greeted her reading of the morning papers, but over the years he had come to see that there was great sense in seeming madness.

'Have you ever had to deal with this sort of thing?' she asked him. She held the bottom half of the paper towards him, so he knew she was not referring to the kidnapping.

'Once, years ago.'

'Where?'

'In Naples. When I was assigned there.'

'What happened?'

'A woman came in to report that she had been raped. She wanted to make an official *denuncia*.' He paused, letting memory return. 'It was her husband.'

Paola's pause was equally long; then she asked, 'And?'

'The questioning was done by the commissario I was assigned to at the time.'

'And?'

'He told her to think about what she was doing, that it would cause her husband a great deal of trouble.'

This time Paola's silence was enough to spur him on.

'After she listened to him, she said she needed time to think about it, and she left.' He could still remember the set of the woman's shoulders as she left the office where the questioning had taken place. 'She never came back.'

Paola sighed, then asked, 'Have things changed much since then?'

'A bit.'

'Are they any better?'

'Minimally. At least we try to have female officers do the first interview.'

'Try?'

'If there are any on duty when it happens, when they come in.'

'And if there aren't?'

'We call around and see if a woman can come on duty.'

'And if not?'

He wondered how breakfast had somehow become an inquisition. 'If not, then they are interviewed by whoever's available.'

'That means, I suppose, that men like Alvise or Lieutenant Scarpa could do the questioning.' She made no attempt to disguise her disgust.

'It's not really questioning, Paola, not like when we have a suspect.'

She pointed at the *Gazzettino*, her fingernail tapping out a quick triple beat on the second headline. 'In a city where *this* is possible, I hate to think of what *any* sort of questioning is like.'

He was just at the point of opposition when she, perhaps sensing this, changed her tone entirely and asked, 'How's your day look? Will you be home for lunch?'

Relieved, aware that he was tempting fate but helpless to stop himself, he answered, 'I think so. Crime seems to be on holiday in Venice.'

'God, I wish I could say the same about my students,' she said with tired resignation.

'Paola, you've only been back at work six days,' he couldn't prevent himself from saying. He wondered how she had managed to monopolize the right to complain about work. After all, he had to deal, if not on a daily basis, then at least with upsetting frequency, with murder, rape and battery, while the worst thing that could happen in her classroom was that someone would ask the identity of the Dark Lady or forget what happened at the end of *Washington Square*. He was about to say something to this effect when he caught the expression in her eyes.

'What's the matter?' he asked.

'Huh?' He knew evasion when he heard it, saw it.

'I asked you what was the matter.'

'Oh, difficult students. The usual stuff.'

Again, he recognized the signs that she was reluctant to discuss something. He pushed back his chair and got to his feet. He came to her side of the table, braced his hand on her shoulder, and bent to kiss the top of her head.

'I'll see you at lunch.'

'I'll live in that single hope,' she answered and leaned forward to sweep up the spilled sugar.

Left alone at the table, Paola was faced with the decision of whether to finish reading the paper or to wash the dishes: she chose the dishes. That task finished, she glanced at her watch and saw that her only class of the day began in less than an hour, and so she went back to the bedroom to finish dressing, her mind absorbed, as was often the case, with the writing of Henry James, though in this case it was only to the extent that he might have influenced Edith Wharton, whose novels were to be the subject of her lecture.

She had been lecturing, recently, on the theme of honour and honourable behaviour and the way it was central to Wharton's three great novels, but she was preoccupied with whether the concept still had the same meaning for her students; indeed, whether it had any meaning for her students. She had wanted to talk about this with Guido that morning, for she respected his opinions on the subject, but the headline had diverted her.

After decades, she could no longer feign not to notice his usual response to her coffee sermons: that quickened desire to leave the table. She smiled to herself at the term he'd invented and at the affection with which he generally used it. She knew she responded too quickly and too strongly to many stimuli; indeed, in a moment of high anger, her husband had once drummed out a damning list of just which subjects would push her until she was past reason hunted. She refused to dwell upon his catalogue, its accuracy still enough to cause her a tremor of nervousness.

The first autumn chill had fallen on the city the day before so Paola took a light woollen jacket from the closet, picked up her briefcase and left the apartment. Though she walked through the city of Venice to reach her classroom, it was New York that was on her mind, the city where the drama of the lives of the

5

women in Wharton's novels had played out a century ago. Attempting to navigate the shoals of social custom, old and new money, the established power of men, and the sometimes greater power of their own beauty and charm, her three protagonists found themselves perpetually buffeted against the hidden rocks of honour. But passage of time, Paola reflected, had vaporized from the common mind any universal agreement on what constituted honourable behaviour.

Certainly the books did not suggest that honour triumphed: in one case it cost the heroine her life; another lost her happiness because of it; the third triumphed only because of a constitutional inability to perceive it. How, then, to argue for its importance, especially to a class of young people who would identify – if indeed students were any longer capable of identification with characters who were not in film – only with the third?

The class went as she had expected, and she found herself, at the end of it, tempted to quote to them from the Bible, a book for which she had no special fondness, the bit about those who have eyes and fail to see, ears and fail to hear, but she refrained, realizing that her students would be as insensitive to the evangelist as they had proven themselves to be to Wharton.

The young people filed from the room, and Paola busied herself replacing papers and books in her briefcase. The failure of her profession no longer troubled her to the extent it had years ago, when she had first realized how incomprehensible much of what she said, and probably of what she believed, was to her students. During her seventh year of teaching, she'd made a reference to the *Iliad* and, in the face of general blankness, had discovered that only one of the students in the class had any memory of having read it, and even he was utterly incapable of understanding the concept of heroic behaviour. The Trojans had lost, hadn't they, so who cared how Hector had behaved?

'The times are out of joint,' she whispered to herself in English and then started in surprise, realizing that someone was standing next to her, one of the students, a young girl, now probably convinced that her professor was mad.

'Yes, Claudia?' she asked, fairly certain that was the girl's name. Short, dark of hair and eye, the girl had a creamy white complexion that looked as though she had never been out in the sun. She'd taken a class with Paola the year before, seldom spoken, made frequent notes, and done very well in her exams, leaving Paola with a vague overall impression of a bright young woman handicapped by shyness.

'I wonder if I could speak to you, Professoressa,' the girl said.

Remembering that she could be acerbic only with her own children, Paola did not ask her if that was not what they were doing. Instead, she clipped shut her briefcase and said, turning to face the girl, 'Certainly. What about? Wharton?'

'Well, sort of, Professoressa, but not really.'

Again, Paola refrained from pointing out that only one of these answers could be true. 'What about, then?' she asked, but she smiled when she asked the question, unwilling to make this usually silent girl reluctant to go on. To avoid any suggestion that she might be eager to leave, Paola removed her hand from her briefcase, leaned back against the desk, and smiled again.

'It's about my grandmother,' the girl said, glancing at Paola inquisitively, as if to ask if she knew what a grand-mother was. She looked towards the door, back at Paola, then back to the door. 'I'd like to get an answer about something that's bothering her.' Having said that, she stopped.

When it seemed that Claudia was not going to continue, Paola picked up her briefcase and made slowly towards the door. The girl eeled around her and opened it, stepping back to allow Paola to pass through first. Pleased by this sign of respect and displeased with herself for being so,

7

Paola asked, not that she could see it mattered much but thinking that the answer might provide the girl with a reason to give further information, 'It is your mother's or your father's mother?'

'Well, really neither, Professoressa.'

Promising herself a mighty reward for all the unpronounced replies this conversation, if that's what it was, had so far cost her, Paola said, 'Sort of an honorary grandmother?'

Claudia smiled, a response which seemed to manifest itself primarily in her eyes and was all the sweeter for that. 'That's right. She's not my real grandmother, but I've always called her that. Nonna Hedi. Because she's Austrian, you see.'

Paola didn't, but she asked, 'Is she related to your parents, a great-aunt or something?'

This question obviously made the girl uncomfortable. 'No, she's not, not in any way.' She paused, considered, then blurted out, 'She was a friend of my grandfather's, you see.'

'Ah,' Paola replied. This was all growing far more complicated than the girl's simple request had seemed to suggest, and so Paola asked, 'And what is it that you wanted to ask about her?'

'Well, it's really about your husband, Professoressa.'

Paola was so surprised that she could only echo the girl's remark, 'My husband?'

'Yes. He's a policeman, isn't he?'

'Yes, he is.'

'Well, I wonder if you'd ask him something for me, well, something for my grandmother, that is.'

'Certainly. What would you like me to ask him?'

'Well, if he knows anything about pardons.'

'Pardons?'

'Yes. Pardons, for crimes.'

'Do you mean an amnesty?'

'No, that's what the government does when the jails are full and it's too expensive to keep people there: they just let them all out and say it's because of some special event or something. But that's not what I'm talking about. I mean an official pardon, a formal declaration on the part of the state that a person wasn't guilty of a crime.'

As they talked, they had progressed very slowly down the stairs from the fourth floor, but now Paola stopped. 'I'm not sure I understand much of this, Claudia.'

'That doesn't matter, Professoressa. I went to a lawyer and asked him, but he wanted five million lire to give me an answer, and then I remembered that your husband was a policeman, so I thought that maybe he could tell me.'

Paola let a quick nod serve for understanding. 'Could you tell me exactly what it is you want me to ask him, Claudia?'

'If there is any legal process by which a person who has died can be given a pardon for something they were put on trial for.'

'Only put on trial for?'

'Yes.'

The edges of Paola's patience showed through as she asked, 'Not convicted and sent to prison for?'

'Not really. That is, convicted but not sent to prison.'

Paola smiled and placed a hand on the girl's arm. 'I'm not sure I understand this. Convicted but not sent to prison? How can that happen?'

The girl glanced over the railing and at the open door to the building, almost as if Paola's question had spurred her to consider flight. She looked back at Paola and answered, 'Because the court said he was mad.'

Paola, careful not to inquire about who the person might be, considered this before she asked, 'And where was he sent?'

'To San Servolo. He died there.'

Like everyone else in Venice, Paola knew that the island of San Servolo had once been the site of the madhouse, had served that purpose until the Basaglia Law closed the

9

madhouses and either freed the patients or removed them to less horrendous locations.

Sensing that the girl would not tell her, Paola asked anyway. 'Do you want to tell me what the crime was?'

'No, I don't think so,' the girl said and started down the steps. At the bottom she turned and called back to Paola, 'Will you ask him?'

'Of course,' Paola answered, knowing that she would, as much now for her own curiosity as for any desire to do a favour for this girl.

'Then thank you, Professoressa. I'll see you in class next week, then.' With that Claudia walked to the door, where she paused and looked up at Paola. 'I really liked the books, Professoressa,' she called up the stairway. 'It broke my heart when Lily died like that. But it was an honourable death, wasn't it?'

Paola nodded, glad that at least one of them seemed to have understood.

2

Brunetti, for his part, gave little thought to honour that morning, busy as he was with the task of keeping track of minor crime in Venice. It seemed at times as though that were all they did: fill out forms, send them off to be filed, make up lists, juggle the numbers and thus keep the crime statistics reassuringly low. He grumbled about this, but when he considered that accurate figures would require even more paperwork, he reached for the documents.

A little before twelve, just as he was beginning to think longingly of lunch, he heard a knock on his door. He called out, '*Avanti*,' and looked up to see Alvise.

'There's someone to see you, sir,' the officer said with a smile.

'Who is it?'

'Oh, should I have asked him who he was?' Alvise asked, honestly surprised that such a thing could be expected of him.

'No, just show him in, Alvise,' Brunetti said neutrally.

Alvise stepped back and waved his arm in obvious

imitation of the white-gloved grace of traffic officers in Italian movies.

The gesture led Brunetti to believe that no less a personage than the President of the Republic might be entering, so he pushed back his chair and started to get to his feet, if only to maintain the high level of civility Alvise had established. When he saw Marco Erizzo come in, Brunetti walked around his desk and took his old friend by the hand, then embraced him and patted him on the back.

He stepped back and looked at the familiar face. 'Marco, how wonderful to see you. God, it's been ages. Where have you been?' It had been, how long, a year, perhaps even two, since they'd spoken, but Marco had not changed. His hair was still that rich chestnut brown, so thick as to cause his barber difficulty, and the laugh lines still radiated in happy abundance from around his eyes.

'Where do you think I've been, Guido?' Marco asked, speaking Veneziano with the thick Giudecchino accent his classmates had mocked him for almost forty years ago, when he and Brunetti had been at elementary school together. 'Here, at home, at work.'

'Are you well?' Brunetti asked, using the plural and thus including Erizzo's ex-wife and their two children as well as the woman he now lived with and their daughter.

'Everyone's good, everyone's happy,' Marco said, an answer that had become his standard response. Everything was always fine, everyone was always happy. If so, then what had brought him to the Questura this fine October morning, when he certainly had more urgent things to do running the many shops and businesses he owned?

Marco glanced down at his watch. 'Time for *un'ombra*?'

For most Venetians, any time after eleven was time for *un'ombra*, so Brunetti didn't hesitate before assenting.

On the way to the bar at the Ponte dei Greci, they talked about nothing and everything: their families, old friends, how stupid it was that they so seldom saw one another for longer than to say hello on the street before hurrying off to whatever it was that occupied their time and attention.

Once inside, Brunetti walked towards the bar, but Marco put a hand on his elbow and pulled him to a bench at a booth in front of the window; Brunetti sat opposite him, sure he'd find out now what it was that had brought his friend to the Questura. Neither of them had bothered to order anything, but the barman, from long experience of Brunetti, brought them two small glasses of white wine and went back to the bar.

'*Cin cin*,' they both said and took small sips. Marco nodded in appreciation. 'Better than what you get in most bars.' He took another small sip and set the glass down.

Brunetti said nothing, knowing that this was the best technique to induce a reluctant witness to speak.

'I won't waste our time, Guido,' Marco said in a different, more serious, voice. He took the short stem of his wine glass between the thumb and forefinger of his right hand and moved the glass in a small circle, a gesture instantly familiar to Brunetti. Ever since he'd been a small boy, Marco's hands had always betrayed his nervousness, whether it was by breaking the points of his pencils during exams or plucking at the top button of his shirt whenever he had to speak to a girl he liked. 'Are you guys like priests?' Marco asked, glancing up for an instant, then back at the glass.

'Which guys?' Brunetti asked, honestly confused by the question.

'Cops. Even if you're a commissario. I mean, if I tell you something, can it be like it used to be when we were kids and went to confession: the priest couldn't tell anyone?'

Brunetti sipped at his wine to hide his smile. 'I'm not sure it's the same thing, Marco. They weren't allowed to tell, no matter what we told them, no matter how bad it was. But if you tell me about a crime, I'll probably have to do something about it.'

'What sort of crime?' When Brunetti didn't answer, Marco went on, 'I mean, how big a crime would it have to be before you had to tell?'

The urgency in Marco's voice showed this was not some sort of parlour game, and so Brunetti considered the question before he answered, 'I can't say. That is, I can't give you a list of things I'd have to report. Anything serious or anything violent, I suppose.'

'And if nothing's happened yet?' Marco asked.

Brunetti was surprised by this question from Marco, a man who had always lived in the real, the concrete. It was very strange to hear him posing a hypothetical question; Brunetti wondered if he'd even ever heard Marco use a complex grammatical structure, so accustomed was he to his use of the simple declarative.

'Marco,' he said, 'why don't you just trust me and tell me what it is and then let me think about how to handle it?'

'It's not that I don't trust you, Guido. God knows I do; that's why I came to talk to you. It's just that I don't want to get you into any sort of trouble by telling you something you might not want to know about.' He looked in the direction of the bar, and Brunetti thought he was going to call for more wine, but then he looked back, and Brunetti realized Marco was checking to see if anyone could hear what they were saying. But the other men at the bar seemed busy with their own conversation.

'All right, I'll tell you,' Marco said. 'And then you can decide what to do with it.'

Brunetti was struck by how similar Marco's behaviour, even the rhythm of his speech, was to that of so many suspects he had questioned over the years. There always came a point where they gave in and stopped resisting their desire to make it clear just how it was or had been or what had driven them to do what they had done. He waited.

'You know, well, maybe you don't know that I bought a new shop near Santa Fosca,' Marco began and paused for Brunetti to respond.

'No, I didn't.' Brunetti knew better than to give anything but a simple answer. Never ask for more, never request clarification. Just let them talk until they run themselves out and have nothing else to say: that was when you began to ask questions.

'It's that cheese shop that belonged to the balding guy who always wore a hat. Nice guy; my mother used to go to his father when we lived over there. Anyway, last year they tripled his rent so he decided to retire, and I paid the *buon' uscita* and took over the lease.' He glanced at Brunetti to see that he was following. 'But because I want to sell masks and souvenirs, I've got to have show windows so people can see all the stuff. He just had that one on the right side where he had the provolone and scamorza, but there's one on the left, too, only his father closed it up, bricked it over, about forty years ago. But it's on the original plans, so it can be opened up again. And I need it. I need two windows so people can see all the junk and take a mask home to Düsseldorf.'

Neither he nor Brunetti needed to comment upon the folly of this, nor on the fact that so much of what would be sold in his shop as 'original Venetian handcrafts' was made in third world countries where the closest the workers ever came to a canal was the one behind their houses that served as a sewer.

'Anyway, I took over the lease and my architect drew up the plans. That is, he drew them up a long time ago, as soon as the guy agreed I could take over, but he couldn't present them in the Comune until the lease was in my name.' Again he looked at Brunetti. 'That was in March.' Marco raised his right hand in a fist, shot up his thumb, repeated 'March,' and then counted out the months. 'That's seven months, Guido. Seven months those bastards have made me wait. I'm paying the rent, my architect goes into the planning office once a week to ask where the permits are, and every time he goes, they tell him that the papers aren't ready or something has to be checked before I can be given the permissions.'

Marco opened his fist and laid his hand flat on the table, then put the other beside it, fingers splayed open. 'You know what's going on, don't you?' he asked.

'Yes,' Brunetti said.

'So last week I told my architect to ask them how much they wanted.' He looked across, as if curious to see if Brunetti would register surprise, perhaps shock, at what he was telling him, but Brunetti's face remained impassive.

'Thirty million.' Marco paused for a long time, but Brunetti said nothing. 'If I give them thirty million, then I'll have the permissions next week and the workers can go in and start the restorations.'

'And if you don't?' Brunetti asked.

'God knows,' Marco said with a shake of his head. 'They can keep me waiting another seven months, I suppose.'

'Why haven't you paid them before this?' Brunetti asked.

'My architect keeps saying it isn't necessary, that he knows the men on the planning commission and it's just a question of lots of requests before mine. And I've got problems with other things.' Brunetti thought for a moment that Marco would tell him about them, too, but all he said was, 'No, all you need to know about is this one.'

Brunetti remembered the time, a few years ago, when a chain of fast food restaurants had done extensive restorations in four separate locations, keeping their crews working day and night. Almost before anyone knew it, certainly before anyone had any idea that they were going to open, there they were, in business, the odour of their various beef products filling the air like summer in a Sumatran slaughterhouse.

'Have you decided to pay them?'

'I don't have much of a choice, do I?' Marco asked tiredly. 'I already spend more than a hundred million lire a year for a lawyer as it is, just keeping ahead of the lawsuits people bring against me in the other businesses and trying to resolve them. If I bring a civil suit against people who work for the city for wilfully preventing me from running my business or whatever crime my lawyer can think of to charge them with, it would just cost me more and drag on for years, and in the end nothing would happen anyway.'

'Why did you come to me, then?' Brunetti asked.

'I wondered if there was anything you could do? I mean, if I marked the money or something . . .' Marco's voice petered out and he tightened his fists. 'It's really not the money, Guido. I'll make that back in a couple of months; so many people want to buy that junk. But I'm just sick to death of having to do business this way. I've got shops in Paris and Zurich, and none of this shit goes on there. You apply for building permission, they process your papers, and when they're ready they give you the permissions and you begin the work. No one's there, sucking at your tit.' His fist smashed down on the table. 'No wonder this place is such a mess.' His voice rose, suddenly high-pitched and sharp as, for a moment that frightened Brunetti, Marco seemed to lose all control. 'No one can run a business here. All these bastards want to do is suck us dry.' Again, his hand came smashing down on the table. The two men and the bartender looked over at them, but none of this was new in Italy, so they nodded in silent agreement and went back to their own conversation.

Brunetti had no idea whether Marco's condemnation was of Venice in particular or Italy in general. It hardly mattered: he was right either way.

'What are you going to do?' Brunetti asked.

Implicit in his question, and both men knew it, was the acknowledgement that there was no way Brunetti could help. As a friend he could commiserate and share Marco's anger, but as a policeman he was impotent. The bribe would be paid in cash and so, as is the way with cash, it would leave no traces. If Marco made an official complaint against someone working in the planning commission, he might just as well close up his shops and go out of business, for he would never obtain another permit, no matter how minor, no matter how urgent.

Marco smiled and shifted to the end of the bench. 'I just wanted to let off steam, I guess. Or maybe I wanted to push your nose in it, Guido, since you work for them, sort of, and if that was the reason, then I'm sorry and I apologize.' His voice sounded normal, but Brunetti watched his fingers, this time folding the four corners of a paper napkin into neat triangles.

Brunetti was surprised at how deeply he was offended that any friend of his should consider him as working for 'them'. But, if he didn't work for 'them', then whom did he work for?

'No, I don't think that was why,' he finally said. 'Or at least I hope it wasn't. And I'm sorry, too, because there's nothing I can do. I could tell you to make *una denuncia*, but I might as well tell you to commit suicide, and I don't think I want to do that.' He wondered how Marco could continue to open new businesses if this was the sort of thing he met at every turn. He thought about that restless boy, the one with the big dreams, who had shared his school bench for three years in a row, and he remembered how Marco could never sit still for long, yet he always managed to find the patience to complete one task before rushing off to another. Maybe Marco was programmed like a bee and had no option but to work at something and fly off to something new as soon as he'd finished.

'Well,' Marco began, slipping out of the bench and getting to his feet. He reached into his pocket, but Brunetti held up a monitory hand. Marco understood, took his hand out of his pocket and extended it to the still-sitting Brunetti.

'Next time, mine?'

'Of course.'

Marco glanced at his watch. 'I've got to run, Guido. I've got a shipment of Murano glass,' he began, placing a light smile and heavy emphasis on 'Murano', 'coming in from the Czech Republic and I've got to be at the Customs to see it gets through without any trouble.'

Before Brunetti could rise from the bench, Marco was gone, walking quickly, as he had always walked, off to some new project, some new scheme.

3

Though Brunetti and Paola listened, after dinner, to each other's account of the day, neither of them saw much of a connection between the two events; certainly neither of them connected the stories they'd heard to the idea of honour or its demands. Paola, in sympathy with Marco, said she'd always liked him, surprising Brunetti into saying, 'But I thought you didn't.'

'Why's that?'

'I suppose because he's so different from the sort of person you tend to like.'

'Specifically?'

'I always thought you considered him something of a hustler.'

'He is a hustler. That's precisely why I like him.' When she saw his confusion, she explained, 'Remember, I spend most of my professional life in the company of students or academics. The first are usually lazy, and the second are always self-satisfied. The first want to talk about their delicate sensibilities and wounded souls, some sudden injury to which has prevented them from completing what they were meant to do for class; and the second want to talk about how their last monograph on Calvino's use of the semicolon is going to change the entire course of modern literary criticism. So someone like Marco, who talks about tangible things, about making money and running a business, and who has never, once, in all these years, tried to impress me with what he knows or where he's been or burdened me with long stories of his suffering; someone like Marco's a glass of prosecco after a long afternoon spent drinking cold camomile tea.'

'Cold camomile tea?' he inquired.

She smiled. 'I threw it in for the effect achieved by the contrast with the prosecco. It's a technique of artful exaggeration, akin to the *reductio ad absurdum*, that I've picked up from my colleagues.'

'Who, I imagine, are not at all like prosecco.'

She closed her eyes and put her head back in an attitude of exquisite pain, the sort usually observed in pictures of Saint Agatha. 'There are days when I'm tempted to steal your gun and take it with me.'

'Who would you use it on, students or professors?'

'Surely you're joking,' she said in feigned astonishment.

'No, who?'

'On my colleagues. The students, poor babies, they're just young and callow and will grow up, most of them, and turn into reasonably pleasant human beings. It's my colleagues I long to destroy, if only to put a stop to the endless litany of self-congratulation I have to listen to.'

'All of them?' he asked, accustomed to hear her denounce particular people and thus surprised at her scope.

She considered this, as if she knew there were six bullets in his gun and she was preparing a list. After a while she said, not without a certain disappointment, 'No, not all of them. Maybe five or six.'

'But that's still half of your department, isn't it?'

'Twelve on the books, but only nine teach.'

'What do the other three do?'

'Nothing. But it's called research.'

'How can that be?'

'One of them is aggressive and probably gaga; Professoressa Bettin had what is described as a crisis of nerves and has been put on medical leave until further notice, which probably means until she retires; and the Vice-Chairman, Professore Della Grazia, well, he's a special case.'

'What does that mean?'

'He's sixty-eight and should have retired three years ago, but he refuses to leave.'

'But he doesn't teach?'

'He can't be trusted with female students.'

'What?'

'You heard me. He can't be trusted with female students. Or, for that matter,' she added after a reflective pause, 'with female faculty.'

'What does he do?'

'With the students it's a kind of dirty-minded subtext to everything he says during his tutorials, well, when he still used to have them. Or he'd read graphic descriptions of sex in his classes. But always from the classics, so no one could complain, or if they did, he'd take on an attitude of shocked disdain, as if he were the only protector of the Classical tradition.' She paused for him to respond, but when he didn't she went on: 'With the younger faculty members I've been told that he blocks their chance of promotion unless there's an exchange of sex. He's the Vice-Chairman of the department, so he gets to approve promotions or, in some cases, disapprove them.'

'You said he's sixty-eight,' Brunetti said, not without a certain disgust.

'Which, if you think about it, just gives you some idea of how long he's got away with it.'

'But no longer?'

'To a lesser degree, at least since he was taken out of the classroom.'

'What does he do?'

'I told you, research.'

'What does that mean?'

'It means he collects his salary and, when he decides to leave, he'll collect a generous bonus and then an even more generous pension."

'Is all of this common knowledge?'

'Among the faculty, certainly; probably among the students, as well.'

'And nothing is done about it?'

As soon as he spoke, he knew what she was going to answer, and she did. 'It's no different from what Marco told you today. Everyone knows these things go on, but no one is willing to take the risk of making a formal complaint because of the consequences. To be the first one to make this public would be professional suicide. They'd be sent to some place like Caltanissetta and made to teach a class in something like . . .' He watched her attempting to formulate a subject of sufficient horror. 'Elements of Bardic Verse in Early Catalan Court Poetry.'

'It's strange,' he said. 'I suppose we've all come, more or less, to expect this sort of thing in a government office. But we all think, or maybe we hope – or maybe I do, anyway – that it's somehow different in a university.'

Paola repeated her imitation of Saint Agatha and soon after they went to bed.

In the morning, over coffee, Paola asked, 'Well?'

Brunetti knew exactly what this referred to: the answer he had not given the previous evening, when Paola had told him

23

about the request of her student, and so he said, 'It depends on what the crime was that was committed, and what the sentence was.'

'She didn't say what the crime was, only that he was convicted and sent to San Servolo.'

Idly stirring his coffee, Brunetti asked, 'And the woman's Austrian? Did she say who the man was?'

Paola thought back to her hurried conversation with the girl, trying to remember details. 'No, but she did say the woman was an old friend of her grandfather, so I assume she's talking about him.'

'What's the girl's name?' Brunetti asked.

'Why do you need to know that?'

'I could ask Signorina Elettra to see if there's anything in the files.'

'But the old woman isn't related to her,' Paola protested, somehow reluctant to give the girl up to police investigation, no matter how delicate and no matter how well intended that investigation might be. Who knew the consequences of introducing her name into the police computer?

'Presumably her grandfather would be,' Brunetti said, sounding far more pedantic than he wanted to but irritated that his wife had brought this homework back with her.

'Guido,' Paola said in a voice she herself found unusually firm, 'all she wanted to know was whether it was theoretically possible that a pardon could be granted. She didn't ask for a police examination, just for information.' Paola, a professor of the old school, could not shake herself of the belief that, in some way, she functioned *in loco parentis* to her students, a belief which hardened her resolve not to reveal the girl's name.

He set his cup down. 'I don't think I can do anything until I know what he was convicted of, this man who is or is not her grandfather.' If things like this had ever come up in any of his university law classes, he had long since forgotten. 'If it was something minor, like theft or assault, a pardon would hardly be necessary, especially after all this time, but if it was a major crime, like murder, then perhaps, perhaps . . .' He considered further. 'Did she say how long ago it happened?'

'No, but if he was sent to San Servolo, then it had to be before the *Legge Basaglia*, and that was in the Seventies, wasn't it?' Paola said.

Brunetti considered this. 'Umm,' he muttered. After a long silence, he said, 'It'll be hard, even if we learn his name.'

'We don't need to know his name, Guido,' Paola insisted. 'All the girl wants is a theoretical answer.'

'Then the theoretical answer is that no other kind of answer is possible until I know what the crime was.'

'Which means no answer is possible?' Paola asked acerbically.

'Paola,' Brunetti said in much the same tone, 'I'm not making this up. It's like asking me to put a value on a painting or a print without letting me see it.' Both of them, later, were to recall this comparison.

'Then what am I supposed to tell her?' Paola asked.

'Tell her exactly what I've said. It's what any lawyer of good conscience . . .' he began, ignored Paola's raised eyebrows at this most absurd of possibilities, and went on, 'would tell her. What is it that schoolmaster in that book you're always quoting says? "Facts, facts, facts"? Well, until I have the facts or anyone else has the facts, that's the only answer she's going to get.'

Paola had been weighing the cost and consequences of further opposition and had decided they were hardly worth it. Guido was acting in good faith, and the fact that she didn't much like his answer didn't make it any less true. 'Good, I'll tell her,' she said. 'Thank you.' Smiling, she added, 'It makes me feel like that other Dickens character and makes me want to tell her that she's saved five million lire in lawyer's costs and should go right out and spend it on something else.'

'You can always find whatever you're looking for in a book, can't you?' he asked with a smile.

Instead of a simple answer, something she seldom gave him, Paola said, 'I think it was Shelley who said that poets are the unacknowledged legislators of the world. I don't have any idea if that's true or not, but I do know that novelists are the unacknowledged gossip-mongers of the world. No matter what it is, they thought of it first.'

He pushed back his chair and stood. 'I'll leave you to the contemplation of the splendours of literature.'

He leaned down to kiss her head and waited for her to come up with another literary reference, but she did not. Instead, she reached behind with one hand and patted him on the back of his calf, then said, 'Thank you, Guido. I'll tell her.'

4

Because the requests for information came from what might be termed minor players in their lives, both Brunetti and Paola forgot about them or at least allowed them to slip to the back of their minds. A police department burdened with the increase in crime resulting from the flood of unregulated immigration from Eastern Europe would no more have concerned itself with the attempt to stamp out minor corruption in a city office than Paola would have turned from rereading *The Golden Bowl* to attend to those semicolons in Calvino.

When Claudia did not show up for the next lecture, Paola realized that she felt almost relieved. She didn't want to be the bringer of her husband's news, nor did she want to grow more involved in the personal life or non-academic concerns of one of her students. She had, as had most professors, done so in the past, and it had always either led nowhere or ended badly. She had her own children, and their lives were more than enough to satisfy whatever nurturing instincts the current wisdom told her she must have.

But the girl was present the following week. During the lecture, which dealt with the parallels between the heroines of James and those of Wharton, Claudia behaved as she always did: she took notes, asked no questions, and seemed impatient with the student questions that displayed ignorance or insensitivity. When the class was over, she waited while the other students left the room and then came up to Paola's desk.

'I'm sorry I wasn't here last week, Professoressa.'

Paola smiled but before she could say anything Claudia asked, 'Did you have time to speak to your husband?'

It occurred to Paola to ask the girl if she thought that perhaps she might not have had occasion to speak to her husband during the last two weeks. Instead, she turned to face Claudia and said, 'Yes, I asked him about it, and he said that he can't give you an answer until he has an idea of the seriousness of the crime for which the man was convicted.'

Paola watched the girl's face register this information: surprise, suspicion, and then a quick assessing glance at Paola, as if to assure herself that no trick or trap lay in her answer. These expressions flashed by in an instant, after which she said, 'But in general? I only want to know if he thinks it's possible or if he knows there's some sort of process that would allow, well, that would allow a person's reputation to be restored.'

Paola did not sigh, but she did speak with a sort of over-patient slowness. 'That's what he can't say, Claudia. Unless he knows what the crime was.'

The girl considered this, then surprised Paola by asking, 'Could I speak to your husband myself, do you think?'

Either the girl was too obsessed with finding an answer to care about the distrust her question showed of Paola or too artless to be aware of it. In either case, Paola's response was a lesson in equanimity. 'I see no reason why you couldn't. If you call the Questura and ask for him, I'm sure he'd tell you when you could go and speak to him.'

'But if they won't let me speak to him?'

'Then use my name. Tell them you're calling for me or that I told you to call. That should be enough to make them put you through to him.'

'Thank you, Professoressa,' Claudia said and turned to leave. As she turned, she bumped her hip against the edge of the desk, and the books she was holding fell to the floor. Bending to pick them up, Paola, with the instinct of every lover of books, had a look at them. She saw a book with a title in German, but because it was upside down she couldn't make it out. There was Denis Mack Smith's history of the Italian monarchy as well as his biography of Mussolini, both in English.

'Do you read German, Claudia?'

'Yes, I do. My grandmother spoke it to me when I was growing up. She was German.'

'Your real grandmother, that is?' Paola said with an encouraging smile.

Still on one knee, arranging the books, the girl shot her a very suspicious glance but answered calmly, 'Yes, my mother's mother.'

Not wanting to be perceived as prying, Paola contented herself with saying only, 'How lucky you were to be raised bilingual.'

'You were, too, weren't you, Professoressa?'

'I learned English as a child, yes,' Paola said and left it at that. She did not add that it had not been from her family but from a succession of English nannies. The less any student knew about her personal life, the better. With a gesture to the Mack Smith books, Paola asked, 'What about you?'

Claudia got to her feet. 'I've spent summers in England.' That, it seemed, was the only explanation Paola was going to get.

'Lucky you,' Paola said in English and then added with a smile, 'Ascot, strawberries, and Wimbledon.'

'It's more like mucking out the stables at my aunt's place in Surrey,' Claudia answered in the same accentless English.

'If your German is as good, it must be quite extraordinary,' Paola said, not without a trace of envy.

'Oh, I seldom get to speak it, but I still like to read in it. Besides,' she said, hefting the books on to her hip, 'it's not as if there were any Italian accounts of the war that are particularly reliable.'

'I think my husband will be pleased to talk to you, Claudia. He's very fond of history, and I've listened to him say for years what you've just said.'

'Really? He reads?' Claudia asked, then, aware of how insulting that sounded, added lamely, 'History, I mean.'

'Yes,' Paola answered, gathering up her papers and resisting the impulse to add that her husband was also able to write. In a voice just as pleasant as previously, she said, 'Usually the Romans and the Greeks. The lies they tell seem to leave him less angry than the ones contemporary historians tell, or so he says.'

Claudia smiled at this. 'Yes, I can understand that. Would you tell him that I'll call him, probably tomorrow? And that I'm very eager to meet him?'

Paola found it remarkable that this attractive young woman seemed to find nothing at all unusual in telling another woman how eager she was to meet her husband. The girl was by no means stupid, so it must result only from a sort of ingenuousness Paola had not seen in a student in quite some time or from some other motive she could not discern.

It went against everything she had learned about the necessity of avoiding involvement with students, but curious now to know what was behind Claudia's request, she said, 'Yes, I'll tell him.'

Claudia smiled and said, quite formally, 'Thank you, Professoressa.'

Bright, apparently widely read, at least trilingual, and respectful to her elders. Considering these things, it occurred to Paola that perhaps the girl had been raised on Mars.

5

Because Paola had told him the night before that the girl wanted to talk to him directly, Brunetti realized who it must be when the guard at the entrance to the Questura phoned him to say that a young woman was downstairs, asking to speak to him.

'What's her name?' Brunetti asked.

There was a pause, after which the guard said, 'Claudia Leonardo.'

'Show her up, please,' Brunetti said and set down the phone. He finished reading a paragraph from a meaningless report on spending proposals, set the paper aside and picked up another, not at all unaware that this would show him to be busy when the girl arrived.

There was a knock, the door opened, and he saw a uniformed arm, quickly withdrawn, and then a young woman. She came into the office, certainly looking far too young to be a university student preparing for her last exams, as Paola had said.

He stood, motioning toward the chair that faced him.

'Good morning, Signorina Leonardo. I'm very glad you found time to come and see me,' he said in a tone he attempted to make sound avuncular.

Her quick glance told him she was accustomed to being patronized by older people; it also showed him how little she liked it. She seated herself, and Brunetti did the same. She was a pretty girl in the way young girls are almost always pretty: oval face, short dark hair and smooth skin. But she seemed bright and attentive in a way they seldom are.

'My wife told me there's something you wanted to discuss with me,' he said when he realized she was leaving it for him to speak.

'Yes, sir.' Her gaze was direct, patient.

'She said you were curious about the possibility of a pardon for something that happened a long time ago and for which, unless I misunderstood what my wife told me, a man was convicted.'

'Yes, sir,' she repeated, her glance so unwavering as to make Brunetti wonder if she were waiting for him to resume patronizing her and was curious only as to what new form it would take.

'She also said that he was sent to San Servolo and died there.'

'That's right.' There was no sign of emotion or eagerness on the girl's face.

Sensing that there would be no warming her with these questions, he said, 'She also told me you were reading the Mack Smith biography of Mussolini.'

Her smile revealed two rows of immaculate teeth and seemed to open her eyes wider, until the dark brown irises were completely surrounded with brilliant, healthy white. 'Have you read it?' she asked, her voice charged with eager curiosity.

'Some years ago,' Brunetti answered, then added, 'I usually don't read much modern history, but I had a

33

conversation at dinner one night with someone who started telling us all about how much better it would be if only he were here again, how much better it would be for all of us if he could . . .'

'Instil some discipline into young people,' she seamlessly completed his phrase, 'and restore order to society.' Claudia had somehow managed a perfect echo of the orotund voice of the man who had spoken in favour of Il Duce and the discipline he had managed to instil into the Italian character. Brunetti threw back his head and laughed, delighted and encouraged by the way her imitation dismissed with contempt the man and his claims. 'I don't remember seeing you there,' he said when he stopped laughing, 'but it certainly sounds like you were at the table and heard him talking.'

'Oh, God, I hear it all the time, even at school,' she said with exasperation. 'It's fine for people to complain about the present. It's one of the staples of conversation, after all. But once you start to mention the things in the past that made the present the way it is, then people begin to criticize you for having no respect for the country or for tradition. No one wants to go to the trouble of thinking about the past, really thinking about it, and what a terrible man he was.'

'I didn't know young people even knew who Il Duce was,' Brunetti said, exaggerating, but not by much, and mindful of the almost total amnesia he had discovered in the minds of anyone, of whatever age, with whom he had attempted to discuss the war or its causes. Or worse, the sort of cock-eyed, retouched history that portrayed the friendly, generously disposed Italians led astray by their wicked Teutonic neighbours to the north.

The girl's voice drew him back from these reflections. 'Most of them don't. This is old people I'm talking about. You'd think they'd know or remember what things were like then, what he was like.' She shook her head in another sign of exasperation. 'But no, all I hear is that nonsense about the trains being on time and no trouble from the Mafia and how happy the Ethiopians were to see our brave soldiers.' She paused as if assessing just how far to go with this conservatively dressed man with the kind eyes; whatever she saw seemed to reassure her, for she continued, 'Our brave soldiers come with their poison gas and machine-guns to show them the wonders of Fascism.'

So young and yet so cynical, he thought, and how tired she must be already of having people point this out to her. 'I'm surprised you aren't enrolled in the history faculty,' he said.

'Oh, I was, for a year. But I couldn't stand it, all the lies and the dishonest books and the refusal to take a stand about anything that's happened in the last hundred years.'

'And so?'

'I changed to English Literature. The worst they can do is make us listen to all their idiotic theories about the meaning of literature or whether the text exists or not.' Hearing her, Brunetti had the strange sensation of listening to Paola in one of her wilder moments. 'But they can't change the texts themselves. It's not like what the people in power do when they remove embarrassing documents from the State Archives. They can't do that to Dante or Manzoni, can they?' she asked speculatively, a question that really asked for an answer.

'No,' Brunetti agreed. 'But I suspect that's only because there are standard editions of the basic texts. Otherwise, I'm sure they'd try, if they thought they could get away with it.' He saw that he had her interest, so he added, 'I've always been afraid of people in possession of what they believe is the truth. They'll do anything to see that the facts are changed and whipped into shape to agree with it.'

'Did you study history, Commissario?' she asked.

Brunetti took this as a compliment. 'If I had, I doubt I would have lasted the course, either.' He stopped and they exchanged a smile, both struck by how immediate and democratic was the union of people who sought and found intellectual solace within the pages of books. He went on, giving no thought to the propriety of saying this to someone who was not a member of the forces of order: 'I still spend most of my time listening to lies, but at least some of the people who tell them to me are presumed to be lying because they're criminals. It's not like having to listen to a lie from someone who holds the chair in history at the university.' He almost added, 'Or the Minister of Justice,' but stopped himself in time.

'That makes the lies they tell all the more dangerous, doesn't it?' she asked instantly.

'Absolutely,' he agreed, pleased that she so immediately saw the consequences. Almost reluctantly, he took the conversation back to where it had been before becoming an examination of historical truth. 'But what is it you wanted to ask me?' When she didn't answer, he continued, 'I think my wife told you that I can't give you any information until I know the details.'

'You won't tell anyone?' she blurted out. The tone in which she asked this reminded Brunetti that the girl was not much older than his own children and that her intellectual sophistication didn't necessarily imply any other sort of maturity.

'No, not if there's no sign of ongoing criminal activity. If what you want to ask about happened far enough in the past, then it's likely that the statute of limitations has run out or a general amnesty has been granted.' Because the information Paola had given him was so vague, he decided to leave it to the girl to tell him more if she chose to do so.

There followed a pause in which Brunetti had no idea what the girl might be thinking. It went on so long that he looked away from her, and his eyes were automatically drawn to the printed words on the paper on his desk. He found himself, in the silence, beginning to read, almost against his will.

More time passed. Finally, she said, 'As I told your wife, it's about an old woman I've always thought of as my third grandmother. I need the information for her. She's Austrian, but she lived with my grandfather during the war. My father's father, that is.' She looked across at Brunetti, checking to see if this explanation would suffice; he met her glance, looking interested but certainly not eager.

'After the war, my grandfather was arrested. There was a trial, and during it the prosecution presented copies of articles he had written for newspapers and journals where he condemned "alien art forms and practices". Brunetti recognized this as the Fascist code for Jewish art or art by anyone who was Jewish. 'Despite the Amnesty, they were still admitted as evidence.'

She stopped. When it became evident that she was not going to say more unless he prodded, he asked, 'What happened at the trial?'

'Because of the Togliatti Amnesty he couldn't be prosecuted for political crimes, so he was charged with extortion. For other things that happened during the war,' she explained. 'At least, this is what my grandmother has told me,' she continued. 'When it looked as if he was likely to be convicted, he had a sort of breakdown, and his lawyer decided to plead insanity.' Anticipating Brunetti's question, she added, 'I wondered about that, but my grandmother said it was a real breakdown, not a fake one like they have today.'

'I see.'

'And the judges believed it, too, so when they sentenced him, they sent him to San Servolo.'

It would have been better to have gone to prison, Brunetti found himself thinking, though this was an idea he decided to spare the girl. San Servolo had been closed decades ago, and it was perhaps best to forget the horrors of what had gone on there for so many years. What had happened, had happened, not only to the other inmates, but probably to her grandfather, and there was no changing it. A pardon, however, if such a thing were possible, might change the way people thought about him. If – he found a cynical voice saying – anyone bothered to think about such things any more or if anyone cared about what had happened during the war.

'And what is it you want to obtain for him? Or your grandmother wants to obtain,' he added, seeking this way to encourage her to be more forthcoming about the source of her request.

'Anything that would exonerate him and clear his name.' Then, lowering both her voice and her head, she added, 'It's the only thing I could give her.' Then, more softly, 'It's the only thing she wants.'

This was an area of the law with which Brunetti was not familiar, so he could consider her request only in terms of legal principles. He lacked the courage, however, to tell the girl that the law as it was enacted was not always the result of those principles. 'I think, in legal terms, what might apply here is a legal reversal or overturning of the original judgment. Once it was determined that the verdict was incorrect, your grandfather would, in effect, be declared innocent.'

'Publicly?' she asked. 'Would there be some official document that I could show my grandmother?'

'If the courts issued a judgment, then there would have to be official notice of it,' was the best answer he could supply.

She considered this for so long that Brunetti finally broke into her silence and asked, 'Was his name the same as yours?'

'No. Mine is Leonardo.'

'But he was your father's father?'

She said simply, 'My parents weren't married. My father didn't acknowledge my paternity immediately, so I kept my mother's name.'

Thinking it best not to comment on this, Brunetti asked only, 'What was his name?'

'Guzzardi. Luca.'

At the sound of the name, the faintest of faint bells sounded in the back reaches of Brunetti's memory. 'Was he Venetian?' he asked.

'No, the family was from Ferrara. But they were here during the war.'

The name of the city brought the memory no closer. While seeming to consider her answer, Brunetti was busy trying to think of whom he could ask about events in Venice during the war. Two candidates sprang instantly to mind: his friend Lele Bortoluzzi, the painter, and his father-in-law, Count Orazio Falier, both men of an age to have lived through the war and both possessed of excellent memories.

'But I still don't understand,' Brunetti said, thinking that a display of confusion would be a better means of obtaining information than open curiosity, 'what the purpose of legal action now would be. The original case should have been passed to the Court of Appeals.'

'That was done at the time, and the conviction was upheld; so was the decision to send him to San Servolo.'

Brunetti assumed a befuddled expression. 'Then I don't understand, not at all, how a reversal of judgment would be possible or why anyone would want one.'

She gave him such a penetrating glance that he wiped the country bumpkin expression from his face and felt distinct embarrassment at having attempted to trick her into revealing the name of this grandmother who wanted to obtain the pardon, a desire he knew was motivated by nothing more than curiosity.

She started to speak, stopped, studied him as if remembering his attempt to appear less intelligent than he was, then finally said, with an asperity far in advance of her years, 'I'm sorry but I'm not at liberty to tell you that. All I've asked you to do,' she went on, and he was struck by the dignity with which she spoke, claiming equality with him and basing that claim on the brotherhood they'd established in their talk about books, 'is to tell me if it's possible to clear his name.' Even before he could ask, she cut him off and added, 'Nothing more.'

'I see,' he said, getting to his feet, uncertain that he could be of much help to her but sufficiently charmed by her youth and sincerity to want to try.

She stood up as well. He came around the desk to approach her, but it was she who was the first to extend a hand. They shook hands. Quickly she went to the door and let herself out of the office, leaving Brunetti with the nagging sense that he had behaved foolishly but also with the desire to discover what the memory was that had awakened at the name Guzzardi.

6

When she was gone, Brunetti pulled the pile of papers that remained on his desk towards him, scribbled his initials on each of them without bothering to read a word, and moved them to his left, whence they would continue to meander through the offices of the Questura. It bothered him not at all to dismiss them thus; he thought it might be an intelligent policy to adopt from now on, or perhaps he could make a deal with one of the other commissari to trade off weeks reading them. He contemplated for a moment the possibility of making the same deal with all of the colleagues he trusted, to diminish this stupid waste of time, but was brought up short by how few names he could put on any such list: Vianello, Signorina Elettra, Pucetti, and one of the new commissari, Sara Marino.

The fact that Marino was Sicilian had at first made Brunetti wary of her, and then the revelation that her father, a judge, had been murdered by the Mafia had made him fear she might be a zealot. But then he had seen her honesty and enthusiasm for work; moreover, Patta and Lieutenant Scarpa both disapproved of her and so Brunetti had come to trust her. Aside from those four – and Sara's name was there only because his gut impulse told him she was an honourable person – there was no one else at the Questura in whom he could place blind trust. Rather than put his security in the hands of colleagues, all sworn to protect and uphold the law, how much sooner would he trust his life, career and fortunes to someone like Marco Erizzo, a man he had just advised to commit a crime.

He decided not to waste any more time sitting and making stupid lists. Instead he would go and talk to his father-in-law, another man he had come to trust, though it was a trust that never failed to make him uneasy. He sometimes thought of Count Orazio Falier as Orazio the Oracle, for he was certain that the myriad connections the Count had spent a lifetime forming could lead to the answer to any question Brunetti might ask about the people or workings of the city. In the past, the Count had passed on to Brunetti intimate secrets about the great and good, information which more often than not called into question both of those adjectives. The one thing he had never revealed, however, was a source, though Brunetti had come to believe implicitly in whatever the Count told him.

He called the Count in his office and asked if he could have a word with him. Explaining that he had an appointment for lunch and was leaving the city immediately afterwards, the Count suggested that Brunetti come over to Campo San Barnaba right then, where they could talk undisturbed about whatever it was Brunetti wanted to know. When he set the phone down, Brunetti realized that the Count's intuition made him nervous. He had assumed that Brunetti would have no other reason to ask to see him than to extract information, though he had mentioned it so casually as to make it impossible for Brunetti to take legitimate offence.

Brunetti left a note on his door, saying he had gone to

question someone and would be back after lunch. The day had grown darker and colder, so he decided to take the vaporetto rather than walk. The Number One from San Zaccaria was jammed with an immense tourist group surrounded by a rampart of luggage, no doubt headed for the train station or Piazzale Roma and the airport. He stepped on board and made for the doors of the cabin, only to find his way blocked by an enormous backpack suspended from the shoulders of an even more enormous woman. It seemed to him that in the last few years American tourists had doubled in size. They had always been big, but big in the way the Scandinavians were big: tall and muscular. But now they were lumpish and soft as well as big, agglomerations of sausage-like limbs that left him with the sensation that his hand would come away slick if he touched them.

He knew it was impossible for human physiology to change at less than glacial speed, but he suspected that some shocking transformation had nevertheless taken place in what was required to sustain human life: these people seemed incapable of survival without frequent infusions of water or carbonated drinks, for they all clutched at their litre-and-a-half-bottles as though they alone offered the possibility of continued life.

A recidivist, he opened his *Gazzettino* and turned his attention to the second section, dedicating himself to its many delights until the vaporetto pulled up at the Ca' Rezzonico stop.

At the end of the long *calle*, he turned right in front of the church, then down into an ever narrower *calle* until he found himself at the immense *portone* of Palazzo Falier. He rang the bell and stepped to the right, placing himself in front of the speaker to announce himself, but the door was opened almost instantly by Luciana, the oldest of the servants who staffed the *palazzo* and who had, by virtue of devotion and the passage of time, become an ancillary member of the family.

'Ah, Dottor Guido,' she said, smiling and putting her hand on his arm to lead him through the doorway. Her instinctive gesture expressed happiness to see him, concern for his well-being, and something close to love. 'Paola? The children?'

Brunetti recalled that it was only a few years ago, when both children already towered over this tiny woman, that she had stopped referring to them as 'the babies'.

'Everyone's fine, Luciana. And we're all waiting for this year's honey.' Luciana's son had a dairy farm up near Bolzano, and every year, for Christmas, she gave the family four one-kilo bottles of the different kinds of honey he produced.

'Is it all gone?' she asked, voice quick with worry. 'Would you like some more?'

He pictured her, if he said yes, catching the first train to Bolzano the next morning. 'No, Luciana, we still have the *acacia*. We haven't opened it yet. And there's still half of the *castagno*, so we should make it until Christmas. So long as we keep it hidden from Chiara.'

She smiled, long familiar with Chiara's wolfish appetite. Unpersuaded by his answer, she said, 'If you run out, let me know, and Giovanni can send some down. It's no trouble.'

With another pat on his arm, she said, 'Il Signor Conte is in his office.' Brunetti nodded, and Luciana turned back toward the steps that led up to the first floor and the kitchen, where she reigned supreme; no one could recall a time when she had not done so.

The door to the Count's office was open when Brunetti arrived, so he entered with only a perfunctory tap on the jamb. The Count looked up and greeted him with a smile so warm Brunetti began to wonder if there was some information the Count wanted in exchange for whatever he could supply.

Brunetti had no idea how old the Count was, nor was it easy to gauge it from the man's appearance. Though his close-cropped hair was white, in combination with his sun-darkened skin, it gave an impression of vibrant, active contrast and removed any suggestion that the colour of his hair was an indication of age. Brunetti had once asked Paola how old her father was, and she had answered only that he'd have to find that out by having a look at the Count's passport; she'd gone on gleefully to explain that he had four of them, from four different countries, all with different dates and places of birth.

The piercing blue eyes and the beaked nose would, Brunetti was certain, appear on all of them; Paola had never said whether the names on the passports were all the same, and he had never had the courage to ask.

The Count crossed the room to meet his son-in-law with a firm handshake and a smile. 'How nice of you to come. Have a seat and something to drink. Coffee? *Un'ombra*?'

'No, thank you,' Brunetti said, taking a seat. 'I know you've got an appointment, so I'll just ask you what I've come for and try to be quick about it.'

Without looking at his watch, the Count said, 'I've got half an hour, so there's plenty of time for a drink.'

'No, really,' Brunetti insisted. 'Maybe after we've talked, if there's time.'

The Count went back around his desk and sat. 'Who is it?' he asked, showing his familiarity with Brunetti.

'An Italian named Luca Guzzardi who was convicted after the war, though I don't know for what crimes, and who, instead of going to prison, was sent to San Servolo, where he died.' Brunetti chose to say nothing about Claudia Leonardo nor to explain the reason for his questions. In any case, the Count usually didn't care why Brunetti wanted to know something; the fact that Brunetti was married to his daughter was sufficient reason to offer him any help he could.

The Count's face remained impassive as Brunetti spoke. When he stopped, the Count pursed his lips and tilted his

45

head to one side, as if listening to a sound from one of the *palazzi* on the other side of the Grand Canal. When he looked back at Brunetti, he said, 'Ah, life really is long.'

Brunetti knew that, like his daughter, the Count would not resist the temptation to elucidate. After a moment, he did so. 'Luca Guzzardi was the son of a business associate of my father. He called himself an artist.' Seeing Brunetti's confusion, he explained, 'The son, not the father.'

Presumably, the Count was arranging the facts in an orderly way so as to tell the story clearly. He went on. 'He was not an artist, though he did have a minor talent as an illustrator. This served him in very good stead, for he became a muralist and poster designer for the party in power before and during the war.' There were times when Brunetti had no choice but to admire the Count's arrogance: just as a man in his position did not call his servants by their first names, so too did he refuse to pronounce the name of the political party that had reduced his country to ruins.

Brunetti, who was familiar with *I Fascisti*, now remembered where he had heard the name Guzzardi, or at least read it: in a book on Fascist art, page after numbing page of well-fed factory workers and bright-eyed maidens with long braids, dedicated, in the most glaring of colours, to the triumph of people just like themselves.

'He was quite active during the war, Luca Guzzardi,' the Count went on, 'both in Ferrara, where his family was originally from – I believe they dealt in textiles – and here, where both he and his father held positions of some importance.'

Brunetti had long since abandoned any idea of asking his father-in-law to explain how he came by the information he provided, but this time the Count supplied it. 'As Paola may have told you, we had to leave the country in 1939, so none of us was here during the first years of the war. I was still a boy, but my father had many friends who remained, and after the war, when the family came back to Venice, he learned, and so did I, what had gone on while we were away from the city. Little of it was pleasant.'

After this brief explanation, he went on, 'Guzzardi *padre* supplied cloth to the Army, for uniforms and, I think, tents. Thus he made a fortune. The son, because of his artistic talents, had some sort of job in propaganda, designing posters and billboards that showed the appropriate pictures of life in our great nation. He was also one of the people appointed to decide which pieces of decadent art should be disposed of by galleries and museums.'

'Disposed of?' Brunetti asked.

'It was one of the diseases that came down from the North,' the Count said drily, and then continued.

'There was a long list of painters who were declared objectionable: Goya, Matisse, Chagall, and the German Expressionists. Many others, as well: it was enough that they were Jewish. Or that the subjects of their paintings weren't pretty or supportive of Party myth. Any evidence had to be removed from the walls of museums, and many people took the precaution of removing paintings from the walls of their houses.'

'Where did they go?' Brunetti asked.

'Well you may ask,' the Count answered. 'Often, they were the first paintings that were sold by people who needed enough money to survive or who wanted to leave the country, though they got very little for them.'

'And the museums?'

The Count smiled, that peculiarly cynical tightening of the lips his daughter had inherited from him. 'It was Guzzardi *figlio* whose job it was to decide which things had to be removed.'

'And was it his job,' Brunetti asked, beginning to see where this might be leading, 'to decide where they were sent and to keep the records of where they were?'

'I'm so glad to see that all of these years at the police have done nothing to affect the workings of your mind, Guido,' the Count said with affectionate irony.

Brunetti ignored the remark, and the Count continued, 'Many things seem to have disappeared in the chaos. It seems though, that he went too far. I think it was in 1942. There was a Swiss family living on the Grand Canal in an old place that had been in their family for generations. The father, who had some sort of title,' the Count said with an easy dismissal of all claims to aristocracy that did not go back more than a thousand years, 'was the honorary consul, and the son was always in trouble for saying things against the current government here, but he was never arrested because of his father, who was very well connected. Finally, I can't remember when it was, the son was found in the attic with two British Air Force officers he'd hidden there. The story was very unclear, but it seems that the Guzzardis had found out about it and one of them sent in the police.' He stopped talking, and Brunetti watched him try to call back these memories from more than half a century ago.

'The police took all of them away,' the Count went on. 'Later, the evening of the same day, both of the Guzzardis paid a call on the father in his *palazzo* and, well, there was a discussion of some sort. At the end of it, it was agreed that the boy would be sent home and the matter dropped.'

'And the airmen?'

'I've no idea.'

'The Guzzardis, then?' Brunetti asked.

'They are reported to have left the *palazzo* that night with a large parcel.'

'Decadent art?'

'No one knows. The consul was a great collector of early master drawings: Tiziano, Tintoretto, Carpaccio. He was also a great friend of Venice and gave many things to the museums.'

'But not the drawings?'

'They were not in the *palazzo* at the end of the war,' the Count explained.

'And the Guzzardis?' Brunetti asked.

'It seems that the Consul had been at school with the man who was sent here as British ambassador right after the war, and the Englishman insisted that something be done about the Guzzardis.'

'And?'

'Guzzardi, the son, was put on trial. I don't remember what the exact charges were, but there was never any question about what would happen. The ambassador was a very wealthy man, you see, as well as a very generous one, and that made him very powerful.' The Count looked at the wall behind Brunetti, where three Tiziano drawings hung in a row, as if to ask them to prompt his memory.

'I don't know that the drawings were ever seen again. The rumour I heard at the time was that Guzzardi's lawyer had made a deal and he would be acquitted if the drawings were given back, but then he had some sort of collapse or seizure during the trial, real or fake I don't know, and the judges ended up convicting him – now that I think about it, it might have been for extortion – and sending him to San Servolo. There was talk that it was all a charade, put on so that the judges could send him there. Then they'd keep him there for a few months, then let him out, miraculously cured. That way, the ambassador would get what he wanted, but Guzzardi wouldn't really be punished.'

'But he died?'

'Yes, he died.'

'Anything suspicious about that?'

'No, not that I can remember ever hearing. But San Servolo was a death pit.' The Count considered this for a moment, then added, 'Not that it's much better with the way things are organized now.'

The window of Brunetti's office looked across to the old men's home at San Lorenzo, and what he saw there was enough to confirm everything he believed about the fate of the old, the mad, or the abandoned who came to be cared for by the current public institutions. He drew himself away from these reflections and glanced at his watch; it was past time for the Count to leave, if he was to be in time for lunch. He got to his feet. 'Thank you. If you remember anything else . . .'

The Count interrupted and finished the thought for him, 'I'll let you know.' He smiled, not a happy smile, and said, 'It's very strange to think about those times again.'

'Why?'

'Just like the French, we couldn't forget what happened during the war years fast enough. You know my feelings about the Germans,' he began, and Brunetti nodded to acknowledge the unyielding distaste with which the Count viewed that nation. 'But to give them credit, they looked at what they did.'

'Did they have a choice?' Brunetti asked.

'With Communists in charge of half the country, the Cold War begun, and the Americans terrified which way they'd go, of course they had a choice. The Allies, once the Nuremberg Trials were over, would never have pushed the Germans' noses in it. But they chose to examine the war years, at least to a certain degree. We never did, and so there is no history of those years, at least none that's reliable.'

Brunetti was struck by how much the Count sounded like Claudia Leonardo, though they were separated by more than two generations.

At the door of the office, Brunetti turned and asked, 'And the drawings?'

'What about them?'

'What would they be worth now?'

'That's impossible to answer. No one knows what they

were or how many of them there were, and there's no proof that it happened.'

'That the Guzzardis took them?'

'Yes.'

'What do you think?'

'Of course they took them,' the Count said. 'That's the sort of people they were. Scum. Pretentious, upstart scum, the usual sort of people who are attracted to that kind of political idea. It's the only chance they'll ever have in their lives to have power or wealth, and so they gang together like rats and take what they can. Then, as soon as the game's up, they're the first to say they were morally opposed all the time but feared for the safety of their families. It's remarkable the way men like that always manage to find some high-sounding excuse for what they did. Then, at the first opportunity, they join the winning side.' The Count threw up one hand in a gesture of angry contempt.

Brunetti could not remember ever seeing the Count pass so quickly from distant, amused contempt into raw anger. He wondered what particular set of experiences had led the Count to feel so strongly about these far-off events. This was hardly the time, however, to give in to his curiosity, so he contented himself with repeating his thanks and shaking the Count's hand before leaving Palazzo Falier to return to his more modest home and to his lunch.

7

In the apartment, he found the children in the middle of an argument. They stood at the door to the living room, voices raised, and barely glanced in Brunetti's direction when he came in. Years of evaluating the tones of their various interchanges told him that their hearts weren't in this one and they were doing little more than going through the motions of combat, rather in the fashion of walruses content to rise to the surface of the water and display their tusks to an opponent. As soon as one backed off, the other would flop down and swim away. The dispute concerned a CD, its ownership as disputed as it was currently divided: Raffi had the disc in his hand, and Chiara held the plastic box.

'I bought it a month ago at Tempio della Musica,' Chiara insisted.

'Sara gave it to me for my birthday, stupid,' retorted Raffi.

Applauding himself for his self-restraint, Brunetti did not suggest that they emulate a previous judgment, cut the squealing thing in two, and have done with it. Instead, he inquired, 'Is your mother in her study?'

Chiara nodded but turned immediately back to combat. 'I want to listen to it now,' Brunetti heard her say as he went down the corridor.

The door to Paola's study was open, so he went in, saying, 'Can I claim refugee status?'

'Hummm?' she asked, looking up from the papers on her desk, peering at him through her reading glasses as though uncertain of the identity of the man who had just walked in unannounced.

'Can I claim refugee status?'

She removed her glasses. 'Are they still at it?' she asked. As formulaic as a Haydn symphony, the children's bickering had moved into an adagio but Brunetti, in expectation of the allegro tempestoso that was sure to come, closed the door and sat on the sofa against the wall.

'I spoke to your father.'

'About what?' she asked.

'This thing with Claudia Leonardo.'

'What "thing"?' she asked, refusing to ask him how he came to know her name.

'This grandfather and his criminal behaviour during the war.'

'Criminal?' Paola repeated, interested now.

Quickly, Brunetti explained what Claudia had told him and what he had learned from her father.

When he was finished, Paola said, 'I'm not sure Claudia would like other people to know about this. She asked if she could talk to you, but I don't think she's the sort of person who'd like her family's business being made public.'

'Talking to your father is hardly making what she told me public,' Brunetti said shortly.

'You know what I mean,' she returned in the same tone. 'I assumed that she spoke to me in confidence.'

'I didn't make the same assumption,' Brunetti said and waited to see Paola's response. 'She came to see me in the

53

Questura, so she knows I'm a policeman. How else am I supposed to answer?'

'As I remember, the question was only a theoretical one.'

'I needed to know more about it to be able to answer her,' Brunetti explained for what seemed the hundredth time, conscious of how similar their conversation had become to the one he'd heard on entering the apartment, which conversation, he was happy to note, appeared to have concluded. 'Look,' he added in an effort at reconciliation, 'your father said he'd try to remember more about what happened.'

'But is there any chance of some sort of legal rehabilitation?' she asked. 'That's all she wants to know.'

'As I said to you before, I can't answer that until I know more.'

She studied him a long time, her right hand fiddling idly with one of the earpieces of her glasses, then said, 'It sounds like you already know enough to be able to give her an answer.'

'That it's impossible?'

'Yes.'

'It probably is,' he said.

'Then why ask my father about it? Is it because you're curious?' When he didn't answer, she said, in a far softer voice, 'Has my knight in shining armour climbed yet again upon the broad back of his noble steed, prepared to ride off in pursuit of justice?'

'Oh, stop it, Paola,' he said with an embarrassed smile. 'You make me sound like such a fool.'

'No, my dear,' she said, picking up her glasses and putting them on again. 'I make you sound like my husband and the man I love.' Hiding whatever expression accompanied these words, she looked at the papers and added, 'Now go into the kitchen and open the wine. I'll be out as soon as I finish correcting this paper.'

Wishing the children could see and then emulate the celerity with which he obeyed their mother's command, Brunetti went to the kitchen and opened the refrigerator. He took out a bottle of Chardonnay and set it on the counter, opened the drawer to search for the corkscrew, then changed his mind, replaced the bottle, and took out one of prosecco. 'The workman is worthy of his hire,' he muttered as he popped the cork. Taking glass and bottle, he retreated to the living room in hopes of finishing that day's *Gazzettino*.

Twenty minutes later, they sat down to lunch. The argument over the CD had apparently been settled, he hoped most fervently in Chiara's favour. She at least still remained browbeaten by her parents into using a Discman: Raffi had last year bought a small stereo system for his room and insisted upon using it to broadcast to the family, and to that part of the world within a fifty-metre radius of their home, a sort of music which made Brunetti think longingly of the symptoms of tinnitus he'd once read about: constant mechanical roaring or buzzing in the ear that blocked out all other sound.

In keeping with the change in season, Paola had made risotto di zucca and into it at the last minute had tossed grated slivers of ginger, its sharp bite softened to amiability by the chunk of butter and the grated parmigiano that had chased it into the pot. The mingled tastes drove all dread of Raffi's music from Brunetti's mind, and the chicken breast grilled with sage and white wine that followed replaced that music with what Brunetti thought must be the sound of angels' singing.

Brunetti set down his fork and turned to his wife. 'Bring me a Braeburn apple, a thin slice of Montasio and a glass of Calvados,' he began, 'and I will cover you in diamonds the size of walnuts, place pearls as white as truffles at your feet, pluck emeralds as large as kiwi fruit . . .'

Chiara cut him off before he could continue. 'Oh, *Papà*, all you ever think about is food.' Coming from someone as voracious as she, this was the basest sort of hypocrisy, but before Brunetti could reproach her, Paola put a large bowl of apples in front of him. 'Besides,' Chiara continued, 'how could anyone wear an emerald as big as a kiwi fruit?'

His plate disappeared, replaced by a clean fruit plate, a small knife and fork.

'*Mamma* would just use it as a paperweight, anyway,' Raffi said, reaching for an apple. He bit into it and asked if he could be excused to go and finish his calculus homework.

'If I hear a single note of that noise before three this afternoon, I will come into your room and drive bamboo shoots into your eardrums, permanently deafening you,' his loving mother said, nodding to him that he could leave the table and letting Brunetti know who had won possession of the CD. Raffi grabbed two more apples and left, quickly followed by Chiara, who slipped away in his wake.

'You spoil him,' Brunetti said, cutting a not particularly thin slice of Montasio. 'I think you should be firmer with him, perhaps begin by threatening to tear out his fingernails.'

'He's only two years younger than some of my students,' Paola said, picking up an apple and beginning to peel away the skin. 'If I began doing any of these things to him, I'm afraid of what I might be led to do to the students. I might be maddened by the smell of teenage blood.'

'It can't be that bad,' Brunetti said in an interrogative voice.

Once the apple was peeled, Paola quickly cut it into eight slices and removed the pieces of core. She jabbed her fork into the first and ate it before she said, 'No, I suppose it's not as bad as what you do. But, believe me, there are days when I long to be locked in a cell: me, two strong policemen, one of the students, and a wide array of fearsome implements.'

'Why is it so bad all of a sudden?' Brunetti asked.

'It's not really all of a sudden. It's more that I've become aware of how bad it's become.'

56

'Give me an example,' he said.

'Ten years ago, I could force them into accepting the fact, or at least giving lip service to the idea, that the culture that formed me, all those books and ideas that our generation grew up on – Plato, Virgil, Dante – that it was superior in some way to whatever fills their lives. Or, if not superior, then at least interesting enough to be worthy of study.' She ate three more pieces of apple and a thin slice of Montasio before she went on. 'But that doesn't happen any more. They think, or at least they seem to think, that their culture, with its noise and acquisitiveness and immediate forgettability is superior to all of our stupid ideas.'

'Like?'

'Like our no doubt ridiculous idea that beauty conforms to some standard or ideal; like our risible belief that we have the option to behave honourably and should take it; and like our idiotic idea that the final purpose of human existence is something more than the acquisition of wealth.'

'No wonder you want the fearsome implements,' Brunetti said and opened the Calvados.

8

Back in his office that afternoon, faintly conscious that he had perhaps dined too well, Brunetti decided he might try to get more information about Guzzardi from Lele Bortoluzzi, another prime source of the sort of information that in more ordered societies would lead to accusations of slander. Ordinarily, he would have made the trip across the city to Lele's gallery, but today Brunetti felt himself weighed down by the Calvados, though he told himself it had been little more than a whisper, and so decided to phone, instead.

'*Sì*,' Lele answered after the second ring.

'*Ciao*, Lele,' Brunetti said, not bothering to give his name. 'I need to pick through your archive again, this time for someone called Luca Guzzardi, who . . .'

'*Quel figlio di mignotta*,' Lele interrupted, his voice shot through with an anger Brunetti was unaccustomed to hearing from the painter.

'So you remember him,' Brunetti said with a laugh, trying to disguise his surprise.

'Of course I remember him,' Lele said. 'Bastard: he got

exactly what he deserved. The only pity is that he died so soon: he should have been kept alive longer, living there like a larva.'

'At San Servolo?' Brunetti asked, though there was little doubt what his friend meant.

'Where he deserved to be. Better than any prison they could have sent him to, the bastard. I'm sorry for the other devils who were kept there: none of them deserved to live like that, worse than animals. But Guzzardi deserved it all, and more.'

Brunetti knew that whatever reason Lele had for this passionate disgust would soon be made clear. Prodding, Brunetti said, 'I never heard you talk about him before. Strange, if you feel so strongly about him.'

Lele continued. 'He was a thief and a traitor, and so was his father. There was nothing they wouldn't do, no one he wouldn't betray.'

Brunetti noticed that Lele's condemnation was so much more forceful than the Count's, but then he recalled that his father-in-law had said he had not been in Venice during the war. Lele had been, for all of it, and two of his uncles had died, one fighting with the Germans and one fighting against them. Brunetti cut into the string of epithets that continued to pour from the phone and said, 'All right, all right, I understand your feelings. Now tell me why.'

Lele had the grace to laugh. 'It must be strange, this anger after so long. I haven't heard his name in, oh, I don't know, twenty years, but all I needed was to hear it, and everything I knew about him came back.' He paused for a moment and then added, 'It's strange, isn't it, how some things just don't go away? You'd think time would have softened some of it. But not with Guzzardi.'

'What hasn't been softened?' Brunetti asked.

'Well, obviously, how much we all hated him.'

'All?'

'My father, my uncles, even my mother.'

'Why?'

'Are you sure you have time to listen?' Lele asked.

'Why else call?' Brunetti asked in response, grateful that Lele hadn't bothered to ask why he was curious about Guzzardi.

By way of answer, Lele began by asking, 'You know my father was an antiquarian, a dealer?'

'Yes,' Brunetti answered. He had a vague memory of Lele's father, an enormous man with a white moustache and beard who had died when Brunetti was still a young boy.

'There were a lot of people who wanted to leave the country. Not that there were many places where they could go, not go and be safe, that is. But at any rate, after the war began, some of them approached my father, asking if he could sell things for them.'

'Antiques?'

'And paintings, and statues, and rare books, just about anything that had beauty and value.'

'What did he do?'

'He acted as agent,' Lele said, as though that explained everything.

'What does that mean, that he acted as agent?'

'Just that. He agreed to find buyers. He knew the market and he had a long list of clients. And in return he took ten per cent.'

'Isn't that normal?' Brunetti asked, aware that he was missing whatever message Lele thought he was conveying.

'There was no such thing as normal during the war,' Lele said, again as though that would explain everything.

Brunetti interrupted. 'Lele, there's too much going on here that I don't understand. Make things clear to me, please.'

'All right. I always forget how little people know, or want to know, about what happened then. It was like this. When people were forced to sell things or were put into positions where they had no choice but to sell things, they had the option of trying to do it themselves, which is always a mistake, or they could turn to an agent. Though that was just as often a mistake.'

'Why?'

'Because some of the dealers had smelled the scent of money, great sums of money, and many of them, once they realized how panicked the sellers were, went mad with it.'

'Went mad how?'

'By raising their percentages. People were desperate to sell and get out of the country if they could. Towards the end, most of them finally realized that they would die if they stayed here. No,' he corrected himself, 'not die: be killed. Be sent off to be murdered. But some of them still lacked the courage to cut and run and leave everything behind them: houses, paintings, clothing, art, papers, family treasures. That's what they should have done, just left it all and tried to get to Switzerland or Portugal, even to North Africa, but too many of them weren't willing to take the loss. But then finally they had no choice.'

'And so?' Brunetti prodded.

'So, in the end, they were forced to sell everything they had, turn it into gold or stones or into foreign currency, into something they thought they could carry out of the country with them.'

'Couldn't they?'

'This is going to take a long time to explain, Guido,' Lele said, almost apologetically.

'Good.'

'All right. It worked, at least many times, it worked like this. They contacted the agents, many of whom were antiquarians, either here or in one of the big cities. Some of the big collectors even tried to deal with Germans, men like Haberstock in Berlin. The word had got around that Prince Farnese in Rome had managed to sell a lot of things through him. But, anyway, people contacted the agents, who came and had a look at what they had to sell, and then they offered to buy what they liked or thought they could sell.' Again, Lele stopped.

Puzzled about what in all of this could have turned Lele pyrotechnic, Brunetti prompted. 'And?'

'And they'd offer a fraction of what the objects were worth and say that's all they could expect to get for them.' Even before Brunetti could ask the obvious question, Lele explained. 'Everyone knew it wasn't worth the trouble to contact anyone else. They'd formed a cartel, and as soon as one of them gave prices, he'd tell all the others what the prices were, and none of them would offer more.'

'But what about men like your father? Couldn't people contact him?'

'By then my father was in prison.' Lele's voice was like ice.

'On what charge?'

'Who knows? What does it matter? He was reported to have made defeatist remarks. Of course he did. Everyone knew we had no chance of winning the war. But he made those remarks only at home, only with us. It was the other agents. They gave his name and the police came around and took him away, and it was made clear to him while he was being questioned that he should no longer work as an agent.'

'For people who wanted to leave the country?'

'Among others. He was never told just whom he shouldn't deal with, but he didn't have to be, did he? My father got the message. By the third beating, he got the message. So when they let him go, and he came home, he no longer attempted to help those people.'

'Jews?' Brunetti asked.

'Primarily, yes. But also non-Jewish families. Your father-in-law's, for example.'

'Are you serious, Lele?' Brunetti asked, unable to disguise his astonishment.

'This is a subject about which I do not joke, Guido,' Lele said with unusual asperity. 'Your father-in-law's father had to leave the country, and he came to my father and asked if he would handle the sale of certain items for him.'

'And did he?'

'He took them. I think there were thirty-four paintings and a large collection of Minutius first editions.'

'He wasn't afraid of the warning he'd just had?'

'He didn't sell them. He gave the Count a certain sum of money and told him he'd keep the paintings and books for him until he came back to Venice.'

'What happened?'

'The family, including your father-in-law, went overland to Portugal and then to England. They were among the lucky ones.'

'And the things your father had?'

'He put them in a safe place, and when the Count and his family came back after the war, he returned all of them.'

'Where did he keep them?' Brunetti asked, not because it made any difference but because the historian in him needed to know.

'I had an aunt who was a Dominican abbess, in the convent over by the Miracoli. She put all of them under her bed.' Brunetti was too amazed to say anything, but Lele explained, anyway. 'Actually, there was a large space beneath the floor of the abbess's bedroom, and she placed her bed directly over the entrance to it. I never thought it polite to ask what an abbess would want to hide there, so I don't know what its original purpose was.'

'We can but hope,' Brunetti observed, recalling childhood tales of the misbehaviour between priests and nuns.

'Indeed. At any rate, it all stayed there until the war was over and the Faliers came home, when my father gave everything back. The Count gave him the money. He also gave him a small Carpaccio, the one that's now in our bedroom.'

After considering all of this, Brunetti said, 'I've never heard about this, not in all the time I've know him.'

'Orazio doesn't talk about what happened during the war.'

Surprised that Lele should speak so familiarly of a man Brunetti had never addressed, not in more than two decades, by his first name, he asked, 'But how do you know about it? From your father?'

'Yes, at least part of it. Orazio told me the rest.'

'I didn't know you knew him that well, Lele.'

'We fought together with the Partisans for two years.'

'But he said he was only a boy when they left Venice.'

'That was in 1939. Three years later, he was a young man. A very dangerous young man. He was one of the best. Or worst, I suppose, if you were a German.'

'Where were you?' Brunetti asked.

'Up near Asiago, in the mountains,' Lele said, paused, and then added, 'Anything else you want to know about this, I think you better ask your father-in-law.'

Taking that as the command it so clearly was, Brunetti went back to the subject at hand. 'Tell me more about your father, before he was arrested.'

'Before that, he'd taken only his ten per cent, and he'd done his best to try to get as much as he could for the things his clients had to sell. And, for whatever it's worth, he never bought anything from them. No matter how good the price they offered him, and no matter how much he wanted to own the object, he refused to buy anything for himself.'

'And Guzzardi?' Brunetti asked, bringing the story back where he wanted it to be.

'They were a perfect team. The father was the money man and the son was the artist.' Lele's voice dribbled acid on the word. 'They got into the antiques business almost by accident. They must have smelled how much money they could make at it. People like that always do. At the beginning, they hired someone to work as an appraiser for them, and because both of them were senior Party members, they had no trouble in getting themselves into the cartel. And before you knew it, people here, and in Padova and Treviso, who wanted to sell things and needed to do it fast, well, they ended up dealing with the Guzzardis. And they sold. The Guzzardis sucked up everything. Like sharks.'

'Did they have anything to do with your father's arrest?'

Lele said, cautious as always, given his belief that all phone conversations were monitored by some agency of the state, 'It's always wise business procedure to eliminate the competition.'

'Did they buy only for themselves or also for clients?'

'When they started out – because neither of them had any taste at all – they bought for clients, people who might have heard that a certain collection was for sale and who didn't want to get their hands dirty by being seen to buy things openly. This happened more and more, the closer it got to the end of the war. People wanted the art works, but they didn't want it to be seen that they'd bought them.'

'And the Guzzardis?' Brunetti asked.

'Toward the end, they are said to have bought only for themselves. By then Luca had developed a fairly good eye. Even my father admitted that. He wasn't stupid, Luca, not at all.'

'What sort of things?'

'The father bought paintings; Luca was interested in drawings and etchings.'

'Is that what Luca was good at?'

'Not particularly, no, I don't think so. But they're very portable, and because there's always more than one etching and because very often painters made a few sketches or drawings before a painting, it's harder to trace them than if they were unique. And they're very easy to hide.'

'I had no idea any of this went on,' Brunetti said when it seemed that Lele had finished speaking.

'Few people do. And even fewer want to know anything about it. That's what we did, right after Liberation: we all decided that we'd forget what had happened during the last decade, especially in the years since the beginning of the war. Besides, we finished on the winning side, so it was even easier to forget. That's what we've had since then, the politics of amnesia. It's what we wanted and it's what we've got.'

Brunetti had seldom heard it better named. 'Anything else?' he asked.

'I could fill a history book with what went on during those years. Then, as soon as the war ended, things went back to business as usual, just like in Germany. Well, no, it took a little longer there because they had to go through all that de-Nazification stuff, not that it served for much. But these pigs, these agents, had their snouts back in the trough almost as soon as the war was over.'

'You make it sound like you know them.'

'Of course I do. A few of them are still alive. One of them even has a portfolio of Old Master drawings in a bank vault, has had it there since he acquired it in 1944.'

'Legally?'

Lele gave a snort of contempt. 'If someone is in fear of his life and sells something, signs a bill of sale – and the Guzzardis were always careful to get them – then the sale's still legal. But if someone were to steal those drawings from the bank vault and give them back to the original owner, I'm sure that would be illegal.' Lele allowed a long pause to draw out from that remark before he said abruptly, 'I'll call you if I think of anything,' and then his voice was gone.

9

Brunetti had the entire afternoon to muse upon what Lele had told him. He'd read little of the history of the last war, but certainly other centuries provided sufficient examples of plundering and profiteering to illustrate all that Lele had said. The sack of Rome, the sack of Constantinople: hadn't both of them been followed by vast transfers of wealth and art and by the collateral destruction of even more? Rome had been left in ruins, and Byzantium smouldered for weeks as the victors devoted themselves to looting. Indeed, the bronze horses that pranced above the entrance of the Basilica had been part of the loot the Venetians brought home. Certainly the defeat of those cities must have been preceded by hysteria on the part of those desperate to escape. In the end, no matter how beautiful or precious, what object had any value in comparison to life? Some years ago he had read an account by a French crusader who had been present at the siege and sack of Constantinople: he'd written that 'so much booty had never been gained in any city since the creation of the world'. But what did that count in the face of the loss of so many lives?

Shortly after seven he pulled himself free from these reflections, moved some paper idly from one side of his desk to the other so as to give the appearance that he had done something that afternoon other than try to make sense of human history, and went home.

He found Paola, predictably, in her study, where he joined her, flopping down on the battered sofa she refused to part with. 'You never told me about your father,' he said by way of introduction.

'Never told you what about my father?' she asked. Judging by both his tone and his manner that this would be a long conversation, she abandoned the notes she was preparing.

'About the war. And what he did.'

'You make it sound as if you'd discovered he's a war criminal,' she observed.

'Hardly,' Brunetti conceded. 'But someone told me today that he fought with the Partisans up near Asiago.'

She smiled. 'So now you know as much as I know.'

'Really?'

'Absolutely. I know that he fought and that he was very young when he was there, but he has never chosen to talk to me about it, and I've never had the courage to ask my mother about it.'

'Courage?'

'From her tone and the way she reacted whenever I brought the subject up, as I did when I was younger, I realized that it was not something she wanted to talk about and that I shouldn't ask him, either. So I didn't, and then I suppose I got out of the habit of being curious about it or wanting to know exactly what he did.' Before Brunetti could respond to this, she added, 'Just like you with your father. All you've ever told me is that he came back from Africa, went off on the Russian campaign and was gone for years, and when he came back everyone who knew him said he wasn't the same person who had marched away. But you've never told me more than that. And your mother, when she talked about it, never said anything more than that he had been gone for five years.'

Brunetti's childhood had been scarred by the results of those five years, for his father had been a man much given to fits of violence that came upon him for no apparent reason. A chance word, a gesture, a book lying on the kitchen table: any of these could set him off into a rage from which only Brunetti's mother could free him. As if possessed of the power of the saints themselves, she could do this merely by placing a hand upon his arm: even the lightest touch sufficed to pull him back from whatever hell he had slipped into.

When not in the grip of these sudden, spectacular moods, he was a quiet man, much given to silence and solitude. Repeatedly wounded in the war, he had been granted a military pension, on which the family tried to live. Brunetti had never understood him and, in a certain sense, had never know him, for his wife always insisted that the real man was the one who marched off to war and not the one who came home. She, by the grace of God or love, or both, loved both of them.

Only once had Brunetti seen evidence of the man his father must have been, the day he came home to announce that he was the only student in his class to have been accepted into the Liceo Classico. When he told his parents, doing his best to hide his bursting pride and fearful how his father would take this news, the older man pushed himself up from the table, where he was helping his wife shell peas, and came to stand beside his son. Placing his hand on Brunetti's cheek, he said, 'You make me a man again, Guido. Thank you.' The memory of his father's smile was enough to call down the stars, and for the first time since his childhood Brunetti had felt himself melt with love for this gentle, decent man.

'Are you listening to me, Guido?' Paola asked, calling him back to her room and her presence.

'Yes, yes. I was just thinking about something.'

'So,' she went on as though there had been no interruption, 'I know as little about what my father did as you know about yours. They fought and they came back, and neither of them wanted to talk about what happened while they were away.'

'Do you think it was so awful, what they had to do?'

'Or what was done to them,' Paola answered.

'There was a difference, though,' he said.

'What?'

'Your father came back to fight voluntarily. Or he must have. Lele said the family got safely to England, so he must have chosen to come back.'

'And your father?'

'My mother always told me he never wanted to join the Army. But he had no choice. They rounded them up, and after they'd trained them to march together without falling over one another, they sent them off to campaign in Africa and Greece and Albania and Russia, sent them off with shoes made out of cardboard because some friend of some friend of someone in the government made a fortune on the contract.'

'He really never talked about it?' Paola asked.

'Not to me, and not to Sergio, no,' Brunetti said.

'Do you think he might have talked to his friends?'

'I don't think he had any friends,' Brunetti said, admitting to what he had always thought of as the great tragedy of his father's life.

'Most men don't, do they?' she asked, but there was only sadness in her tone.

'What do you mean? Of course we have friends.' In the face of her visible sympathy, Brunetti could not keep the indignation from his voice.

'I think most men don't, Guido, but you know that's what I think because I've said it so many times. You have what the Americans call "pals", men you can talk to about sports or politics or cars.' She considered what she had said. 'Well, since you live in Venice and work for the police, I guess you can substitute guns and boats for cars. Things, always things. But in the end it's the same: you never talk about what you feel or fear, not the way women do.'

'Are we talking about lack of friends or the fact that we don't talk about the same things women do? I'm not sure they're the same.'

This was an old battle, and Paola apparently was in no mood to fight it again that evening, not with Brunetti in so fragile a mood and not with a long class to prepare for the following morning. 'There aren't going to be too many evenings like this one left, do you think?' she asked, holding the remark out as a flag of truce. 'Shall we get a glass of wine and go out and sit on the terrace?'

'The sun's already set,' he said, not willing to give in so easily and still stung by the implication that he had no friends.

'We can watch the glow, then. And I'd like to sit beside you and hold your hand.'

'Goose,' he said, moved.

Claudia did not appear in class the following day, a fact which Paola noted but to which she paid little attention. Students were by definition unreliable, though she had to admit that Claudia had seemed not to be. The reason for her absence was made clear to her in a phone call from Brunetti, which reached her at her office at the university later that same afternoon.

'I have bad news for you,' he began, filling her with instant terror for the safety of her family. Sensing that, Brunetti said, voice as calm as he could make it, 'No, it's not the children.' He gave her a moment to register that and then went on, 'It's Claudia Leonardo. She's dead.'

Paola had a flash of memory of Claudia's turning back from the door of the classroom and saying that Lily Bart's death had broken her heart. Please let someone's heart be broken by Claudia's death, she had time to think, before Brunetti went on: 'There was a burglary in her apartment, and she was killed.'

'When?'

'Last night.'

'How?'

'She was stabbed.'

'What happened?'

'What I was told was that her flatmate came back this morning and found her. Claudia was on the floor: it looks as if she came in and found whoever it was and he panicked.'

'With a knife in his hand?' Paola asked.

'I don't know. I'm just telling you what it sounds like for now.'

'Where are you?'

'There. I just got here. I've got Vianello's *telefonino*.'

'Why did you call?'

'Because you knew her and I didn't want you to hear about it some other way.'

Paola let a long silence stretch out between them. 'Was it quick?'

'I hope so,' was the only answer he could give.

'Her family?'

'I don't know. I told you I just got here. We haven't even looked at the place yet.' There was a noise in the background, a voice, two voices, and then Brunetti said, 'I've got to go. Don't expect me before tonight.' And then he was gone.

Gone perhaps from the sound of his wife's voice but not from the presence of death, an apartment in Dorsoduro, not far from the Pensione Seguso but back two streets from the Canale della Giudecca.

He handed the *telefonino* back to Vianello, who put it in the pocket of his jacket. Not for the first time, Brunetti found himself surprised by the sight of Vianello in civilian clothes, the result of his too-long-delayed promotion to Ispettore. Though the wrapping had changed, the contents were the same: reliable, honest, clever Vianello had responded to Brunetti's call, which had caught him at home, just about to spend his day off on a shopping expedition to the mainland with his wife. Brunetti was grateful for Vianello's instinctive willingness to join him: the solid, confident bulk of the man would help him with what was to come.

Vianello had overheard Brunetti's conversation and made no attempt to pretend that he had not. 'Your wife knew her, sir?'

'She was one of her students,' Brunetti explained.

If Vianello thought it strange that Brunetti knew this, he kept it to himself and suggested, 'Shall we go up, sir?'

A uniformed officer stood at the door to the street, another at the top of the second flight of steps, directly before the open door of the apartment. The rest of the building, in which there were three other apartments, might as well have been empty, so profound was the silence that radiated from all the closed doors. Yet Claudia's flatmate was in one of those apartments, he knew, for their landlady had said so when she phoned.

Brunetti did not hesitate at the door but went directly into the apartment. The first thing he saw was her hand, fingers clutched in a death grip among the pieces of fringe at the end of a dark red carpet. A Turkoman, its centre field was filled with hexagonal white ghuls on a deep red field. The design was neat and geometrical, the stylized flowers arranged in rows, white bars creating a border at top and bottom. The pattern was interrupted at one end, where her blood had flowed into the carpet, staining the white with a red just a bit lighter than the red of the carpet. Brunetti saw that one of the flowers had been blotted out; blotted out with her life.

He moved his eyes to the left and saw the back of her head and her neck, white and defenceless. She was turned away, so he walked around to the other side of the room, careful where

73

he set his feet, until he could look down and see her face. It too was white and seemed strangely relaxed. No expression could be read on it, just as no expression could be read on the face of a person who was sleeping. Brunetti wished there were some way he could make this make a difference.

Standing still, he looked around the apartment for signs of violence, but he saw none. A plate holding a few slices of apple, darkened and dry now, stood in the centre of a low table to one side of a print-covered easy chair. On one arm, a book lay face down. Brunetti moved over to the chair and glanced down at the title: *The Faustian Bargain*. It meant nothing to him, as meaningless as the apparent calm with which she had met her death.

'This was no robbery,' Vianello said.

'No, it wasn't, was it?' Brunetti agreed. 'Then what?'

'Lovers' quarrel?' Vianello offered, though it was obvious he didn't believe this. There had been no quarrel here.

Brunetti went over to the door and asked the young officer there, 'Did the flatmate say anything about the door? Was it open or closed?' He noticed that the young man had nicked his chin shaving, though he seemed barely old enough to need to shave.

'I don't know, sir. When I got here, one of the neighbours had already taken her downstairs.'

Brunetti nodded in acknowledgement, then asked, 'The knife? Or whatever it was?'

'I didn't see anything, sir,' he said apologetically, then added, 'Maybe it's under her.'

'Yes, that could be,' Brunetti said and turned back toward Vianello. 'Let's take a look at the other rooms.'

Vianello stuck his hands in the pockets of his trousers; Brunetti did the same. Both had forgotten to bring along disposable gloves but knew they could get them when the medical examiner showed up.

The bedrooms, kitchen and bathroom gave up no

information other than that one of the girls was much neater than the other and that the neat one was a reader: Brunetti was in little doubt as to which would turn out to be which.

Back in the living room, Vianello asked, 'The flatmate?'

Again Brunetti went to the door. Pausing only long enough to tell the officer to come down and get him as soon as the medical examiner arrived, Brunetti led the way downstairs.

Obviously they were anticipated, for an elderly woman stood at the open door to one of the apartments below. 'She's in here, sir,' she said, stepping back and leaving room for Brunetti, and then Vianello, to enter.

Seeing that they were in a small foyer, Brunetti asked softly, 'How is she?'

'Very bad, sir. I've called for my doctor, and he'll come as soon as he can.' She was a short woman, somewhat given to stoutness, with light blue eyes and skin that looked as though it would be as cool and dry as a baby's to the touch.

'Have they lived here long?' Brunetti asked.

'Claudia came three years ago. The apartment's mine, and I rent it to students because I like to have the sound of them around me. Only to girls, though. They keep their music lower, and they stop in sometimes for a cup of tea in the afternoon. Boys don't,' she said in final explanation.

Brunetti had a son at university, so he knew all there was to know about the volume at which students liked to keep their music as well as the unlikelihood that they would stop in for a cup of tea in the afternoon.

Brunetti knew he would have to talk to this woman at length, but he wanted to speak to the girl first, to see if there was anything that would help them begin to look for the killer. 'What's her name, Signora?' he asked.

'Lucia Mazzotti,' she said. 'She's from Milano,' she added, as if this would help Brunetti in some way.

'Will you take me to her?' he asked, making a small signal with his hand for Vianello to stay behind. Even though

Vianello no longer wore his uniform, his size might be enough to make the girl nervous.

The old woman turned and, favouring her right leg, led Brunetti back through a small sitting room, past the open door of the kitchen and the closed door of what must be the bathroom, to the one remaining door. 'I made her lie down,' the woman said. 'I don't think she's asleep. She wasn't just a few minutes ago, when I heard you on the stairs.'

She tapped lightly on the door and, in response to a sound from inside, pushed the door open. 'Lucia,' she said softly, 'there's a man to see you, a policeman.'

She made to step aside, but Brunetti took her arm and said, 'I think it would be better if you stayed with us, Signora.'

Confused, the old woman froze, glancing from Brunetti into the room. 'I think it would be easier for her,' Brunetti whispered.

Persuaded, but still not fully agreeing, the woman stepped into the room and stood to one side of the door, allowing Brunetti to enter.

A young woman with bright red hair lay on top of the covers, leaning back on a plump pillow. Her hands extended on either side of her, palms upwards, and she stared at the ceiling.

Brunetti approached the bed, pulled a chair towards him, and sat, making himself smaller. 'Lucia,' he said, 'I'm Commissario Brunetti. I've been sent to find out what happened. I know that you found Claudia, and I know it must have been terrible for you, but I need to talk to you now because you might be able to help us.'

The girl turned her head and looked at him. Her fine-boned face was curiously slack. 'Help you how?' she asked.

'By telling us what happened when you came home, what you saw, what you remember.' Before she could say anything, he went on, 'And then I'll need for you to tell me anything you can about Claudia that you think might be in some way related to what's happened.'

'You mean to her?'

Brunetti nodded.

The girl rolled her head away from him and returned her gaze to the yellow lampshade that hung suspended from the ceiling.

Brunetti allowed at least a full minute to pass, but the girl continued to stare at the lamp. He turned back to the old woman and raised his eyebrows interrogatively.

She came to stand beside him, putting a firm hand on his shoulder and pushing him back into the chair when he attempted to stand. 'Lucia,' she said, 'I think it would be a good thing if you'd speak to the policeman.'

Lucia turned towards the old woman, then towards Brunetti. 'Is she dead?'

'Yes.'

'Did someone kill her?'

'Yes,' he said.

The girl considered this for some time and then said, 'I got home at about nine. I spent the night in Treviso and came home to change and get my books. I have a class this morning.' She blinked a few times and looked out the window. 'Is it still morning?' she asked.

'It's about eleven,' the old woman said. 'Would you like me to get you something to drink, Lucia?'

'I think I'd like some water,' the girl said.

The woman gripped Brunetti's shoulder again and left the room, again favouring her right leg.

When she was gone, the girl went on, 'I got back and went upstairs and opened the door to the apartment and went in, and I saw her on the floor. At first I thought she'd fallen or something, but then I saw the rug. I stood there and I didn't know what to do. I think I screamed. I must have because Signora Gallante came up and brought me down here. That's all I remember.'

'Was the door locked?' Brunetti asked. 'The door to your apartment?'

She considered this for a moment, and Brunetti could sense her reluctance in having to keep returning to the memory of that scene. Finally she said, 'No, I don't think it was. That is, I don't remember using my key.' There was a long silence, and then she added, 'But I could be wrong.'

'Did you see anyone outside?'

'When?'

'When you got home.'

'No,' she said with a quick shake of her head. 'There wasn't anyone.'

'Even people you know, neighbours,' Brunetti asked and then, at her quick, suspicious glance, he explained, 'They might have seen someone.'

Again she shook her head. 'No, no one.'

These questions, Brunetti knew, were probably less than useless. He'd seen the colour of the blood on the carpet and knew it meant Claudia had been dead for a considerable time. The medical examiner would be able to tell him more accurately, but Brunetti would not be surprised to learn that she had lain there all night. He needed to establish in this girl's mind the importance of answering his questions so that, when he got to the ones that might lead to whoever had done this, she would answer without thinking of the consequences, perhaps for someone she knew.

Signora Gallante came back into the room, saying, 'The doctor's here, sir.'

Brunetti got to his feet and said something he tried to make comforting to the girl, then left the room. Signora Gallante went in with a glass of water in her hand. Behind her came a man who looked far too young to be a doctor, the only proof that he was, the black leather bag, obviously new, that he carried in his right hand.

10

After a few minutes, Signora Gallante came out of the bedroom and approached Brunetti and Vianello. 'The doctor suggested she stay here with me until her parents can get here from Milano and take her home.'

'Have you called them?'

'Yes. As soon as I called you.'

'Are they coming?'

'I spoke to her mother. She's been here a few times to visit Lucia, so she knew who I was. She said she'd call her husband at work, and then she called back and told me they were leaving immediately to come here.'

'How?'

'I didn't ask,' Signora Gallante said, surprised at such a question. 'But the other times they came by car, so I suppose that's how they'll come this time.'

'How long ago did you speak to them?' Brunetti asked.

'Oh, half an hour, perhaps an hour ago. It was right after I went up and found Lucia and brought her down here. I called the police first, and then I called her parents.'

Though this would limit the time Brunetti would have to speak to Lucia and complicate all future contact with her, he said, 'That was very kind of you, Signora.'

'I tried to think of what I'd want to happen if it were one of my granddaughters, and then it was easy.'

Brunetti couldn't stop himself from glancing towards the door of the bedroom. 'What did the doctor say?'

'When I told him that her parents were coming, he said he wouldn't give her a sedative, but he asked me to give her some linden tea with lots of honey. To work against the shock,' she added.

'Yes, that's a good idea,' Brunetti said, hearing footsteps outside the apartment and eager to speak to the medical examiner. 'Perhaps the Ispettore can stay here with you while you do that,' he said, with a significant glance at Vianello, who needed no urging to see to questioning Signora Gallante about Claudia or about anyone who might have visited her in her apartment.

With a polite goodbye, Brunetti left the apartment and went back upstairs. Dottor Rizzardi was already kneeling beside the dead girl, plastic-gloved fingers wrapped around her out-thrust wrist. He glanced up when he heard Brunetti come in and said, 'Not that there's any hope, but it's what the regulations require.' He looked down at the dead girl, removed his hand, and said, 'She's dead.' He allowed silence to expand from those terrible words, then got to his feet. A photographer, who had come in with the doctor, stepped close to the body and shot a few pictures, then moved in a slow circle around her, taking photos from every angle. He moved away and took one last shot from the doorway, then slipped his camera inside its case and went outside to wait for the doctor.

Knowing Rizzardi better than to suggest anything or to point to the colour of the dried blood, Brunetti asked, 'When would you say?'

'Probably some time last night, but it could have been almost any time. I won't know until I have a look at her.' Rizzardi meant 'inside her'. Both of the men knew that, but neither of them could or would say it.

Looking at her again, the doctor asked, 'Presumably, you want to know what did it?'

'Yes,' Brunetti said, moving automatically to stand beside the doctor. Rizzardi handed him a pair of transparent gloves and waited while Brunetti slipped them on.

Working together, the two men knelt and slid their hands under her body. Slowly, with the sort of gentleness with which large men usually handle babies, they raised her shoulder and then her hip and turned her over on to her back.

No knife, no instrument or implement, lay beneath her body, but the sticky holes in the front of her cotton blouse made the cause of death shockingly visible. There were, Brunetti thought at first, four of them, but then he noticed another higher up, near her shoulder. The wounds were all on the left side of her body.

Rizzardi opened the two top buttons of her shirt and pulled it aside. He glanced at the wounds, actually pulled one of them open, reminding Brunetti of some perverse poem Paola had once read to him about the wounds in Christ's body looking like lips. 'Some of these look bad enough,' Rizzardi said. 'Once I've done the autopsy, I'll be able to tell you for sure, but there's little doubt.' He closed the blouse and carefully rebuttoned it. He nodded to Brunetti and they got to their feet.

'I know it's only stupid superstition, but I'm glad her eyes are closed,' Rizzardi said. Then, with no preparation, 'I'd say you're looking for a person who isn't very tall, not much taller than she was.'

'Why?'

'The angle. It looks as if they went in more or less horizontally. If it had been a taller person, they would have gone downward at an angle, depending on how tall the killer was. I can make a rough calculation after I measure them, but that's my first guess.'

'Thanks.'

'It's precious little, I'm afraid.'

Rizzardi moved towards the door, and Brunetti followed in his wake. 'There won't be much more to tell you, but I'll call your office when I'm finished.'

'Do you have the number of Vianello's *telefonino*?'

'Yes,' Rizzardi answered. 'Why don't you have your own?'

'I do. But I keep leaving it at work or at home.'

'Why doesn't Vianello just give you his?'

'He's afraid I'll lose it.'

'My, my, hasn't the sergeant come up in the world since he became an ispettore?' Rizzardi asked, but affection glistened through the apparent sarcasm.

'It took long enough,' Brunetti said with the residual anger he felt at the years it had taken Vianello to be given what he had so long deserved.

'Scarpa?' Rizzardo asked, naming Vice-Questore Patta's personal assistant and showing just how intimate he was with the real workings of the Questura.

'Of course. He managed to block it for years, ever since he got here.'

'What changed things?'

Brunetti gazed away evasively and began to say, 'Oh, I've no . . .' but Rizzardi cut him short.

'What did you do?'

'I threatened Patta that I'd ask for a transfer to Treviso or Vicenza.'

'And?'

'He caved in.'

'Did you think that would happen?'

'No, quite the opposite. I thought he'd be happy to have the chance to get rid of me.'

'And if Patta had refused to promote him, would you have gone?'

Brunetti raised his eyebrows and pulled up the corner of his mouth in another evasion.

'Would you?'

'Yes,' Brunetti said and walked towards the door. 'Call me when you're done, all right?'

Back downstairs, Brunetti found Vianello in the kitchen, sitting opposite Signora Gallante, a white porcelain teapot and a jar of honey between them. Each had a cup of yellow tea. Signora Gallante started to get to her feet when she saw Brunetti, but Vianello leaned across the table and put a hand on her arm. 'Stay there, Signora. I'll get the Commissario a cup.'

He got up and with the sort of ease that usually comes with long familiarity, opened a cabinet and pulled down a cup and saucer. He sat them in front of the now-seated Brunetti and turned back to open a drawer and get him a spoon. Silently, he poured out a cup of linden tea and took his place again across from the Signora.

Vianello said, 'The Signora's just been telling me a bit about Signorina Leonardo, sir.' Signora Gallante nodded. 'She said she was a good girl, very considerate and thoughtful.'

'Oh, yes, sir,' the old woman interrupted. 'She used to come down here for tea once in a while, and she always asked me about my grandchildren, even asked to see pictures of them. They never made any noise, she and Lucia: study, study, study; it seems that's all they ever did.'

'Didn't friends ever visit them?' Vianello asked when Brunetti made no move to do so.

'No. Once in a while I'd see a young person on the steps, a boy or a girl, but they never caused any trouble. You know how students like to study together. My sons always did that when they were in school, but they made a lot more noise, I'm afraid.' She started to smile, but then remembering just what had brought these two men to her table, her smile faded and she picked up her teacup.

'You said you met Lucia's mother, Signora,' Brunetti began. 'Did you ever meet Signor and Signora Leonardo?'

'No, that's impossible. They're both gone, you know.' When she saw Brunetti's confusion, she tried to explain. 'That is, her father's dead. She told me he died when she was just a little girl.'

When Signora Gallante said nothing else, Brunetti asked, 'And the mother?'

'Oh, I don't know. Claudia never spoke about her, but I always had the sense that she was gone.'

'Do you mean dead, Signora?'

'No, no, not exactly. Oh, I don't know what I mean. It's just that Claudia never said she was dead; she just made it sound like she was gone, as if she was somewhere else and was never coming back.' She thought for a moment, as if trying to recall conversations with the girl. 'It was all very strange, now that I think about it. She usually used the past tense when she spoke about her mother, but once she spoke of her as though she were still alive.'

'Do you remember what she said?' Vianello asked.

'No, no, I can't. I'm very sorry, gentlemen, but I just can't. It was something about liking something, a colour or a food or something like that. Not a specific thing like a book or a movie or an actor, just something general; now that I think about it, it might have been a colour, and she said something like, "My mother likes . . ." and then she said the name of the colour, whatever it was, perhaps blue. I really don't remember, but I know I thought at the time how strange it was that she spoke of her as though she were still alive.'

'Did you ask her about it?'

'Oh, no. Claudia wasn't the sort of girl you could ask. If she wanted you to know something, she'd tell you. Otherwise, she spoke of other things or just ignored the question.'

'Did that offend you?' Vianello asked.

'Perhaps at first, but then I realized what she was like and that there was nothing I could do about it. Besides, I liked her so much it didn't matter, didn't matter at all.' Signora Gallante picked up her cup and held it to her mouth, lowering her face as if to drink from it, but then the tears got the better of her and she had to put the cup down and reach for a handkerchief. 'I don't think I want to talk about this any more, gentlemen.'

'Of course, Signora,' Brunetti said, finishing his tea, which had grown cold while they talked. 'I'll just see if the doctor's finished and have a word with Lucia if that's possible.'

Signora Gallante clearly disapproved of this, but she said nothing and busied herself with wiping away her tears.

Brunetti went to the door of the bedroom and knocked, then knocked again. After a time, the door was opened by the doctor, who put his head out and asked, 'Yes?'

'I'd like to speak to Signorina Mazzotti, Dottore, if that's possible.'

'I'll ask her,' the doctor said and closed the door in Brunetti's face. After a few minutes he pulled the door open and his head appeared again. 'She doesn't want to talk to anyone.'

'Dottore, would you explain to her that what we want to do is find the person who killed her friend. I know Signorina Mazzotti's parents are on their way from Milano to take her home, and as soon as that happens it will be very difficult to speak to her.' Brunetti didn't mention the fact that he had the legal right to forbid her to leave the city. Instead, he added, 'We'd be very grateful if she'd agree to talk to us now. It would help us a great deal.'

The doctor nodded his understanding and, Brunetti thought, his sympathy and closed the door again.

When, at least five minutes later, the doctor opened the door again, Lucia Mazzotti stood behind him. She was taller and thinner than he'd thought and now, seeing her full face, he saw just how pretty she was. The doctor held the door for her and she stepped out into the corridor. Brunetti led her into the sitting room and waited while she took a seat on a straight-backed chair. 'Would you like the doctor to stay here while we talk, Signorina?' he asked.

She nodded, then said yes in a very soft voice.

The doctor sat on the edge of a sofa. He set his bag on the floor at his feet and leaned back, silent and still.

Brunetti took another straight-backed chair and placed it about a metre from Lucia's chair, careful to arrange it so that she remained in shadow and his face in the light that came in from the window behind her. He wanted to create as much of an atmosphere of openness as he could between them to relax her into speaking easily. He smiled in what he hoped was a reassuring way. She had the green eyes so common to redheads, red-rimmed now from crying.

'I want to tell you how very sorry I am about this, Signorina,' he began. 'Signora Gallante has been telling us what a sweet girl Claudia was. I'm sure it's very painful for you to lose such a good friend.'

Lucia bowed her head and nodded.

'Could you tell me a little bit about your friendship? How long have you shared the apartment?'

The girl's voice was soft, almost inaudible, but Brunetti, by leaning forward, managed to hear. 'I moved in about a year ago. Claudia and I were enrolled in the same faculty, so we took some classes together, and so when her other flatmate decided to leave school, she asked me if I wanted to take over her room.'

'How long had Claudia been here?'

'I don't know. A year or two before I came.'

'From Milano, is that correct?'

The girl was still looking at the floor, but she nodded in assent.

'Do you know where Claudia came from?'

'I think from here.'

At first Brunetti wasn't sure he had heard her correctly. 'Venice?' he asked.

'Yes, sir. But she was in school in Rome before she came here.'

'But she was renting her own apartment, not living with her parents?'

'I don't think she had any parents,' Lucia said but then, as if aware of how strange that must sound, she looked directly at Brunetti for the first time and added, 'I mean, I think they're dead.'

'Both of them?'

'Her father, yes. I know that because she told me.'

'And her mother?'

Lucia had to consider this. 'I'm not sure about her mother. I always assumed she was dead, too, but Claudia never said.'

'Did it ever strike you as strange that people as young as her parents probably were could both be dead?'

Lucia shook her head.

'Did Claudia have many friends?'

'Friends?'

'Classmates, people who came here to study or perhaps to have a meal or just talk.'

'Some kids from our faculty would come over to study sometimes, but there was no one special.'

'Did she have a boyfriend?'

'You mean a *fidanzato*?' Lucia asked in a tone that made it clear she had not.

'That, or just a boyfriend she went out with occasionally.'

Again, a negative motion of her head.

'Is there anyone at all you can think of that she was close to?'

Lucia gave this some thought before she answered, 'The only person I ever heard her talk about, or talk to on the phone, was a woman she called her grandmother, but who wasn't.'

'Is this the woman called Hedi?' Brunetti asked, wondering what Lucia's response would be to learning that the police already knew about this woman.

Obviously, Lucia found it not at all strange that the police should know, for she answered, 'Yes, I think she was German, or Austrian. That's what they spoke when they talked on the phone.'

'Do you speak German, Lucia?' he asked, using her name for the first time and hoping that his familiarity would sooth her into answering more easily.

'No, sir. I never knew what they were talking about.'

'Were you curious?'

She seemed surprised at the question: whatever could be interesting in conversation between her flatmate and an old foreign woman?

'Did you ever see this woman?'

'No. Claudia went to see her, though. Sometimes she'd bring home cookies or a kind of cake with almonds in it. I never asked about it, just assumed she'd brought it from her.'

'Why did you think that, Lucia?'

'Oh, I don't know. Maybe because no one I know bakes things like that. With cinnamon and nuts.'

Brunetti nodded.

'Can you remember anything Claudia might ever have said about her?'

'What sort of thing?'

'About how it was that she was her, well, her adoptive grandmother? Or where she lived?'

'I think she must live in the city.'

'Why, Lucia?'

'Because the times she brought back the things to eat, she was never gone for a long time. I mean, not time to get to somewhere else and come back.' She considered this for a while and then said, 'It couldn't even have been the Lido. I mean, it could have been, because you can get to the Lido and back in a short time, but I remember Claudia once said – I forget what we were talking about – that she hadn't been to the Lido for years.'

Brunetti started to ask another question, but suddenly Lucia turned to the doctor and asked, 'Doctor, do I have to answer any more questions?'

Without consulting Brunetti for an answer, the young man said, 'Not unless you want to, Signorina.'

'I don't want to,' she said. 'That's all I want to say.' She looked at the doctor when she spoke, ignoring Brunetti entirely.

Resigning himself to the fact that any further questioning would have to be done in Milano or by phone, Brunetti got to his feet and said, 'I'm very grateful for your help.' Then turning to the doctor, 'For yours, too, Dottore.'

To both of them together, he said, 'Signora Gallante has made tea, and I'm sure she'd be very happy to give you some.' He walked towards the door of the apartment, turned back briefly as if about to say something, but changed his mind and left.

11

Vianello joined him on the stairway. 'Shall we go back to the apartment, sir?' he asked.

By way of an answer, Brunetti started back upstairs. The uniformed officer was still at the door when they arrived and said, when they reached the top of the steps, 'They've taken her away, sir.'

'You can go back to the Questura, then,' Brunetti told him and went inside. The rug was still there in the centre of the room, the discoloured fringe lying smooth now, as though someone had combed it. Brunetti took the gloves from the pocket of his jacket and slipped them on again. The grey puffs of powder that covered the surfaces of the furniture offered silent evidence that the technical squad had been through the apartment and had dusted for prints.

No matter how many times Brunetti had gone through the artefacts that no longer belonged to the dead, he could never free himself of the uneasiness with which it filled him. He poked and prodded, fingered, plucked and pried into the material secrets left behind by those taken off by sudden death, and no matter how much he willed himself to remain dispassionate about what he did, he never managed to avoid the rush of excitement that came with the discovery of what he sought: is this what a voyeur feels? he wondered.

Vianello disappeared in the direction of the bedrooms, and Brunetti remained in the living room, conscious of how reluctantly he turned his back on the place where she had lain. Just where it should have been, he found a small book of telephone numbers placed neatly on top of the city phone book and to the left of the telephone. He opened it and began to read. It was not until he got to the Js that he found what might be what he was looking for: 'Jacobs'. He paged through the rest of the book but, aside from listings for 'plumber' and 'computers', 'Jacobs' was the only listing that was not a surname ending in a vowel. Further, the number began with 52 and had no out-of-city prefix written in front of it, as had some of the other numbers. He toyed for a moment with the idea of calling the number, but if Claudia had been dear to this woman, then the telephone was not the way to do it.

Instead, he flipped open the phone book and found the few listings under that letter. There it was, 'Jacobs, H.', with an address in Santa Croce. After that, his instinct that he had already found what was most important prevented him from taking much interest in the rest of his search of the apartment. Vianello, emerging from his search of Lucia's room, said only, 'Signorina Lucia seems to divide her time between histories of the Byzantine Empire and Harmony Romances.'

Brunetti, who had told Vianello about Claudia's visit to his office and her strange request for information, said, 'I think I've found the missing grandmother.'

Reaching into the pocket of his jacket for his *telefonino*, the Inspector asked, 'Would you like to call her first and tell her you're coming?'

Brunetti waved away the offer and resisted the temptation to point out to Vianello that they were standing just beside a telephone and that his phone was unnecessary. 'No. She'd worry if I told her it was the police, and then I'd have to tell her, anyway. Better to go and talk to her directly.'

'Would you like me to come with you?' Vianello asked.

'No, that's all right. Go and have lunch. Besides, it might be better for her if there's only one of us. Before you go, see what you can find out from other people in the building what they know about the girls and if they saw or heard anything last night. Tomorrow we can begin asking questions at the university: my wife might be able to tell me something about the girl, who her friends were, her other professors. When you get back to the Questura, ask Signorina Elettra what she can find out about Claudia Leonardo or this woman, Hedi – I suppose that's Hedwig – Jacobs. She might as well see if there's anything about Luca Guzzardi.'

'She'll be glad of the work, I think,' Vianello said in a tone that failed to be neutral.

'Good. Then tell her I want anything at all she can find, even if it goes back to the war.'

Vianello started to say something else, perhaps about Signorina Elettra, but he stopped and instead said only, 'I'll tell her.'

Brunetti knew that the address in Santa Croce had to be somewhere near San Giacomo dell'Orio, so he walked to the Accademia and took the Number One to San Stae. From there, instinct took over and he soon entered Campo San Boldo. In the *campo* he saw that the numbers were close to the one he was looking for, so he stopped in a *tabacchaio* and asked for directions. When the man said he wasn't sure, Brunetti explained he was looking for an old Austrian woman. The shopkeeper smiled and answered, 'Keeps me in business, Signora Hedi, and keeps me hopping, taking them up to her. Smokes like a Turk. You've walked past her place. Go out, turn right, and hers is the third door'

He did as he was told and saw, beside the second door on

the left, the name 'Jacobs'. As he raised his hand to ring the bell, Brunetti felt a wave of momentary exhaustion sweep over him. He had done this too many times, brought so much terrible news, and he felt an overwhelming reluctance to do it again. How easy it would be if victims never had relatives, were always people who were solitary and unloved and whose death would not radiate out, swamping the small boats around them, washing up more victims on the shoals of life.

Knowing that he was helpless to dismiss this feeling, he waited for it to pass and a few minutes later he rang the bell. After some time, a deep voice, but still a woman's voice, called over the entry phone, 'Who is it?'

'I've come to talk to you, Signora Jacobs,' was the best he could think of.

'I don't talk to people,' she answered and replaced the phone.

Brunetti rang the bell again, keeping his finger on it until he heard her demand, 'Who are you?' The tone was peremptory, without uncertainty or fear.

'I'm Commissario Guido Brunetti, Signora, from the police. I've come to talk to you.'

There followed a long pause. Finally, she asked, 'About what?'

'Claudia Leonardo.'

The noise he heard, or thought he heard, could simply have been static; it could just as easily have been her breathing. The door snapped open and he went in. The floor of the entrance hall was green with mould, lit only by a dim bulb in a filthy glass case. He started up the stairs, the green of the mould growing lighter as he rose. At the first landing there was another bulb, no brighter, which dimly illuminated the octagonal marble medallions that patterned the floor. A single door, a thick metal *porta blindata*, stood open to his left and just inside it was a tall, painfully stooped woman, her white hair arranged in an elaborate crown of braids of the sort he was familiar with from photos from the Thirties and Forties. She leaned forward, her hands wrapped around the ivory handle of a walking stick. Her eyes were grey with just the faintest touch of the cloudiness of age, but no less filled with suspicion for that.

'I'm afraid I have very bad news for you, Signora Jacobs,' he said, halting outside the door. He watched her face for some response, but she gave none.

'You better come inside to give it to me so I can be sitting down when I hear it,' she said. The longer sentence exposed the Teutonic underpinnings of her speech. 'It's my heart, and I'm not at all steady on my feet any more. I need to sit.'

She turned back into the apartment. Brunetti closed the door and followed her. His first breath proved to him that the tobacco dealer was right: if he could have walked into an ashtray, the smell would have been no stronger. He wondered when a window had last been opened in this apartment, so pervasive was the sour smell.

She led him down a wide corridor, and at first Brunetti kept his eyes on her retreating back, concerned that even the thought of bad news might cause her to falter or fall. But she seemed to proceed steadily, if slowly, so he began to pay attention to his surroundings. Looking around him, he stopped dead, assaulted by the beauty he saw spread around him as if by a profligate hand.

The walls on either side of the corridor were crowded with rows of paintings and drawings, lined up shoulder to shoulder like people waiting for a bus. Like those random waiters, the paintings in no way resembled one another: he saw what had to be a small Degas of the familiar seated dancer; what looked like a pear but only a pear as Cézanne could paint a pear; a thick-lidded Madonna of the Sienese school; and what was surely one of Goya's drawings of a firing squad.

As he stood, petrified as Lot's wife, a voice said from

somewhere to his left, 'Are you going to come and tell me what it is you have to say, Commissario?'

He turned away from the pictures, eyes skimming over what might have been a tiny Memling, a set of Otto Dix drawings, and an unidentifiable and particularly unerotic nude, and followed the voice into the living room. Again his senses were assaulted: the smell was heavier, thicker, so strong that he could feel it beginning to sink into the cloth of his jacket; and the objects on display had lost even the negligible order imposed upon those along the walls of the corridor. One entire wall was covered with Persian or Indian miniatures in gold frames: there must have been thirty of them. The wall to his left held three tiles that even his eye could distinguish as Iznik as well as a large collection of other Middle Eastern ceramic plates and tiles, but the same wall also held a life-sized wooden crucifix. To his right he saw pen and ink drawings, but before he could begin to examine them closely, his attention was drawn to the old woman as she sank heavily into a velvet-covered armchair.

The chair stood in the centre of a carpet that appeared to be an Esfahani: only fine silk would give the luminous sheen in the small portion at the far end that he could see. All trace of silk, in fact all trace of anything at all, was obscured by a wide arc of ground-in ash that spread in a half-circle beneath and in front of her chair. Automatically, with a gesture that seemed as instinctive and rhythmic as breathing, she took a blue packet of Nazionali from the top of the table beside her and lit one with a cheap plastic lighter.

After she had inhaled deeply, she said, 'Will you tell me now what it is you've come to tell me?'

'It's Claudia Leonardo,' he said. 'She's been killed.'

The hand with the cigarette fell, as if forgotten, beside her. She closed her eyes and, had her spine permitted it, her head would have fallen against the back of the high chair. Instead, the gesture merely raised her head until she was looking directly across at him. When he noticed that the angle seemed difficult for her, he moved a chair opposite her and sat down so that she could lower her head and still see him clearly.

'Oh, God. I thought it couldn't happen,' she said under her breath, perhaps not even conscious that she had spoken out loud. She stared a moment longer at Brunetti, then raised a hand with an effort and covered her eyes.

Brunetti was about to ask her what she meant when he noticed smoke rising from beside her. Immediately, he stood and moved towards her. She seemed not the least interested in the sudden, possibly menacing, action. Brunetti picked up the cigarette and stabbed with his foot at the smouldering patch of silk.

Signora Jacobs seemed entirely unaware that he was there, or of what he was doing. 'Are you all right, Signora?' he said, placing one hand on her shoulder. She gave no sign that she heard him. 'Signora,' he repeated, increasing the pressure of his hand.

The hand she held across her eyes slapped down on to her lap, but her eyes remained closed. He moved away from her a little, willing her to open them. When she did, she said, 'In the kitchen. Pills on the table.'

He ran towards the back of the apartment and down another corridor, this one lined with books. He saw a sink through a door on the left, tossed her cigarette into it and grabbed the single bottle of pills that stood on the table. He paused to fill a glass with water and went back to her. He handed her the bottle and waited while she opened it and tipped out two white pills the size of aspirin. She put them into her mouth and held up a hand to reject the proffered glass of water. She closed her eyes again and sat, utterly quiet. When he saw her relax and some hint of colour begin to seep into her face, he was unable to resist the temptation to look again at the walls.

He was used to manifestations of great wealth, though his perhaps stubborn insistence that the family live on their salaries alone kept the opulence of the Falier family at bay. Nevertheless a few paintings – personal possessions of Paola's, like the Canaletto in the kitchen – had managed to slip into the house, in the manner of homeless cats on rainy nights. He was familiar with his father-in-law's collection, as well as those of some of the Count's friends, to make no mention of what he had observed in the homes of wealthy suspects he had questioned. Nothing he had previously seen, however, could have prepared him for this grandiose promiscuity: paintings, ceramics, carvings, prints jostled one another as if competing for pride of place. Order did not exist, but beauty overwhelmed him.

He glanced at Signora Jacobs and saw that she was looking at him as she groped for her cigarettes. He moved around the chair and sat down again while she lit a cigarette and drew on it deeply, almost defiantly. 'What happened?'

'Her flatmate came home this morning and found her in the apartment. She was dead, probably killed some time yesterday evening.'

'How?'

'Stabbed'

'Who did it?'

'It might have been a thief or a burglar.' Even as he spoke, he realized how unconvincing this sounded.

'Things like that don't happen here,' she said. Without bothering to look to see if there were an ashtray beside her, she flicked the ash from her cigarette on to the carpet at her feet.

'No, they usually don't, Signora. But so far we've found nothing that might suggest another explanation.'

'What have you found?' she demanded, surprising him by the speed with which she had recovered her composure.

'Her address book.'

Intelligence flared in her pale eyes. 'And I just happened to be the first person you came to see?'

'No, Signora. I came to see you because, in a sense, I already knew about you.'

'Knew what about me?' she asked, unsuccessfully attempting to disguise the alarm anyone in Italy would feel at the idea that the police knew something about them.

'That Claudia thought of you as her grandmother and that you wanted her to find out about obtaining an official reversal of the conviction of someone who had died on San Servolo.' He saw no reason to hide this from her: sooner or later he would have to question her about this and he might as well begin now, while the shock of what she had just learned might lower her resistance to answering questions of any sort.

She dropped the cigarette on to the carpet and stamped it out, then immediately lit another. Her gestures were slow and careful: she must be, he estimated, well into her eighties. She took three hungry puffs at the cigarette, as though she had not just finished the other. Without asking, Brunetti got up and went to a table behind her and returned with the lid of a jar, which seemed to serve as an ashtray. He set it beside her.

Not bothering to thank him, she said, 'Are you the person she talked to?'

'Yes.'

'I told her to go to a lawyer. I offered to pay for it.'

'She did. He told her it would cost her five million lire.'

She sniffed at the sum, condemning it to eternal insignificance. 'So she came to you?'

'In a way, Signora. First she went to my wife, who is one of her professors at the university, and asked her to ask me. But Claudia was apparently not satisfied with the answer I asked my wife to give her, so she came to the Questura to ask me directly.'

'Yes, she'd do that,' the woman said with a smile that barely touched her lips but warmed her voice. 'What did you tell her when you spoke to her?'

'Essentially what I'd told my wife: that I couldn't give an answer until I had a clearer idea of the crime involved.'

'Did she tell you who it was for?' the woman asked, this time failing to keep the suspicion from her voice.

'No,' Brunetti said. It was a lie, but taking unfair advantage of a sick old woman in shock at the death of someone she loved was just part of the job, after all.

The woman turned her eyes away from him and looked at the wall to her right, the one covered with ceramics. It seemed to Brunetti that she did not see them and was unaware of any of the objects in the room. When she hadn't spoken for a long time, he was no longer sure that she was aware of his presence.

Finally she turned back to him. 'I think that's all,' she said.

'I beg your pardon?' Brunetti asked politely, genuinely not understanding what she meant.

'That's all. That's all I want to know, and that's all I want to say to you.'

'I wish it were that simple, Signora,' he said with real sympathy. 'But I'm afraid you have little choice. This is a murder investigation, and you have the duty to answer questions put to you by the police.'

She laughed. It was a noise devoid of all possibility of amusement or pleasure, but it seemed the only response she could find to a statement which was, to her, so obviously absurd.

'Signor Commissario,' she said, 'I am eighty-three years old, and as my need for those pills ought to have shown you, I am in poor health.' Before he could respond, she went on, 'Even more fortunate, at least in the face of my refusal to speak to you further, is the fact that there does not exist the doctor who would not certify that any questions you might ask me in this matter would put my life at risk.'

'You make it sound as if you don't believe it,' he observed.

'Oh, I do believe it. I was raised in a school far harder than you Italians have any concept of, and I therefore have never been a crybaby, but, believe me, if you could feel how my heart is pounding now, you would know that this is true. Your questions would put my life at risk. I mention the doctor only to make clear to you the lengths to which I will go in order not to continue to speak to you.'

'Is it the questions that would put your life in danger, Signora, or the answers?'

Suddenly aware that her cigarette had gone out, she tossed it to the floor and reached for the packet. 'You can see yourself out, Commissario,' she said, her voice rich with the command that lingers after a youth spent in a house where there are many servants.

12

Brunetti's work had exposed him to the many forms in which despair manifested itself, and so he wasted no more time in what he knew would be a vain attempt to persuade Signora Jacobs to tell him more about the murdered girl.

He left her apartment and decided to walk back to the Questura, using the time to wonder how, even if, the old woman and her link to the Guzzardis might be connected to Claudia's death. Why should criminal actions committed decades before the girl's birth be connected to what might have been a simple robbery gone wrong? Simple thieves, the voice of experience and habitual scepticism whispered in his ear, do not carry knives, and simple thieves do not murder the people who discover them at their work; push them aside, perhaps, in attempting to flee, but not stab them until they are dead.

He found himself looking across at the campanile of San Giorgio, studying the angel who perched atop it, restored now after having been blasted to flame by lightning some years ago. Realizing that he must have walked past the

Questura without noticing where he was, he turned and went back towards San Lorenzo. The officer at the door saluted him normally and gave no sign that he had seen his superior walk by a few minutes ago.

Brunetti paused outside Signorina Elettra's office and peered inside, relieved to see an abundance of flowers on the windowsill. A step further confirmed his hope that more of them stood on her desk: yellow roses, at least two dozen of them. How he had prayed in the last months that she be returned to her shameless depredation of the city's finances by claiming these exploding bouquets as ordinary office expenses. Every bud, every blossom was rich with the odour of the misappropriation of public funds; Brunetti breathed in deeply and sighed in relief.

She sat, as he had hoped, behind her desk, and he was happy to see she was wearing a green cashmere sweater; he was even happier to see that she was reading a magazine. 'What is it today, Signorina?' he asked, '*Famiglia Cristiana*?'

She looked up but she did not smile. 'No, sir, I always give that to my aunt.'

'Is she religious?' Brunetti inquired.

'No, sir. She has a parakeet.' She shut the magazine, preventing him from seeing what it was. He hoped it was *Vogue*.

'Has Vianello told you?' he asked.

'Poor girl. How old was she?'

'I'm not sure, no more than twenty.'

Neither commented on the awful waste.

'He said she was one of your wife's students.'

Brunetti nodded. 'I've just been to see an old woman who knew her.'

'Do you have any idea of what happened?'

'It could have been a robbery.' When he saw her reaction, he added, 'Or it could have been something else entirely.'

'Such as?'

'Boyfriend. Drugs.'

'Vianello said you had spoken to her,' Signorina Elettra said. 'Does either of those seem possible?'

'My first impulse is to say no, but I don't understand the world any more. Anything is possible. Of anyone.'

'Do you really believe that, sir?' she asked, and her tone suggested that her question held greater significance than his remark, which he had made without thinking.

'No,' he said after some thought. 'I suppose I don't believe it. In the end, there are some people it makes sense to trust.'

'Why?'

He had no idea where this line of questioning had come from nor where it might lead them, but he sensed the seriousness with which she was pursuing it. 'Because there are some people, still, who can be trusted absolutely. We have to believe that's so.'

'Why?'

'Because if we don't find at least someone we can trust absolutely, then, well, we're made less by not having them. And by not having the experience of trusting them.' He wasn't exactly sure what he meant by this, or perhaps he was just doing a bad job of explaining what it was he did mean, but he knew he felt that he would be a lesser man if there were no one into whose hands he would put himself.

Before he could say or she could ask anything else, the phone rang. She answered it, 'Yes, sir.' She glanced at Brunetti, and this time she did smile. 'Yes, he's just come in, sir. I'll send him in.'

Brunetti wasn't sure if he were relieved or disappointed to have their conversation cut off like this, but he didn't think he could linger to continue it, not once Vice-Questore Patta had been alerted to his arrival.

'If I'm not out in fifteen minutes,' he said, 'call the police.'

She nodded and opened the magazine.

*

Patta sat at his desk, seeming neither pleased nor displeased and looking, as he always did, so suited to a position of responsibility and authority that his promotion could have been the result of natural law. Seeing him, Brunetti realized how used he was to searching for signs of what was to come in Patta's expression, like an augur examining the kidneys of a freshly slaughtered chicken. 'Yes, sir,' he said, taking the seat towards which Patta waved him.

'What's all this about a dead girl, Brunetti?' Patta asked, short of a demand but somewhere past a question.

'She was stabbed to death some time last night, sir. I'll know more about the time after Dottor Rizzardi gives me his report.'

'Did she have a boyfriend?' Patta asked.

'Not that either her landlady or her flatmate knew of,' Brunetti replied calmly.

'Have you excluded the possibility of robbery?' Patta asked, surprising Brunetti by the suggestion that he did not want to attribute her death to the most obvious cause.

'No, sir.'

'What have you done?' Patta asked, not forgetting to come down heavily on the second word.

Deciding that intentions and deeds were interchangeable, at least while he was speaking to his superior, Brunetti said: 'I've got men questioning the neighbours, asking if they saw anything last night; Signorina Elettra is checking phone records for the girls' apartment; I've already interviewed the girl she shared the apartment with, but she was still too shocked to be of much help; and we've begun asking her friends at the university what they know about her.' Brunetti hoped he'd succeed in getting all of these things in train that afternoon.

'Is that inspector of yours working on this with you?' Patta asked.

Brunetti bit back a remark about the possible ownership of

Lieutenant Scarpa and contented himself with a simple, 'Yes, sir.'

'Right, then, I want you to get this taken care of as quickly as possible. The *Gazzettino* is sure to splash it all over the front page; I just hope the nationals don't pick it up. God knows, enough girls get themselves stabbed to death in other places and no one pays attention. But it's still something of a sensation here, so I suppose we have to prepare ourselves for some bad publicity, at least until people forget about it.' Sighing as if in resignation to yet another of the cares of office, Patta pulled some folders toward him and said, 'That will be all, Commissario.' Brunetti stood but found himself unable to leave. He stood so long that Patta finally looked up at him and said, 'Yes, what is it?'

'It's nothing sir. All this bad publicity is a shame, though.'

'Yes, it is, isn't it?' Patta agreed and turned his attention to the first folder. Brunetti devoted his to getting out of Patta's office without opening his mouth.

He recalled, then, something he had seen with Paola, it must have been four years ago. They'd been at an exhibition of the paintings of the Colombian painter, Botero, she drawn to the wild exuberance of his portraits of fat, pie-faced men and women, all possessed of the same tiny rosebud mouth. In front of them was a teacher with a class of children who couldn't have been more than eight or nine. As he and Paola came into the last room of the exhibition, they heard the teacher say, 'Now, *ragazzi*, we're going to leave, but there are a lot of people here who don't want to be disturbed by our noise or talking. So what we're all going to do,' she went on, pointing to her own mouth, which she pursed up into a tight, tiny circle, 'is make *la bocca di Botero*.' Delighted, the children all placed single fingers on their lips and drew their mouths into tight imitations of those in the paintings as they tiptoed giggling from the room. Since then, whenever either he or Paola knew that to speak might be indiscreet, they invoked '*la bocca di Botero'*, and no doubt thus saved themselves a great deal of trouble, to make no mention of time and wasted energy.

Signorina Elettra had apparently finished the magazine, for he found her leafing through the papers in a file. 'Signorina,' he began, 'I've a number of things I'd like you to do.'

'Yes, sir?' she said, closing the file and making no attempt to cover either the CONFIDENTIAL sticker that ran in bold red letters down the left side of the front cover nor Lieutenant Scarpa's name, which appeared across the top.

'A little light reading?' he inquired.

'Very,' she said with audible disdain, pushing the file to the side of her desk. 'What is it you'd like me to do, sir?'

'Ask your friend at Telecom to see if he can get you a list of calls to and from their phone, and see if either she or Lucia Mazzotti – the flatmate – has a *telefonino*. And see what you can find out about Claudia: if she has a credit card or a bank account. Any financial information would help.'

'Did you search her apartment?' she interrupted to ask.

'Not well, not then. But a team will take care of it this afternoon.'

'Good, then I'll have them bring me any papers they find.'

'Yes. Good,' he said.

'Anything else?' she asked.

'No, not that I can think of now. We don't know much yet. If you find anything interesting in the papers, follow it up.' He read her expression and explained, 'Letters from a boyfriend. If people write letters any more, that is.' Even before she could ask, he said, 'Yes, tell them to bring you her computer, as well.'

'And you, sir?' she asked.

Instead of answering, he looked at his watch, suddenly aware of how hungry he was. 'I'm going to call my wife,' he said. He turned away, saying, 'Then I'll be in my office, waiting for Rizzardi.'

The doctor didn't call until well after five, by which time Brunetti was cranky from hunger and annoyed at sitting and waiting.

'It's me, Guido,' Rizzardi said.

Speaking without impatience, Brunetti asked only, 'And?'

'Two of the stab wounds would have killed her: both of them nicked the heart. She would have died almost instantly.'

'And the killer? Do you still think it was someone short?'

'Well, not someone tall, certainly not as tall as you or I. Perhaps a bit taller than the girl herself. And right handed.'

'Does this mean it could have been a woman?' Brunetti asked.

'Of course, though women usually don't kill like this.' After a moment's reflection, the pathologist added, 'Women don't usually kill at all, do they?'

Brunetti grunted in agreement, wondering if Rizzardi's remark could be interpreted as a compliment to the sex, and, if so, what that said about human nature. The doctor's next remark called him back from these reflections. 'I think she was a virgin.'

'What?' Brunetti asked.

'You heard me, Guido. A virgin.'

There was silence as they considered this, then Brunetti asked, 'Anything else?'

'She didn't smoke, appeared to be in excellent health.' He paused here and Brunetti had an instant to hope that Rizzardi wouldn't say it. But he did. 'She could have lived another sixty years.'

'Thanks, Ettore,' Brunetti said and replaced the receiver.

Irritable once again, Brunetti felt he could relieve his feelings only by activity, so he walked down to the crime lab, where he asked to see the things brought in from Claudia Leonardo's apartment.

'Signorina Elettra has her address book,' said Bocchese, the chief technician, placing a number of plastic bags on his desk.

As Brunetti picked the bags up by the corners, Bocchese said dismissively, 'You can touch anything you want. I've dusted the lot, but there's only two sets of prints on everything, hers and her flatmate's.'

Brunetti opened a large envelope which itself contained a number of papers and smaller envelopes. There were the usual things: gas and electric bills, an invitation to a gallery opening, phone bills, credit card receipts. Toward the back of the small packet of papers he found a bank statement, and he read down through the column of deposits. On the first of each month, ten million lire was deposited in Claudia's account. He checked, and there was the same deposit every month since the beginning of the year. It took little skill in arithmetic to arrive at the annual total, a staggering amount to find in a student's account. Yet it wasn't *in* the account: her current balance was little more than three million lire, which meant that this young girl had, during the course of the last ten months, disposed of almost a hundred million lire.

He studied the statement: on the third of every month, money was transferred from Claudia's account to that of Loredana Gallante, the landlady. The utilities were paid by direct debit. And, each month, with no particular pattern in the date or amount, large transfers in varying amounts were made, though they were listed only as 'Foreign transfers'.

The monthly deposits were explained as 'Transfer from foreign source'. Nothing more. He extracted the bank statement from the stack of papers and asked Bocchese, 'Do I have to sign for this?'

'I think you better, Commissario,' Bocchese replied, opening a drawer and pulling out a thick ledger. He flipped it open, wrote something, then turned the book towards Brunetti. 'Sign here, sir. With the date, as well, if you don't mind.' Neither of them commented on Bocchese's continuing, but unsuccessful, attempts to have a photocopy machine assigned to his office.

Brunetti did as he was told, folded the bank statement and slipped it into his jacket pocket.

The banks were already closed, and when he went back to her office he saw that Signorina Elettra had already left. Her magazine was lying closed and face down on her desk, but Brunetti could not bring himself to flip it over to read the cover. He did, however, move around her desk and bend over to read the title on the spine. *Vogue*. He smiled, glad to see this small piece of evidence that Signorina Elettra was once again devoting to Vice-Questore Patta precisely the amount of attention she judged him to deserve.

13

It wasn't until next morning that Brunetti could begin to satisfy his curiosity about the flow of money into and out of Claudia Leonardo's account. This was quickly handled by a phone call to the local office of the Banca di Perugia. For years, Brunetti had been intrigued to observe that, of all the people made nervous by a phone call from the police, bankers seemed to suffer the most. It led him to wonder what it was they got up to behind their broad desks or inside their thick-walled vaults. Before he could pursue this idea further, he was connected to the Director, who passed him along to one of the tellers, who asked for the account number. It took only a few minutes for her to explain that the transfers came in from a bank in Geneva and had been coming in on the first of every month since the account was opened three years ago, presumably when Claudia came to Venice to begin her studies.

Brunetti thanked her and asked that he be faxed copies of all statements for the last three years, which the teller said would arrive that same morning. Again, he hardly needed paper and pencil to calculate the sum: almost four hundred million lire, and now there remained less than three million in the account. How could a young girl spend over three hundred million lire in three years? He cast his memory back to the apartment, hunting for signs of great expenditure, but he recalled none. In fact, his guess would be that the flat was rented already furnished, for surely a woman of Signora Gallante's generation would have bought the huge mahogany wardrobes he'd seen in both bedrooms. Rizzardi would have noticed and commented upon any sign of drug use, but what other than drugs could absorb such huge sums of money?

He called down to Bocchese, who told him the names of the officers who had searched the apartment, but when he spoke to them they said that neither girl's clothing had seemed out of the ordinary in quality or quantity and thus could not explain the disappearance of so much money.

For a moment he was tempted to call Rizzardi and ask if he had checked the body for evidence of drug use but stopped himself by imagining what the doctor's response would be. If he'd said nothing, then there was nothing.

He called Paola at home. 'It's me,' he said unnecessarily.

'And what can I do for me?' she asked.

'How would you spend three hundred and sixty million lire in three years?' he asked.

'My own or stolen?' she asked, making it clear that she assumed this to be a work-related question.

'What difference does that make?'

'I'd spend stolen money differently.'

'Why?'

'Because it's different; that's all. I mean, it's not as if I would have worked for it or struggled to earn it. It's like money you find on the street or win on the lottery. You spend it much more easily, or at least I think you would.'

'And how would you spend it?'

'Is that a general "you", as in "a person" or is it for me, personally?'

'Both.'

'For me, personally, I'd buy first editions of Henry James.'

Ignoring this reference to the person Brunetti had, over the course of years, come to view as the other man in his wife's life, Brunetti asked, 'And if you were just a person in general?'

'That would depend on the person, I guess. The most obvious is drugs, but the fact that you're calling me to ask for ideas suggest you've already excluded that possibility. Some people would buy expensive cars or designer clothes, or, oh, I don't know, vacations.'

'No, it was taken out month by month, seldom in one big lump,' he said, remembering the pattern of deposit and withdrawal in Claudia's account.

'Expensive restaurants? Girls?'

'It was Claudia Leonardo,' he said soberly.

This stopped Paola for a moment, then she said, 'She'd probably give it away.'

'Do what?'

'Give it away,' Paola repeated.

'Why do you say that?'

There was a long pause. 'I really don't know. I've got to admit that: I've no idea why I said it. I suppose it's my reaction to things she said in class or wrote in her papers, just a general feeling that she had a social conscience, the way so few of them seem to these days.'

Brunetti's reflections were cut off by Paola's question: 'Where did the money come from?'

'A Swiss bank.'

'I think it was Alice in Wonderland who was wont to say, "Curiouser and curiouser."' After another pause, Paola asked, 'Is that how much – three hundred and sixty million in three years?'

'Yes. Any more ideas?'

'No. In a way, it's difficult to think of her in terms of money or a great deal of money. She was so, oh, I don't know, simple. No, that's the wrong word. She had a complex mind, at least from what I knew of her. But one would just never, somehow, associate her with money.'

'Why?'

'She didn't seem interested in it, not at all. In fact I remember noticing, when she'd comment on why characters in novels did things, that she was always slightly puzzled that people could be led to do things by greed, almost as if she didn't understand it, or it didn't make any human sense to her. So, no, she wouldn't spend it on anything she wanted for herself.'

'But that's just books,' he said.

'I beg your pardon,' Paola said, not calmly.

'I mean, you said it was comments she'd make about characters in books. How can that show you what she'd behave like in real life?'

He heard her sigh, but her answer, when it came, showed no lack of patience or sympathy. 'When we tell people about what's happened to our family or our friends we can judge pretty accurately how decent they are by the way they respond, can't we?'

'Of course.'

'It's no different just because the people you're talking about are characters in a book, Guido. You should know that by now, that is if you've paid any attention to anything I've said during the last twenty years.'

He had, and she was right, but he didn't want to have to say so. 'Give it some thought, would you?' he asked. 'What she could have done with it?'

'All right. Will you be home for lunch?'

'Yes. It should be at the regular time.'

'Good. Then I'll cook something special.'

'Marry me,' he implored.

She hung up without answering.

He took the bank statement down to Signorina Elettra, who today wore a pair of jeans and a white shirt starched to pert attention. At her throat she wore a light blue scarf that could have been cashmere but could just as easily have been gossamer.

'Pashmina?' he asked, gesturing towards the scarf.

Her look suggested disdain for his ignorance, but her voice was calm. 'If I might quote the latest French *Vogue*, sir, pashmina, is "mega-out".'

'And so?' he asked, not at all cast down by her remark.

'Cashmere and silk,' she said, as one would speak of thorns and nettles.

'It's much what my wife says about literature: one is always safe with the classics.' He laid the bank statement on her desk. 'Ten million lire was transferred into Claudia Leonardo's account every month from a bank in Geneva,' he said, sure that this would capture her attention.

'From which bank?'

'It doesn't say. Does that make a difference?'

She placed a finger on the bank statement and slid it closer. 'It does if I want to find out about it. It's much easier for me to do research at the private banks.'

'Research?' he inquired.

'Research,' she repeated.

'Could you find out about this?'

'The bank or the original source?' she asked.

'Both.'

She picked up the statement. 'I could try. It might take some time. If it's a private bank, well, even if it's something hard to break into like Bank Hofmann, I should still be able to find something, Commissario.'

'Good. I'd like this to start to make some sort of sense.'

'It never will, though, will it?'

'No, I suppose not,' he agreed as he turned away.

Back in his office he decided to try his father-in-law again, to see if he'd had time to learn anything. But when he called, he was told that the Count had gone to Paris for the day, which left him no choice but to call Lele Bortoluzzi and see if there was anything further he could remember. There was no answer at his studio, so he tried the painter at home, where he found him.

After they exchanged pleasantries, Brunetti asked, 'Do you remember a woman called Hedi – Hedwig – Jacobs, who . . .?'

Lele broke in, 'You still asking about Guzzardi, eh?'

'Yes. And now about Frau Jacobs.'

'I think that "Frau" is a courtesy title,' Lele said. 'There was never a Herr Jacobs in evidence.'

'Did you know her?' Brunetti asked.

'Yes, but not well. We talked occasionally if we met some-where. The thing I remember most is that someone as decent as she could be so gone on a person like Guzzardi. Anything he said was marvellous and anything he did was beyond question.' The painter's voice grew reflective. 'I've seen lots of people lose their heads for love, but usually they maintain a little bit of sense. Not her, though. She would have gone down to hell for him if he'd asked her to.'

'But they never married?' Brunetti prodded.

'He already had a wife, and a son, just a little kid then. He kept them both on a string, the wife and the Austrian. I'm sure they knew about each other, but, given what I know about Guzzardi, I'd guess they had no choice but to accept things the way they were.'

'Did you know them?'

'Who? The women, or the Guzzardis?'

'Any of them?'

'I knew the wife better. She was a cousin of my god-mother's son.' Brunetti wasn't at all sure just how close a link that would have constituted in Lele's family, but the ease and familiarity with which the painter identified the relationship suggested it was no indifferent bond.

'What was she like?' Brunetti asked.

'Why do you want to know all of this?' Lele asked, making no attempt to disguise the fact that Brunetti's curiosity had aroused his own.

'Guzzardi's name has come up in relation to something I'm working on.'

'Can you tell me what?'

'It doesn't matter,' Brunetti answered.

'All right,' Lele said, accepting this. 'The wife put up with it, as I said. After all, they were difficult times and he was a powerful man.'

'And when he wasn't powerful any more?'

'You mean after the war? When they arrested him?'

'Yes.'

'She dropped him, as fast as she could. I think I remember being told that she took up with a British officer. I can't remember now. Anyway, she left the city with her son, and with the soldier.'

'And?'

'I never heard a thing about her again, and I would have, if she'd come back.'

'And the Austrian?'

'You have to understand that I was really little more than a kid myself then. What was I when the war ended? Eighteen? Nineteen? And a lot of time has passed, so much of what I remember is a mixture between what I really saw and heard and what, over the years, I've heard people say. The older I get, the harder it is to distinguish between the two.'

Brunetti wondered if he was going to be treated to a meditation on age, but then Lele continued, 'I think I saw her first at a gallery opening. But that was before she met him.'

'What was she doing in Venice?'

'I forget exactly, but I have a vague memory that it had

something to do with her father. He worked here or had an office here. Something like that, I think.'

'Do you remember anything about her?'

'She was lovely. Of course, I was more than ten years younger than she was, so I might as well have lived on the moon as far as she was concerned, but I remember that she was beautiful.'

'And was she drawn to him by his power, too, like the wife?' Brunetti asked.

'No, that was the strange thing. She really loved him. In fact I always had the impression, or else the belief was there, in the air, as it were, that she had different ideas from his but put up with his because she loved him.'

'And when he was arrested? Do you remember anything about that?'

'No, not clearly. I think she tried to buy his way out, either as a return for favours or with money. At least there was a rumour that she did.'

'But if he went to San Servolo, then she wasn't very successful, was she?'

'No, he'd made too many enemies, the bastard, so no one could help him, not in the end.'

'What had he done that was so bad?' Brunetti asked, still bemused by the ferocity of Lele's feelings and thinking of the enormities committed by so many men, most of whom had danced away from the war and from any trace of guilt.

'He stole what was most precious from a lot of people.'

Brunetti waited, hoping that Lele himself would hear just how weak this sounded. At last he asked, 'He's been dead, what, more than forty years?'

'So what? It doesn't change the fact that he was a bastard and deserved to die in a place where people ate their own shit.'

Once again taken aback by Lele's anger, Brunetti found it difficult to respond. The painter, however, spared him further awkwardness by saying, 'This has nothing to do with you, Guido. You can ask anything you want about him.' After a pause, he added, 'It's because he touched my family.'

'I'm sorry that happened,' Brunetti said.

'Yes, well,' Lele began but found no way to finish the sentence and so left it at that.

'If you think of anything else about her, would you call me?'

'Of course. And I'll ask around, see what anyone else can remember.'

'Thanks.'

'It's nothing, Guido.' Briefly it seemed as if Lele were going to say something more, but he made an affectionate farewell and put down the phone.

Lunch, indeed, was something special. Perhaps it was talk of three hundred and sixty million lire that had driven Paola to excess, for she had bought an entire sea bass and baked it with fresh artichokes, lemon juice and rosemary. With it she served a platter the size of an inner tube filled with tiny roast potatoes, also lightly sprinkled with rosemary. Then, to clear the palate, a salad of rucola and radicchio. They finished with baked apples.

'It's a good thing you have to go to the university three mornings a week and can't do this to us every day,' Brunetti said as he declined a second helping of apples.

'Am I meant to take that as a compliment?' Paola asked.

Before Brunetti could answer, Chiara asked for another apple with sufficient enthusiasm to confirm that her father's remark had indeed been a compliment.

The children astonished their parents by offering to do the dishes. Paola went back to her study and Brunetti, taking with him a glass of grappa, followed her shortly after. 'We really ought to get a new sofa, don't you think?' he said, kicking off his shoes and stretching out on the endangered piece of furniture.

'If I thought I'd ever find anything as comfortable as that one,' Paola said, 'I suppose I'd buy it.' She studied the sofa and her supine husband for some time then said, 'Perhaps I could just have it re-covered.'

'Umm,' Brunetti agreed, eyes closed, hands clasped around the stem of his glass.

'Have you found out anything?' Paola asked, not at all interested in the papers that awaited her.

'Only the money. And Rizzardi said she was a virgin.'

'In the third millennium,' Paola exclaimed, unable to hide her surprise. *'Mirabile dictu.'* After a time, she amended this to, 'Well, perhaps not so astonishing.'

Eyes still closed, Brunetti asked, 'Why?'

'There was a kind of simplicity about her, a complete lack of sophistication. Maybe you could call it artlessness, maybe innocence,' she said, then added, 'whatever that is.'

'That sounds very speculative,' Brunetti observed.

'I know,' she admitted. 'It's just an impression.'

'Do you still have her papers?'

'The ones she wrote for me?'

'Yes.'

'Of course. They're all in the archive.'

'Would it make any sense to look through them?'

Paola considered this for a long time before answering. 'Probably not. If I read them now, or you did, we'd be looking for things that might not necessarily be there. I think it's enough to trust my general impression that she was a decent, generous girl who tended to believe in human goodness.'

'And who was consequently stabbed to death.'

'Consequently?'

'No, I just said that,' Brunetti admitted. 'I'd hate to think one was the consequence of the other.' Though both of them prided themselves in seeing these same qualities in their daughter, neither of them, perhaps out of modesty, though more likely out of superstitious fear, dared to say it. Instead, Brunetti placed his glass on the floor and drifted off to sleep, while Paola put on her glasses and drifted into the sort of trance state that the reading of student papers is bound to induce in the adult mind.

14

He stopped in Signorina Elettra's office when he got back to the Questura and found her on the phone, speaking French. She held up her hand to signal to him to wait, said something else, laughed, and hung up.

He refused to ask about the call and said, 'Has Bocchese brought up those papers?'

'Yes, sir. And I've got people working on it.'

'What does that mean?'

'My friend is going to have a look,' she said, nodding in the direction of the phone, 'but I doubt he'll have anything for me until after the banks close.'

'Geneva?' he asked.

'*Oui.*'

Manfully, he resisted the temptation either to comment or to inquire further. 'I'll be in my office,' he said and went back upstairs.

He stood at the window, gazing at the two yellow cranes that rose above the church of San Lorenzo. They'd been there for so long that Brunetti had come to think of them almost as a pair of angel wings soaring up from either side of the church. He thought they'd been there when he first came to the Questura, but surely no restoration could possibly take that long. Had he, he wondered, ever seen them move, or were they ever in a position different from the one in which they were today? He devoted a great deal of time to these considerations, all the while letting the problem of Claudia Leonardo percolate in some other part of his mind.

The angel wings, he realized, reminded him of an angel that appeared in a painting that hung on the wall behind Signora Jacobs's chair, a painting of the Flemish school, the angel jaundiced and unhappy as if it had been appointed guardian of a person of limitless rectitude and found the assignment dull.

He dialled Lele's number again. When the painter answered, Brunetti said only, 'Has there ever been talk that the Austrian woman might have those paintings and drawings in her home?'

He thought Lele would ask him why he wanted to know, but the painter answered simply, 'Of course, there's always been talk. No one, so far as I know, has ever been inside, so it's only talk, and you know how those things are. People always talk, even if they don't know anything, and they always exaggerate.' There was a long pause, and Brunetti could almost hear Lele turning this over in his mind. 'And I expect,' he went on, 'that if anyone did get inside and see anything he wouldn't say so.'

'Why not?'

Lele laughed, the same old cynical snort Brunetti had heard for decades. 'Because they'd hope that if they kept quiet no one else would be curious about what she might have.'

'I still don't understand.'

'She's not going to live for ever, you know, Guido.'

'And?'

'And if she's got things, she might want to sell some of them before she dies.'

'Do people talk about where they might have come from?' Brunetti asked.

'Ahhh.' Lele's long sigh could be read as satisfaction that Brunetti had finally thought to ask the right question or as a sign of his delight in human weakness.

'That can't be far to look, can it?' the painter finally asked by way of response.

'Guzzardi?'

'Of course.'

'From what you've said about her, she doesn't seem the kind of person who would have anything to do with that sort of thing.'

'Guido,' Lele said with unaccustomed severity, 'your years with the police should have taught you that people are far more willing to profit from a crime than to commit it.' Before Brunetti could object, Lele went on, 'Dare I mention the good Cardinal and Prince of the Church currently under investigation for collusion with the Mafia?'

Brunetti had spent decades listening to Lele in this vein, but he suddenly had no patience for it, and so he cut him off. 'See what you can find out, all right?'

Apparently feeling no ill will at having been so summarily interrupted, the painter asked only, 'Why are you so curious?'

Brunetti himself didn't know or couldn't see the reason clearly. 'Because there's nothing else I can think of,' he admitted.

'That's not the sort of remark that would make me have much confidence in public officials,' Lele said.

'Is there anything that could ever make you have confidence in public officials?'

'The very idea,' the painter said and was gone.

Brunetti sat and tried to think of a way to get back into

123

Signora Jacobs's apartment. He pictured her slumped in her chair, drawing the smoke into her lungs with desperate breaths. He summoned the scene up from memory, examining it as though it were part of the puzzle, 'What's Wrong with this Picture?' Ash-covered carpet, windows a long distance in time from their last cleaning, the Iznik tiles, what could only have been a celadon bowl on the table, the blue packet of Nazionali, the cheap lighter, one shoe with a hole worn through in front by her big toe, the drawing of a Degas dancer. What was wrong with this picture?

It was so obvious that he called himself an idiot for not having registered it sooner: the dissonance between wealth and poverty. Any one of those tiles, just one of those drawings, could have paid to have the entire place restructured, not just cleaned; and anyone in possession of one of those prints would certainly not have to content themselves with the cheapest cigarettes on the market. He searched his memory for other signs of poverty, tried to remember what she had been wearing, but no one pays much attention to old women. He had only the vaguest impression of something dark: grey, brown, black, a skirt or dress, at any rate something that had come down almost to her feet. He couldn't even remember if her clothing had been clean or not, nor if she had worn jewellery. He hoped he would remember his own inability to remember details the next time he grew impatient with a witness to a crime who had difficulty in describing the perpetrator.

The phone startled him from this reverie.

'Yes,' he said.

'You might like to come down here, sir,' Signorina Elettra said.

'Yes,' he repeated, without bothering to ask if she'd had an answer from her friend in Geneva. *Genève*, that is.

When he reached her office, her smile was proof that she had. 'It came from a gallery in Lausanne called Patmos,' she said as he came in. 'It was paid into an account in Geneva each month to be transferred here, to her account.'

'Any instructions?'

'No, only that it was to be sent to her account.'

'Have you spoken to them?' he asked.

'Who, the bank or the gallery?' she asked.

'The gallery.'

'No, sir. I thought you'd want to do that.'

'I'd rather it be done in French,' he said. 'People always feel safer in their own language.'

'Who shall I say I am, sir?' she asked as she reached for the phone and punched 9 to get the outside line.

'Tell them you're calling for the Questore,' Brunetti said.

This is exactly what she did, though it served no purpose. The Director of the gallery, to whom the call was eventually passed, refused to divulge any information about the payments until in possession of an order from a Swiss court to do so. From Signorina Elettra's expression, Brunetti inferred that the Director had not been at all polite in conveying this information.

'And now?' Brunetti asked when she explained what she had been told and the manner in which it had been said.

Signorina Elettra closed her eyes and raised her eyebrows for an instant, as if to remark upon the triviality of the problem that now confronted her. 'It's rather like what the police are always telling people in movies: either they can do it the easy way or the hard way. Monsieur Lablanche has chosen the hard way.'

'For himself or for us?' Brunetti asked.

'For us, at the beginning,' she explained. 'But, depending on what we find, perhaps for himself, as well.'

'Should I ask what you're going to do?'

'Since some of it is illegal, sir, it might be better if you refrained from doing so.'

'Indeed. Will it take long?'

'No longer than it would take you to go down the *fondamenta* and have a coffee. In fact,' she said, glancing at her watch, 'I'll just do this and join you in a few minutes.'

Like Adam, he fell. 'Is it really that easy?'

Signorina Elettra appeared to be in a philosophical mood, for by way of answer she said, 'I once asked a plumber who came to fix my water heater, and who did it in three minutes, how he dared to charge me eighty thousand lire for turning a little knob. He told me it had taken him twenty years to learn which knob to turn. And so I suppose it's like that: it can take minutes, but I've spent years learning which knob to turn.'

'I see,' Brunetti said and went down to the bar at the Ponte dei Greci for a coffee. He was subsequently joined there by Signorina Elettra, though she was longer than twenty minutes.

When she had a coffee in front of her, she said, 'The gallery is run by two brothers, the grandsons of the founder. The Swiss police are very interested in some of their recent acquisitions, especially those from the Middle East, as three pieces in their catalogue were once in the possession of private owners in Kuwait. Or so the Kuwaitis claim; unfortunately, they don't have photos or bills of sale, which means they probably got them illegally in the first place themselves.' She sipped at the coffee, added a bit more sugar, sipped again and set the cup down.

'The grandfather was in charge of the gallery during the war and seems to have received quite a number of paintings from Germany, France and Italy. All, of course, with impeccable pedigrees: bills of sale and Customs declarations. There was an investigation after the war, of course, but nothing came of it. The gallery is well known, successful and rumoured to be very discreet.'

When it seemed likely that she had nothing more to say about the gallery, Brunetti asked, 'And the bank transfers?'

'As you said, every month, ten million lire. It's been going on since she was sixteen.'

That, Brunetti thought, would make more than half a billion lire, with still only three million in the bank. 'How is it possible,' Brunetti began, 'for that much money to come into the country from a foreign source and for no investigation of it to be made?'

'But you don't know that, do you, sir?' she asked. 'Maybe she declared it and paid tax on it, incredible as that would be. Or perhaps the bank had a discreet arrangement and the money went unreported, or the report went unread.'

'But isn't it automatic that the Finanza learns when this much money is coming into the country?'

'Only if the bank wants them to know, sir.'

'That's hard to believe,' Brunetti protested.

'Most of the things banks do are hard to believe.'

He recalled that, before coming to work at the Questura, Signorina Elettra had worked for Banca d'Italia, and so must know whereof she spoke.

'How could someone find out where the money went after it was deposited into her account here?'

'If the bank explained it or if access to the account were possible.'

'Which is easier?'

'Did they volunteer the information when you spoke to them? Presumably, you told them that she was dead.'

Brunetti thought back to the careful formality of the Director. 'No, he passed me to a teller, and she sent me a copy of the deposits and withdrawals to the account, though the large transfers weren't explained.'

'Then I think it might be wise for us to check their records ourselves,' Signorina Elettra suggested.

There was no doubt in Brunetti's mind about the illegality of this. The fact didn't make him hesitate for an instant. 'Could we go back now and have a look?'

'Nothing easier, sir,' she said and finished her coffee.

Back at Signorina Elettra's office, they studied the new information she called up on her computer screen and discovered that Claudia Leonardo had, during the course of the last few years, transferred the bulk of her money to various places around the globe: Thailand, Brazil, Ecuador and Indonesia were but a few of the places the money had gone. There was no pattern to the transfers, and the sums varied from two million to twenty. The total, however, was well in excess of three hundred million lire. Other sums had gone in the form of *assegni circolari* to various recipients. There was no pattern here, either, but there was a similarity of purpose, for all were charitable organizations of one sort or another: an orphanage in Kerala, Médecins sans Frontières, Greenpeace, an AIDS hospice in Nairobi.

'Paola was right,' Brunetti said aloud. 'She gave it all away.'

'That's a strange thing for someone her age to do, isn't it?' Signorina Elettra asked. 'If this is the right figure,' she said, pointing to a total she had calculated at the bottom of the page, 'it's close to half a billion lire.'

He nodded.

'None of it went on taxes, did it?' she asked. 'Not if these amounts went to charities.'

They considered the figures for a moment, neither of them truly understanding anything beyond the total sum and the places it had been sent.

'Was there any mention of a notary or a lawyer?' Brunetti suddenly asked.

'In those, you mean?' she asked, gesturing at the girl's papers, still fanned out on the top of her desk.

'Yes.'

'No. But I haven't checked all the numbers in her address book. Shall I?'

'How? By calling them all?' he said, picking up the book and opening it to the As.

Did he see her eyes close for the merest fraction of a second? He couldn't be sure. While he was still trying to decide, she took the book from him and said, 'No, sir. There's a way Telecom can find the name and address of any number that's listed. All they've got to do is punch in the phone number and the program gives them the name instantly.'

'Is this something I could do by calling them?' he asked.

'It's a public service in other countries, but here, the only ones who have access are Telecom, and I doubt they'd let you have access to the information without a court order.' After a moment, she added, 'But my friend Giorgio has given me a copy of the program.'

'Good. Then would you check all the numbers and see if any are lawyers or notaries?'

'And then?'

'And then I want to talk to them.'

'Would you like me to make appointments if I find them?'

'No, I prefer to appear unannounced.'

'Like a mugger?' she asked.

' "Like a lion" might be a more flattering way to put it, Signorina, but perhaps your image is closer to the truth.'

15

It wasn't until after six that Signorina Elettra brought him the fruits of her labours with Giorgio's pirated program. Placing a sheet of paper on his desk, she couldn't prevent a smile from crossing her face. 'Here it is, sir. Only the number was written in her book; no name. But it's a notary.'

Brunetti glanced at the paper. 'Really?' he asked when he saw the name, one he remembered even from his childhood. 'I thought Filipetto had died, years ago.'

'No, sir, that was his son who died. Cancer of the pancreas. It must be about six or seven years ago. He'd taken over from his father, but he had time before he died to transfer the practice to his nephew, his sister's son.'

'The one who was in that boat accident a few years ago?' Brunetti asked.

'Yes. Massimo.'

'Is the old man still in practice?'

'He couldn't still work if he transferred the practice to his son; besides, the address listed is different from Sanpaolo's office.'

130

He got to his feet, folded the paper in four, and slipped it into the inner pocket of his jacket.'

'Have you ever met him?' Signorina Elettra asked.

'Once, years ago, when he was still practising.' Then he asked her, 'Do you know him?'

'My father dealt with him, years ago. It went very badly.'

'For whom? Your father or Dottor Filipetto?'

'I think it would be impossible to find anything that ever went badly for a Filipetto, either the son or the father,' she said, then added mordantly, 'aside from his pancreas, of course.'

'What was it about?'

She considered this for a while, then explained, 'My father had part ownership of a restaurant that had tables alongside a canal. Dottor Filipetto lived on the third floor, above the restaurant, and he claimed that the tables obstructed his view of the other side of the canal.'

'From the third floor?'

'Yes.'

'What happened?'

'Filipetto was an old friend of the judge who was assigned to the case. At first, my father and his partner didn't worry because the claim was so absurd. But then he learned that both the judge and Filipetto were Masons, members of the same lodge, and once he knew that, he knew he had no choice but to settle the case out of court.'

'What was the settlement?'

'My father had to pay him a million lire a month in return for his promise not to file another complaint.'

'When was this?'

'About twenty years ago.'

'That was a fortune then.'

'My father sold his share in the restaurant soon after that. He never mentions it now, but I remember, at the time, how he spoke Filipetto's name.'

For Brunetti this story recalled many he had heard, over the course of years, concerning Notaio Filipetto. 'I think I'll go along and see if he's at home.'

On the way out he stopped in the officers' room and found Vianello, who had been forced to remain at his desk there even after his promotion, Lieutenant Scarpa having refused to assign him a desk among the other *ispettori*.

'I'm going over to Castello to talk to someone. Would you like to come along?'

'About the girl?' Vianello asked.

'Yes.'

'Gladly,' he said, getting to his feet and grabbing his jacket from the back of his chair. 'Who is it?' Vianello asked as they emerged from the Questura.

'Notaio Gianpaolo Filipetto.'

Vianello did not stop in his tracks, but he did falter for an instant. 'Filipetto?' he asked. 'Is he still alive?'

'It would seem so,' Brunetti answered. 'Claudia Leonardo had his phone number in her address book.' They reached the *riva* and turned right, heading for the Piazza, and as they walked Brunetti also explained the pattern of money transfers and, listing the charities, their final destinations.

'It hardly sounds like the sort of thing a Filipetto would be involved in,' Vianello observed.

'What, giving this much money to charity?'

'Giving anything to charity, I'd say,' Vianello answered.

'We don't know there's any connection between him and her money,' Brunetti said, though he didn't for an instant believe this.

'If ever there is a Filipetto and money, there is a connection,' Vianello said, pronouncing it as a truth Venetians had come to learn through many generations.

'You have any idea how old he could be?' Brunetti asked.

'No. Close to ninety, I'd say.'

'Seems a strange age to be interested in money, doesn't it?'

'He's a Filipetto,' Vianello answered, effectively silencing any speculation Brunetti might have felt tempted to make.

The address was in Campo Bandiera e Moro, in a building just to the right of the church where Vivaldi had been baptized and from which, according to common belief, many of the paintings and statues had disappeared into private hands during the tenure of a previous pastor. They rang, then rang again until a woman's voice answered the speaker phone, asking them who it was. When Brunetti said it was the police, coming to call on Notaio Filipetto, the door snapped open and the voice told them to come to the first floor.

She met them at the door, a woman composed of strange angularities: jaws, elbows, the tilt of her eyes all seemed made of straight lines that sometimes met at odd angles. No arcs, no curves: even her mouth was a straight line. 'Yes?' she asked, standing in the equally rectangular doorway.

'I'd like to speak to Notaio Filipetto,' Brunetti said, extending his warrant card.

She didn't bother to look at it. 'What about?' she asked.

'Something that might concern the Notaio,' Brunetti said.

'What?'

'This is a police matter, Signora,' Brunetti said, 'and so I'm afraid I can discuss it only with the Notaio.'

Either her emotions were easy to read, which Brunetti thought might not be the case, or she wanted them to see how greatly she disapproved of his intransigence. 'He's an old man. He can't be disturbed by questions from the police.'

From behind her, a high voice called out, 'Who is it, Eleonora?' When she did not answer, the voice repeated the question, then, as she remained silent, asked it again. 'Who is it, Eleonora?'

'You'd better come in. You've upset him now,' she said, backing into the apartment and holding the door for them. The voice continued from some inner place, repeating the same question; Brunetti was certain that it would not stop until the question was answered.

Brunetti saw her lips tighten and felt a faint sympathy for her. The scene reminded him of something, but the memory wouldn't come: something in a book.

Silently, she led them towards the back of the apartment. From behind, she was equally angular: her thin shoulders were parallel with the floor, and her hair, streaked heavily with grey, was cut off in a straight line just above the collar of her dress.

'I'm coming, I'm coming,' she called ahead of them. Either in response to the sound of her voice or perhaps, like a clock running down, the other voice stopped.

They arrived at an enormous archway; two inlaid wooden doors stood open on either side. 'He's in here,' she said, preceding them into the room.

An old man sat at a broad wooden desk, a semicircle of papers spread out around him. A small lamp to his left threw a dim light on the papers and kept the upper half of his face in shadow.

His mouth was thin, his lips stretched back over a set of false teeth that had grown too large as the flesh of his face was worn away by age. Heavy dewlaps, so long as to remind Brunetti of those of a hound, hung from both sides of his mouth; the skin below hung in wattles, bunched loosely over his collar.

Brunetti was aware that the man was looking at them, but the light did not reach Filipetto's eyes, so it was impossible for him to read the man's expression. '*Sì?*' the old man asked in the same high-pitched tone.

'Notaio,' Brunetti began, stepping a bit closer so as to afford himself a better view of Filipetto's entire face, 'I'm Commissario Guido Brunetti,' he began, but the old man cut him off.

'I recognize you. I knew your father.'

Brunetti was so surprised that it took him a moment to recover, and when he did he thought he saw a faint upturning of those thin lips. Filipetto's face was long and thin, the skin waxlike. Sparse tufts of white hair adhered to his speckled skull, like down on the body of a diseased chick. As Brunetti's eyes adjusted to the light, he saw that Filipetto's own were hooded and vulpine, the irises tinged the colour of parchment.

'He was a man who did his duty,' Filipetto said in what was clearly meant to be admiration. He said nothing more, but his lips kept moving as he sucked them repeatedly in and out against his false teeth.

The comment confirmed Brunetti's memory of the man and was all he needed. 'Yes, he was, sir. It was one of the things he tried to teach us.'

'You have a brother, don't you?' asked the old man.

'Yes, sir, I do.'

'Good. A man should have sons.' Before Brunetti could respond to this, though he had no idea what he could say, Filipetto asked, 'What else did he teach you?'

Brunetti was vaguely aware that the woman was still standing in the doorway and that Vianello had automatically pulled himself up straighter, as close to a stance of military attention as he could achieve while wearing a yellow tie.

'Duty, honour, devotion to the flag, discipline,' Brunetti recited, doing his best to remember all the things he had always found most risible in the pretensions of Fascism, but pronouncing them in earnest tones. At his side, he sensed Vianello growing even straighter, as if bolstered by the invigorating force of these ideas.

'Sit down, Commissario,' Filipetto said, ignoring Vianello. 'Eleonora, hold his chair,' he commanded. She came from the door and Brunetti forced himself to wait as would a man accustomed to the service of women. She pulled out a chair opposite the old man and Brunetti sat in it, not bothering to thank her.

'What is it you've come about?' Filipetto asked.

'Your name has come up, sir, in an investigation we're conducting. When I read it, I . . .' Brunetti began, coughed a nervous little laugh, then looked over at the old man and said, 'Well, I remembered the way my father always spoke of you, sir, and I, to tell the truth, I couldn't resist the opportunity finally to meet you.'

To the best of Brunetti's memory, the only time he had ever heard his father mention Filipetto's name was when he raged against the men who had been most guilty of plundering the state's coffers during the war. Filipetto's name had not been at the top of the list, a place always reserved for the man who had sold the Army the cardboard boots that had cost Brunetti's father six toes, but it had been there, his name among those others who had made the effortless passage from wartime profiteering to post-war prominence.

The old man glanced idly at Vianello and, observing the smile of approval with which he greeted his superior's last remark, Filipetto said, 'You can sit down, too.'

'Thank you, sir,' Vianello said and did as he was told, though he was careful to sit up straight, as if attentive and respectful to whatever further truths would be revealed during this conversation between men who so closely mirrored his own political ideals.

Brunetti used the momentary distraction caused by Filipetto's remark to Vianello to look at the papers in front of the old man. One was a magazine containing photos of Il Duce in various, but equally fierce, postures. The rest were documents of some sort, but before he could adjust his eyes to try to read them, Filipetto demanded his attention.

'What investigation is this?' he asked.

'Your name,' Brunetti began, assuming that a phone number was as good as a name, 'was found among the papers of a person who died recently, and I wanted to ask you if you had any dealings with her.'

136

'Who?' he asked.

'Claudia Leonardo,' Brunetti said.

Filipetto made no sign that the name meant anything to him and once again looked at the papers, but the radar of long experience told Brunetti that it was not unfamiliar to him. Given the coverage the murder had had in the papers, it was unlikely that anyone in the city would be unfamiliar with her name.

'Who?' the Notary asked, head bowed.

'Claudia Leonardo, sir. She died – she was murdered – here in the city.'

'And how did my name come to be among her effects?' he asked, looking again at Brunetti but not bothering to inquire how or why Claudia had been killed.

'It doesn't matter, sir. If you've never heard of her, then there's no need to continue with this.'

'Do you want me to sign something to that effect?' Filipetto asked.

'Sir,' Brunetti answered hotly, as if unable to disguise his surprise, 'your word is more than enough.'

Filipetto looked up then, his teeth bared in a smile of open satisfaction 'Your mother?' he asked. 'Is she still with us?'

Brunetti had no idea what Filipetto meant by this: whether his mother was alive, which she was; whether she was still sane, which she was not; or whether she still held true to the political ideas that had cost her husband his youth and his peace. As she had never held those ideas in anything but contempt, Brunetti felt secure in answering the first question, 'Yes, sir, she is.'

'Good, good. Though there are many people now who are beginning to realize the value of what we tried to do, it's comforting to know that there are still people who are faithful to the old values.'

'I'm sure there will always be,' Brunetti said, without a trace of the disgust he felt at the idea. He stood, leaving the chair where it was, and leaned across the table to shake the old man's hand, cold and fragile in his own. 'It's been an honour, sir,' he said. Vianello nodded deeply, unable to convey his complete agreement in any other way.

The old man raised a hand and waved towards the woman, who was still standing at the doorway. 'Eleonora, make yourself useful. See the Commissario out.' He gave Brunetti a valedictory smile and again bent his head over his papers.

Eleonora, her connection to the old man still unexplained, turned and led them to the front door of the apartment. Brunetti made no attempt to penetrate the veil of silent resentment she had wrapped so tightly about herself during this interview and at the door did no more than mutter his thanks before preceding Vianello down the stairs and out into the *campo*.

16

'Enough to choke a pig,' was Vianello's only comment as they walked out into the cool evening air.

'Well he *did* make the trains run on time,' Brunetti offered.

'Yes, of course. And, in the end, what's a couple million dead and a country in ruins if the trains run on time?'

'Exactly.'

'God, you think they're all dead and then you turn over a rock and you find one's still under there.'

Brunetti grunted in assent.

'You can understand young people believing all that shit. After all, the schools don't teach them anything about what really happened. But you'd think people who lived it, who were adults all during it and who saw what happened, you'd think they'd realize.'

'I'm afraid it costs people too much to abandon what they believe,' Brunetti offered by way of explanation. 'If you give your loyalty and, I suppose, your love to ideas like that then it's all but impossible to admit what madness they are.'

'I suppose so,' Vianello conceded, though it sounded as if

he weren't fully persuaded. They walked side by side, reached the *riva* and turned up toward the Piazza.

'It's strange, sir,' Vianello began, 'but for the last few years – and I think it's happening more and more often – I meet someone and they say things, and I come away from talking to them thinking that they're crazy. I mean really crazy.'

Brunetti, who had had much the same experience, asked only, 'What sort of things?'

Vianello paused over this for a long time, suggesting that he had perhaps never before revealed this to anyone. 'Well, I talk to people who say they're worried about the hole in the ozone layer and what will happen to their kids and future generations, and then they tell me that they've just bought one of those monster cars, you know, the ones like the Americans drive.' He walked on, in step with Brunetti, considered a moment, then continued. 'This isn't even to mention religion, with Padre Pio being cured by a statue they flew over his monastery in a plane.'

'What?' Brunetti asked, having thought this was something Fellini invented for a film.

'What I'm trying to say is that it doesn't matter which story they tell about him. He was a nut, and they want to make him a saint. Yes,' Vianello said, his ideas clarified, 'it's things like that, that people can believe all of that, that makes me wonder if the whole world isn't mad.'

'My wife maintains that she finds it easier to accept human behaviour if she thinks of us as savages with *telefonini*,' Brunetti said.

'Is she serious?' Vianello asked, his tone one of curiosity, not scepticism.

'That's always a very difficult thing to judge, with my wife,' Brunetti admitted, then, turning the conversation back to their recent visit, he asked, 'What did you think?'

'He recognized the name, that's for sure,' Vianello said.

Brunetti was glad to see his own intuition confirmed. 'Any ideas about the woman?'

'I was paying more attention to the old man.'

'How old do you think she is?' Brunetti asked him.

'Fifty? Sixty? Why do you ask?'

'It might help in figuring out how she's related to him.'

'Related, as in relative?'

'Yes. He didn't treat her like a servant.'

'He told her to pull out your chair,' Vianello reminded him.

'I know; that's what I thought at first. But it's not the way people treat servants: they're politer with them than with their families.' Brunetti knew this because, for decades, he had observed the way Paola's family treated their servants, but he didn't want to explain this to Vianello.

'His name wasn't listed in her address book, was it?' Vianello asked.

'No, only the phone number.'

'Has Signorina Elettra checked the phone records to see how often the girl call him?'

'She's doing that now.'

'Be interesting to know why she called him, wouldn't it?'

'Especially as he said he didn't know her,' Brunetti agreed.

They found themselves in the Piazza, and it was only then that Brunetti realized that he had been leading Vianello away from his house. He stopped and said, 'I'm going to go up and take the Number One. Would you like a drink?'

'Not around here,' Vianello said, his eyes taking in the Piazza and its hosts of pigeons and tourists, one as annoying as the other. 'Next thing, you'll be suggesting we go to Harry's Bar.'

'I don't think they let anyone in who isn't a tourist,' Brunetti said.

Vianello guffawed, as Venetians often do at the thought of going to Harry's Bar, and said he'd walk home.

Brunetti, with farther to go, walked up to the vaporetto

stop and took the Number One towards San Silvestro. He used the trip to gaze inattentively at the façades of the *palazzi* they passed, thinking back over his visit to Filipetto. The room had been so dim that he had not observed much, but nothing he had seen there suggested wealth. Notaries were believed to be among the richest people in the country, and the Filipettos had been notaries for generations, each one succeeding to the studio and practice of the one before him, but no sign of wealth had been evident in the room or what Brunetti could see of its furnishings.

The old man's jacket had been worn bald at the ends of the cuffs; the woman's clothing was undistinguished by any quality other than drabness. Because he had been taken directly to see Filipetto, he had not gained any idea of the total size of the apartment, but he had had a glimpse down the central corridor, and it suggested the existence of many rooms. Besides, a poor *notaio* was as inconceivable as a celibate priest.

At home, though Paola did not ask if there had been any progress, he could sense her curiosity, so he told her about Filipetto while she was dropping the pasta into boiling water. To the left of the pot simmered a pan of tomatoes with, as far as he could identify, black olives and capers. Before she could comment, he asked, 'Where'd you get such big capers?'

'Sara's parents were on Salina for a week, and her mother brought me back half a kilo.'

'Half a kilo of capers?' he asked, astonished, 'It'll take us years to eat them.'

'They're salted, so they'll keep,' Paola responded and then said, 'You might like to ask my father about him.'

'Filipetto?'

'Yes.'

'What does he know?'

'Ask him.'

'How long will the pasta . . .' Brunetti began, but she cut

him off saying, 'Wait to call him until after dinner. It might take some time.'

Because of Brunetti's eagerness to make the call, the capers, to make no mention of the pasta, went less appreciated than they might ordinarily have been. The instant he finished his barely tasted dessert, Brunetti returned to the living room and made the call.

At the mention of Filipetto, the Count surprised Brunetti by saying, 'Perhaps we could talk about this in person, Guido.'

Without hesitation, Brunetti asked, 'When?'

'I'm leaving for Berlin tomorrow morning and I won't be back until the end of the week.'

Before the Count could suggest a later date, Brunetti asked, 'Have you time now?'

'It's after nine,' the Count said, but only as an observation, not as a complaint.

'I could be there in fifteen minutes,' Brunetti insisted.

'All right. If you like,' the Count said and put down the phone.

It took Brunetti less than that, even including the time he spent explaining to Paola where he was going and then listening to her greetings and best wishes to her parents, given as though she didn't speak to them at least once a day.

The Count was in his study, wearing a dark grey suit and a sober tie. Brunetti sometimes wondered if the midwife who had delivered the heir to the Falier title had been taken aback by the emergence of a tiny baby already wearing a dark suit and tie, a thought he had never dared voice to Paola.

Brunetti accepted the grappa the Count offered him, nodded in appreciation of its quality, settled himself on one of the sofas, and asked directly, 'Filipetto?'

'What do you want to know about him?'

'His phone number was listed in the address book of the

young woman who was murdered last week. I'm sure you've read about it.'

The Count nodded. 'But surely you don't suspect Notaio Filipetto of having murdered her,' he said with a small smile.

'Hardly. I doubt that he's able to leave his apartment. I spoke to him earlier this evening and told him about the number, but he denied knowing her.' When the Count made no response, Brunetti added, 'My instinct is that he did know her.'

'That's very like the Filipettos,' the Count said. 'They lie by impulse and inclination, all of them, the whole family, and always have.'

'That's a sweeping condemnation, to say the least,' Brunetti commented.

'But none the less true.'

'How long have you known them?' Brunetti asked, interested in fact as well as opinion.

'All my life, probably, at least by reputation. I don't think I had anything to do with them directly until I was back here after the war, when they served as notary, occasionally, when my family bought property.'

'Working for you?'

'No.' The Count was emphatic. 'For the sellers.'

'Did they ever work for you?'

'Once,' the Count said tersely. 'At the very beginning.'

'What happened?'

The Count waited a long time before answering, sipped at his grappa, savoured it, and went on. 'You'll understand if I don't explain in detail,' he said, a genuflection to their mutual belief that only the most minimal explanation of any financial dealing should ever be given to anyone. Brunetti thought of Lele's refusal to discuss anything of importance on the phone and wondered if suspicion were now a genetic trait peculiar to Italians. 'Our purchase of a particular property was based on Filipetto's examination of the records of ownership, and he assured us that it belonged to one of the heirs. My father went ahead and paid a certain amount to the heir.' The Count paused here, allowing Brunetti time to conclude that the payment had been in cash, not recorded, most probably illegal, and hence the reason for his refusal to discuss the matter on the phone. 'And then, when the case had to be decided in court, it turned out that, not only did this person have no legal right to the property, but Filipetto was fully aware of that fact and had probably always been. I never learned whose idea the payment was, his or the heir's, but I'm certain it was divided equally between them.' Brunetti was surprised at how calm the Count's voice and expression remained. Perhaps after a lifetime spent swimming in the shoals of business, a shark was just another sort of fish. 'Since that time,' the Count went on, 'I have had no dealings with him.'

Brunetti glanced at his watch and saw that it was after ten. 'What time do you have to leave tomorrow?' he asked.

'It doesn't matter. I don't need much sleep any more. That need, like so many desires, seems to decrease with age.'

The Count's reference to age sent Brunetti's thoughts to Signora Jacobs. 'There's an old Austrian woman mixed up in this somehow,' he said. 'Hedwig Jacobs. Do you know her?'

'The name's familiar,' the Count said, 'but I can't remember how it is I might have known her. How is she involved?'

'She was Guzzardi's lover.'

'Poor woman, even if she is an Austrian.'

'Austrian or not, she remained loyal to him,' Brunetti said, surprised at his speed in leaping to the old woman's defence. When the Count didn't respond, Brunetti added, 'It was fifty years ago.'

The Count considered that for some time and then sighed and said, 'Yes.' He got up, went to the drinks cabinet and came back with the bottle of grappa. He poured them both another glass, set the bottle on the table between them and returned to his seat. 'Fifty years,' the Count repeated, and Brunetti was struck by the sadness with which he spoke.

Perhaps it was the hour, the strange intimacy of their sitting together in the silent *palazzo*, perhaps it was nothing more than the grappa, but Brunetti felt himself filled almost to overflowing with affection for this man he had known for decades, yet never really known.

'Are you proud of what you did during the war?' Brunetti asked impulsively, as surprised at the question as was the Count.

If he thought his father-in-law would have to consider before he answered, Brunetti was mistaken, for the answer came instantly. 'No, I'm not proud. I was at the beginning, I suppose. But I was young, little more than a boy. When the war finished I wasn't even eighteen yet, but I'd been living and acting like a man, or like I thought a man was supposed to act, for more than two years. But I had the moral age,' the Count began, paused for a moment and gave Brunetti a smile that seemed strangely sweet, 'of a boy, or the ethical age of a boy, if you will.'

He looked down and studied the carpet at his feet and flicked one errant strand of the fringe back into place; Brunetti was reminded of Claudia Leonardo and the circumstances of her death. The Count's voice summoned him back. 'No one should ever be proud of killing a man, especially men like the ones we killed toward the end.' He looked up at Brunetti, willing him to understand. 'I suppose everyone has an image of the typical German soldier: a blond giant with the death's head insignia of the SS on his shoulder, wiping the blood from his bayonet after putting it through the throat of, oh, I don't know, a nun or someone's mother. The men I was with said they saw some of those at the beginning, but at the end, they were just terrified boys dressed in mismatched jackets and trousers and calling them

146

a uniform, and carrying guns and hoping they were a real army because they did.

'But they were just boys, frightened out of their wits at the thought of death, just like we were.' He sipped at his grappa, then cradled the glass between his hands. 'I remember one of the last ones we killed.' His voice was calm, dispassionate, as if far removed from the events he was describing. 'He might have been sixteen at the most. We had a trial, or what we called a trial. But it was just like what they say in American movies: "Give him a fair trial and then hang him." Only we shot him. Oh, we thought we were important, such heroes, playing at being lawyers and judges. He was a kid, absolutely helpless, and there was no reason we couldn't have kept him as a prisoner. They surrendered a week later. But by then he was dead.'

The Count turned away and glanced toward the window. Lights were visible on the other side of the Canal, and he looked at them while he continued. 'I wasn't part of the squad that shot him, but I had to lead him up to the wall and give him the handkerchief to tie around his eyes. I'm sure someone had read about that in some book or seen it in a movie. It always seemed to me, even then, that it would be better to let them see the men who were going to kill them. They deserved that much. Or that little. But maybe that's why we did it, so that they couldn't see us.'

He paused for a long time, perhaps considering the explanation he'd just given, then went on. 'He was terrified. Just as I reached up to cover his eyes, he wet his pants. I felt no pity for him then; I suppose I even felt good about it, that we had so reduced this German to such shameful terror. It would have been kinder to ignore it, but there was no kindness in me then, nor in any of us. I looked down at the stain on his pants and he saw me looking. Then he started to cry, and I understood enough German to understand what he said. "I want my mother. I want my mother," and then he couldn't stop sobbing. His chin was down on his chest, and I couldn't tie the handkerchief around his eyes, so I moved away from him, and they shot him. I suppose I could have used the handkerchief to wipe away his tears but, as I said, I was a young man then, and there was no pity in me.'

The Count turned away from the lights and back towards Brunetti. 'I looked down at him after they shot him, and I saw his face covered with snot, and his chest with blood, and the war ended for me then, in that instant. I didn't think about it, not in big terms, I suppose not in anything I could call ethical terms, but I knew that what we had done was wrong and that we'd murdered him, just as much as if we'd found him sleeping in his bed, in his mother's house, and cut his throat. There was no glory in what we were doing, and no purpose whatsoever was served by it. The next day, we shot three more. With the first one I was party to it and I still thought it was right, but after that, even when I realized what we were doing, I still didn't have the courage to try to stop the others from doing it because I was afraid of what would happen to me if I did. So, to answer your question again, no, I'm not proud of what I did in the war.'

The Count emptied his glass and set it on a table. He stood. 'I don't think there's anything more I want to say about this.'

Brunetti stood and, compelled by an impulse that surprised him, walked over to the Count and embraced him, held him in his arms for a long moment, then turned and left the study.

17

Paola was asleep when he got home, and though she swam up long enough to ask him how it had gone with her father, she was so dull that Brunetti simply said that they'd talked. He kissed her and went to see if the kids were home and in bed. He opened Raffi's door after knocking lightly and found his son lying face down, sprawled in a giant X, one arm and one foot hanging off the edge of the bed. Brunetti thought of the boy's heritage: one grandfather come back from Russia with only four toes and half a spirit, the other willing executioner of unarmed boys. He closed the door and checked on Chiara, who was neatly asleep under unwrinkled covers. In bed he lay for some time thinking about his family, and then he slept deeply.

The next day he went first to Signorina Elettra's office, where he found her besieged by regiments of paper advancing across her desk.

'Am I meant to find all of that promising?' he asked as he came in.

'What was it Harold Carter said when he could finally see into the tomb, "I see things, marvellous things"?'

'Presumably you don't see golden masks and mummies, Signorina,' Brunetti responded.

Like a croupier raking in cards, she swept up some of the papers on her right and tapped them into a pile. 'Here, take a look: I've printed out the files in her computer.'

'And the bank records?' he asked, pulling a chair up to her desk and sitting beside her.

She waved disdainfully at a pile of papers on the far side of her desk. 'Oh, it was as I suspected,' she said with the lack of interest with which one mentions the obvious. 'The bank never called the attention of the Finanza to the deposits, and it seems they never troubled to ask the bank.'

'Which means what?' he asked, though he had a fair idea.

'The most likely possibility is that the Finanza simply never bothered to cross-check her statements with the reports on money transfers arriving in the country.'

'And that means?' he asked.

'Negligence or bribery, I'd say.'

'Is that possible?'

'As I have told you upon more than one occasion, sir, when you are dealing with banks, anything at all is possible.'

Brunetti deferred to her greater wisdom and asked, 'Was this difficult for you to get?'

'Considering the laudable reticence of the Swiss banks and the instinctive mendacity of our own, I suppose it was more difficult than usual.'

Brunetti knew the extent of her friendships, and so let it go at that, always uneasy at the thought of the information she might some day be asked to provide in return, and whether she would.

'These are her letters,' Signorina Elettra said, handing him the pile of papers. 'The dates and the sums mentioned correspond to bank transfers made from her account.'

He read the first, to the orphanage in India, saying that she hoped her contribution would help the children have better lives, and then one to a home for battered women in Pavia, saying much the same thing. Each letter explained that the money was being given in memory of her grandfather, though it did not give his name nor, for that matter, her own.

'Are they all like this?' he asked, looking up from the page.

'Yes, pretty much. She never gives her name or his, and in each case she expresses the hope that the enclosed cheque will help people have a better life.'

Brunetti hefted the pile of papers. 'How many are there?'

'More than forty. All the same.'

'Is the amount always the same?'

'No, they vary, though she seemed to like ten million lire. The total is close to the amount that went into her account.'

He considered what a fortune one of these transfers would be to an Indian orphanage or for a shelter for battered women.

'Are there any repeated donations?'

'To the orphanage in Kerala and the AIDS hospice. Those seemed to be her favourites but, so far as I can see, all of the others are different.'

'What else?' he asked.

She pointed to the closest pile. 'There are the papers she wrote for her literature classes. I haven't had time to read through all of them, though I must say her dislike of Gilbert Osmond is quite ferocious.'

It was a name he'd heard Paola use; she shared Claudia's dislike. 'What else?' he asked.

Indicating a thick pile to the left of her computer. Signorina Elettra said, 'Personal correspondence, none of it very interesting.'

'And that?' he asked, pointing to the single remaining sheet.

'It would cause a stone to weep,' she said, handing it to him.

'I, Claudia Leonardo,' he read, 'declare that all of the worldly goods of which I am in possession should, at my death, be sold and the profits distributed to the charities listed below. This is hardly enough to make up for a life of rapacious acquisition, but it is, if nothing else, an attempt to do so.' Below were listed the names and addresses of sixteen charities, among them the Indian orphanages and the women's home in Pavia.

'"Rapacious acquisition"?' he asked.

'She had three million, six hundred thousand lire in the bank when she died,' was Signorina Elettra's only reply.

Brunetti read through the will again, pausing at 'rapacious acquisition'. 'She means her grandfather,' he said, finally perceiving the obvious.

Signorina Elettra, who had heard from Vianello some of the history of Claudia's family, agreed instantly.

He noticed that there was no signature on the paper. 'Is this your print-out?' he asked.

'Yes.' Before he could ask, she said, 'There was no copy among her papers.'

'That makes sense. People that young don't think they're going to die.'

'And they usually don't,' Signorina Elettra added.

Brunetti put the will down on the desk. 'What was in the personal correspondence?'

'Letters to friends and former classmates, letters to an aunt in England. These were in English, and she usually talked about what she was doing, her studies, and asked about her aunt's children and the animals on her farm. I really don't think there's anything in them, but you can take a look if you want.'

'No, no, that's all right. I trust you. Any other correspondence?'

'Just the usual business things: the university, the rough draft of what looks like a letter of application for a job, but there's no address on it.'

'A job?' Brunetti interrupted. 'She was being sent more than a hundred million lire a year: why would she want a job?'

'Money isn't the only reason people work, sir,' Signorina Elettra reminded him with sudden force.

'She was a university student,' Brunetti said.

'What does that mean?'

'She wouldn't have had time to work, at least not during the academic year.'

'Perhaps,' Signorina Elettra conceded with a scepticism suggesting a certain measure of familiarity with the academic demands made by the university. 'Certainly there was no change in her finances that would indicate she had another source of income,' she said, pushing some of the papers aside until she found Claudia Leonardo's bank account. 'Look, she was still drawing out the same amounts every month when she died. So she didn't have any other income.'

'Of course she might have been working for nothing, as a volunteer or an apprentice,' Brunetti said. 'It's a possibility.'

'You just said she was a university student, sir, and wouldn't have had the time.'

'It could have been part time,' Brunetti insisted. 'Do you remember anything in the letters that suggests she might have been working?'

Signorina Elettra considered this for a while and finally said, 'No, nothing, but I wasn't looking for anything specific when I read the letters.' Without asking, she picked up the copies of Claudia Leonardo's letters, divided the pile in two, and handed half to Brunetti.

He moved his chair back from her desk, stretched out his legs and began to read. As he read his way through these records of Claudia's truncated life, he recalled a present an aunt of his had once, decades ago, given him for Christmas. He had been disappointed when he opened the matchbox and found nothing more than what looked like a bean made out of paper. Unable to disguise his disappointment, he had asked his aunt, 'But what's this for?' and in answer she had filled a pan with water and told him to put the bean into it.

When he did, it swam magically on the surface of the water and then, under his marvelling eyes, gradually began to move and twist around, as the water unfurled what seemed like hundreds of tiny folds, each one pulling another one open after it. When it was finally still, he found himself gazing down at a perfect white carnation, the size of an apple. Before the water could soak and ruin it, his aunt plucked it out and set it on the windowsill, in the pale winter sun, where it stood for days. Each time Brunetti looked at it, he recalled the magic that had turned one thing into such a wonderfully different other.

Much the same process took place as he read Claudia's words and heard her natural voice. 'These poor Albanians. People hate them as soon as they learn where they're from, as though their passports (if the poor devils even have passports) were pairs of horns.' 'I can't stand to hear my friends complain about how little they have. We live, all of us, better than the Emperors of Rome.' 'How I long to have a dog, but who could make a dog live in this city? Perhaps we should all keep a pet tourist, instead.' Nothing she said was particularly insightful, nor was the language distinguished, but then that pale dollop of compressed paper had hardly merited a second glance; yet how it had blossomed.

After about ten minutes he looked up and asked, 'Found anything?'

She shook her head and kept reading.

After another few minutes he observed, 'She seemed to spend a great deal of time in the library, didn't she?'

'She was a student,' Signorina Elettra said, looking up from the papers. Then she added, 'But, yes, she did, didn't she?'

'And it never sounds like she's doing research there, I'd say.' Brunetti asked, turning back a page and reading out,

' "I had to be at the library at nine this morning, and you know what a horror I am that early, enough to frighten anyone away."'

Brunetti set the page down. 'Seems a strange concern, doesn't it? Turning people away?'

'Especially if she's going there to read or study. Why would it matter?' Though Signorina Elettra's question was rhetorical, both of them considered it.

'How many libraries are there in the city?' Brunetti asked.

'There's the Marciana, the Querini Stampalia, the one at the university itself and then those in the *quartieri* and maybe another five.'

'Let's try them,' Brunetti said, reaching for the phone.

Just as quickly, Signorina Elettra opened the bottom drawer of her desk, pulled out the phone book and flipped to 'Comune di Venezia'. One after the other, Brunetti called the city libraries in Castello, Canareggio, San Polo and Giudecca, but none of them had an employee or a volunteer working there called Claudia Leonardo nor, when he called them, did the Marciana, the Querini Stampalia, or the library of the university.

'Now what?' she asked, slapping the directory shut. Brunetti took it from her and looked under the B's. 'You ever heard of the Biblioteca della Patria?' he asked.

'Of the what?' she asked.

'Patria,' he repeated and read out the address, saying, 'Sounds like it might be down at the end of Castello.' She pressed her lips together and shook her head.

He dialled the number and, when a man answered, asked if someone named Claudia Leonardo worked there. The man, speaking with a slight accent, asked him to repeat the name, told him to hold on a moment, and set the phone down. A moment later he was back and asked, 'Who's calling, please?'

'Commissario Guido Brunetti,' he answered, then asked, 'And Claudia Leonardo?'

'Yes, she worked here,' the man said, making no reference to her death.

'And you are?' Brunetti asked.

'Maxwell Ford,' he answered, all the Italianate softness of his voice slipping away to reveal the Anglo-Saxon bedrock. In response to Brunetti's demanding silence, he explained, 'I'm co-director of the Library.'

'And where, exactly, is this library?'

'It's at the very end of Via Garibaldi, across the canal from Sant'Anna.'

Brunetti knew where it must be, but he had no memory of ever having been conscious of the existence of a library in that area. 'I'd like to talk to you,' Brunetti said.

'Of course,' the man answered, his voice suddenly much warmer. 'Is it about her death?'

'Yes.'

'A terrible thing. We were shocked.'

'We?' Brunetti asked.

A brief pause, and then the man explained, 'The staff here at the library.' When Ford spoke Italian his accent was so slight as almost not to be there.

'It should take me about twenty minutes to get there,' Brunetti said and put the phone down.

'And?' Signorina Elettra asked.

'Signor Ford is the co-director of the Biblioteca, but seemed uncertain at first about whether she worked there or not.'

'Anyone would be nervous, being asked about someone who was murdered.'

'Possibly,' Brunetti said. 'I'll go and talk to him. What about Guzzardi?' he asked.

'A few things. I'm trying to check on some houses he owned when he died.'

Brunetti had been moving towards the door, but he stopped and turned back.

'Were there many?'

'Three or four.'

'What happened to them?'

'I don't know yet.'

'How did you learn about them?'

'I asked my father.' She waited to see what Brunetti would say in response, but he had no time to talk to her about this now: he was reluctant to keep Signor Ford waiting. In fact, he already regretted having called and told the library director he was coming: people's response to the unexpected arrival of the police on their doorstep was often as illuminating as anything they subsequently said.

Brunetti walked back towards the Arsenale, turning and choosing bridges by instinct as he allowed the tangled story of Claudia Leonardo and her grandfather to take shape, evaporate, and then reform in his mind. Facts, dates, pieces of information, fragments of rumour swirled around, blinding him so that it wasn't until he found himself at the entrance to the Arsenale, the goofy lions lined up on his left, that he came back to the present. At the top of the wooden bridge he allowed himself a moment to gaze through the gateway into what had once been the womb of Venice's power and the ultimate source of her wealth and dominion. With only manpower and hammers and saws and all those other tools with strange names that carpenters and boat builders use, they had managed to build a ship a day and fill the seas with the terrible power of their fleet. And today, with cranes and drills and endless sources of power, there was still no sign that the burnt-out Fenice would ever be rebuilt.

He turned both from these reflections and the gateway and continued, weaving back towards Via Garibaldi and then, keeping the canal on his left, down towards Sant'Anna. When he saw the façade of the church, he realized he had no memory of ever having been inside; perhaps, like so many others in the city, it didn't function any longer as a church. He wondered how much longer they could continue to serve as places of worship, now that there were so few worshippers and young people were bored, as were his own children, by the irrelevance of what the Church had to say to them. Brunetti would not much regret its passing, but the thought of what little there was to replace it unsettled him. Again, he had to summon himself back from these thoughts.

He crossed the small bridge on his left and saw, on his right, a single long building the back of which faced the church. He turned into Calle Sant'Anna and found himself in front of an immense green *portone*. To the right were two bells: 'Ford', and 'Biblioteca della Patria'. He rang the one for the library.

The door snapped open and he walked into an entrance hall that must have been five metres high. Enough light filtered in from the five barred windows on the canal to illuminate the enormous beams, almost as thick as those of the Palazzo Ducale, that spanned the ceiling. The floor was of brick, set in a simple herringbone pattern. He noticed that, towards the back door and particularly around the stairs that ran down to the water gate, the bricks glistened slickly with a thin coat of dark moss.

There was only one set of steps. At the first landing a short, thickset man dressed in a very expensive dark grey suit waited at the door. A bit younger than Brunetti, he had thinning reddish hair the curious dappled colour such hair turns on its way to white. 'Commissario Brunetti?' he asked and extended his hand.

'Yes. Signor Ford?' Brunetti asked in return, shaking hands.

'Please come in.' Ford stepped back and stood just inside the door, holding it open for Brunetti.

He entered and glanced around. A row of windows looked out over the canal, towards the opposing flank of the church. To his left, at the far end, more windows looked out over what Brunetti knew must be the Isola di San Pietro.

Four or five long tables, each of them bearing green-shaded reading lamps, were placed around the room, and glass-fronted bookcases lined the walls between the windows. The other walls were covered with framed photos and documents, and in a glass case in one corner objects Brunetti could not identify lay exposed on three shelves.

The room had ceilings as high as those in the entrance hall, and from many of the beams hung flags and standards which Brunetti did not recognize. To his left a long, glass-topped case, like the ones used in museums, contained a number of notebooks, all of them spread open so that the exposed pages could be read.

'I'm glad you came,' Ford said, making towards a door on the right. 'Please come into my office. We can talk there.'

As no one was in the reading room, Brunetti didn't understand why this was necessary, but he followed Ford as requested. His office, carved into the angle of the building farthest from the Isola di San Pietro, had windows on two sides, though those on the shorter wall looked across at the shutters of the house across the *calle*.

Here, too, the walls between the windows were filled to the height of a man with bookshelves; half contained box files, rather than books.

Taking the seat offered him, Brunetti began by asking, 'You said Claudia Leonardo worked here?'

'Yes, she did,' Ford answered. He sat opposite Brunetti, declining the opportunity to place himself behind his desk and thus in some sort of position of authority. He had light brown eyes and a straight nose and was, at least by English standards, a handsome man.

'For how long?'

'About three months, perhaps a bit less than that.'

'What did she do here?'

'She catalogued entries, helped readers with research questions . . . all the jobs it's normal for a librarian to do.'

Ford's voice was level as he answered Brunetti's questions, as if to suggest he found them understandable and expected.

'Presumably, as a student at the university, she hadn't been trained as a librarian. How did she know how to do all of this?'

'She was very bright, Claudia,' Ford said with his first smile. His eyes grew sad as he heard himself praising the young girl. 'And, really, once a person knows the basic principles of research, it's all pretty much the same.'

'Doesn't the Internet change all of that?' Brunetti asked.

'Of course, in some fields. But the information we have here at the Library and the sort of things our borrowers are interested in, well, I'm afraid most of it isn't available on the Internet.'

'What sort of things?'

'Personal accounts of the men who served in the war or in the Resistance. Names of people who were killed. Places where small battles or skirmishes were fought. That sort of thing.'

'And who is interested in this information?'

Ford's voice grew more animated as the subject turned to material he was familiar with, the death of young men more than fifty years ago, and away from the recent death of a young girl. 'Very often we get requests from the relatives of men who were reported as lost or who were listed as having been captured. Sometimes, in the journals or letters of men who fought in the same place or who were perhaps captured at the same time, some mention is made of the missing men. Because most of the information we have is unpublished, this is the only place people can find it. And find out what happened to their relatives.'

'But doesn't the Archivio di Stato provide this sort of information?' Brunetti asked.

'I'm afraid the Archives provide very little information of this sort. And I choose the verb intentionally: provide. Of course, they have the information, but they seem reluctant to provide it. Or, if they do, it's only after heartbreaking delays.'

'Why?' Brunetti asked.

'Only God knows why,' Ford answered, making no attempt to disguise his exasperation. 'I can tell you only how it works or, more accurately, doesn't work.' As with any historian warming to his subject, Ford's voice grew more animated. 'The process of making a request is unnecessarily complicated and, to be fair, the Archive functions at its own pace.' When Brunetti did not ask for illumination of this last, Ford offered it anyway. 'I've had people come here who made official requests as long ago as thirty years. One man even brought me a folder of correspondence concerning his attempt to discover the fate of his brother, who was last heard from in 1945. The file was filled with standard letters from the Archive, saying that the request was being processed through the proper channels.' Brunetti made a noise that displayed interest, and the Englishman continued. 'The worst part of this one was that the original letters asking for information, the ones from the family, were all signed by his father. But he died abut fifteen years ago without hearing anything, so the son took over.'

'Why did he come to you?'

Ford looked uncomfortable. 'I don't think it's right to boast about what we do and so I try not to, but we have found records for many people who failed to get information from the Archive, and so the word has got round that we might be able to help.'

'Is there a charge for your services?'

Ford seemed genuinely surprised by the question. 'Absolutely not. The Library receives a small grant from the state, but the bulk of our money comes from private contributions and from a private foundation.' He hesitated, then continued. 'The question is offensive, Commissario. Excuse me for saying that, but it is.'

'I understand, Signore,' said Brunetti with a small bow in his direction, 'but I ask you to understand that I am here, in a sense, as a researcher myself, and so I have to ask everything that occurs to me. But I assure you I meant no offence.'

Ford accepted this with a small bow of his own, and the atmosphere between them grew warmer.

'And Claudia Leonardo?' Brunetti asked. 'How is it that she came to work here?'

'She came, originally, to do research, and then when she learned what we were doing here she asked if she could work as a volunteer. It really wasn't more than a few hours a week. I could check my records if you want,' Ford said, starting to get to his feet. Brunetti waved him back with a motion of his hand.

'She quickly became familiar with our resources,' the Englishman continued, 'and just as quickly she became very popular with many of our borrowers.' Ford looked down at his hands, searching for a way to say what he wanted to say. 'Many of them are very old, you see, and I think it did them a lot of good to have someone around who was not only helpful, but who was very . . .' he trailed away.

'I think I understand,' Brunetti said, himself unable to use any of the words which might do justice to Claudia's youth and spirit without causing himself pain. 'Do you have any idea how she came to learn of the Library in the first place?'

'No, not at all. She showed up here, asking if she could consult our records, and as she was interested in our material she came back often and then, as I said, she asked if there were any way she could be of help.' He cast his memory back to the young girl and her request. 'We do not have a large grant from the state, and many of our borrowers are poor, so we were very happy to accept her offer.'

'We?' Brunetti inquired. 'You said you were co-director. May I inquire who the other director is?'

'Of course,' Ford said, with a smile at his own

forgetfulness. 'My wife. It was she, in fact, who established the Library. When we married, she suggested I take over half of her duties.'

'I see,' said Brunetti. 'To get back to Claudia, did she ever talk of her friends, perhaps a boyfriend?'

Ford considered this. 'No, nothing I can remember exactly. She might have talked of a boy – I like to think that young girls do – but I can't honestly say that I have a memory of anyone specific.'

'Her family, perhaps? Other friends?'

'No, nothing at all. I'm very sorry, Commissario. But she was much younger, and I have to confess that, unless they're talking about history or some other subject I find interesting, I don't pay too much attention to what young people say.' His grin was embarrassed, almost self-effacing, but Brunetti, who shared his opinion of the conversation of the young, saw no reason for him to feel embarrassed.

He could think of nothing else to ask and so got to his feet and extended his hand. 'Thank you for your time and your help, Signor Ford,' Brunetti said.

'Do you have any idea . . .?' the other man asked, unable to phrase the question.

'We're continuing the investigation,' came Brunetti's formulaic response.

'Good. It's a terrible thing. She was a lovely girl. We were all very fond of her.'

There seemed nothing Brunetti could add to that, so he followed Ford from the office and through the empty reading room. Ford offered to see him to the entrance, but Brunetti politely said he would go downstairs alone. He let himself out into the pale light of a late autumn day with little to do save go home for lunch, taking with him only the feeling of the senseless loss of a young life which his time with Ford had brought so forcefully back to him.

18

At home, Paola greeted him with the news that he'd had two calls from Marco Erizzo, asking that he call back as soon as possible. Beside the phone she had written the number of Marco's *telefonino*, and Brunetti called it immediately, though he could see through the door that his family was already seated at the table, steam rising from their tagliatelle.

On the second ring, Marco answered with his name.

'It's me, Guido. What is it?'

'Your men are looking for me,' Marco said in an agitated voice. 'But I'd rather you came and got me and took me in.'

Thinking that Marco had perhaps been watching too much television, Brunetti asked, 'What are you talking about, Marco? What men? What have you done?'

'I told you what was happening, didn't I?'

'About the permits? Yes, you told me. Is that what this is about?'

'Yes.' There were noises in the background, a blast of static on the line. Brunetti asked when the line cleared, 'What happened?'

'It was the architect,' Marco said. 'That bastard. He was the one. The permits were ready three months ago, but he kept telling me they weren't and that if we made some minor changes to the plans, maybe they'd finally approve them. And then, like I told you, he said someone in the Comune wanted thirty million lire. And all this time I was paying him for every new set of plans he drew up and for all the time he said he spent working for me.' His voice stopped, cut off by rage.

'How did you find out?'

'I was having a drink with Angelo Costantini yesterday, and a friend of his came in, and when he introduced us, this guy recognized my name and said he works in the planning office and asked me when I was going to come in and pick up the permissions.' He paused to allow Brunetti to express shock or disapproval, but Brunetti's attention was devoted to his tagliatelle, now covered with an upended plate in what he hoped would be a successful attempt to keep them warm.

'What did you do, Marco?' he asked, his attention still distracted by his quickly cooling lunch.

'I asked him what he was talking about, and he said that the architect told them – it must have been two months ago – that I wanted him to make some more changes to the plans so he needed to discuss them with me before he submitted the final drawings.'

'But if they were already approved, why didn't they just call you?'

'They called the architect. He's lucky I didn't kill him.'

Brunetti suddenly understood the reason for the call. 'What happened?'

'I went to his office this morning,' Marco said, then stopped.

'And what did you do?'

'I told him what I'd heard, what the guy at the planning office told me.'

'And then?'

'Then he told me I must have misunderstood what he meant and that he'd go over there and straighten things out this morning.' He heard Marco breathe deeply in an attempt to control his anger. 'But I told him I knew what was going on and that he was fired.'

'And?'

'And he said I couldn't fire him until the job was finished and if I did he'd sue me for breach of contract.'

'And?'

The pause was one Brunetti had often heard from his children, so he knew to wait it out. 'So I hit him,' Marco finally said. Another pause, and then he said, 'He sat there, behind his big desk, with plans and projects laid out on it, and he told me he'd sue me if I tried to fire him. And I lost my temper.'

'What happened?'

'I went around his desk; I just wanted to get my hands on him . . .' Brunetti imagined Marco saying this before a judge and cringed. 'He stood up and came towards me.'

When it seemed that this was the only explanation Marco was going to give, Brunetti said, 'Tell me exactly what you did, Marco,' using the same tone he used with the kids when they came home from school with bad reports.

'I told you. I hit him.' Before Brunetti could speak, Marco went on, 'It wasn't very hard. I didn't even knock him down, just sort of shoved him away from me.'

'Did you hit him with a fist?' Brunetti asked, thinking it necessary to determine just what 'shove' might mean.

After a long pause, Marco said, 'Sort of.'

Brunetti left that and asked, 'Where?'

'On his jaw, or his nose.'

'And?'

'He just sort of fell back in his chair.'

'Was there any blood?'

166

'I don't know.'

'Why not?'

'I left. I watched him sit back down and then I left.'

'Why do you think my men are after you, then?'

'Because that's the sort of man he is. He'd call the police and say I tried to kill him. But I wanted you to know what really happened.'

'Is this what really happened, Marco?'

'Yes, I swear it on my mother's head.'

'All right. What do you want me to do?'

There was real surprise in Marco's voice when he said, 'Nothing. Why should I want you to do anything? I just wanted you to know.'

'Where are you now?'

'In the restaurant.'

'The one near Rialto?' Brunetti asked.

'Yes. Why?'

'I'll be there in five minutes. Wait for me. Don't do anything and don't talk to anyone. Do you understand me, Marco? Not to anyone. And don't call your lawyer.'

'All right,' Marco said sulkily.

'I'll be there,' Brunetti said and put the phone down. He went back to the table, lifted the cover from his plate and breathed in the savoury aroma of grated smoked ricotta and eggplant. He set the cover gently back in place, kissed Paola on the top of her head and said, 'I've got to go and see Marco.'

As he let himself out of the door, he heard Chiara saying, 'OK, Raffi, you can have half.'

The restaurant was full, tables covered with things, marvellous things: one couple sat with lobsters the size of dachshunds in front of them, while to the left a group of businessmen were eating their way through a platter of seafood that would have fed a Sri Lankan village for a week.

Brunetti went straight into the kitchen, where he found

Marco talking to Signora Maria, the cook. Marco came over to Brunetti. 'Do you want to eat?' he asked.

This was one of the best restaurants in the city, and Signora Maria was a woman whose genius had provided Brunetti with endless pleasure. 'Thanks, Marco, but I had lunch at home,' he said. He took Marco by the arm and pulled him away from the disappointment in Maria's eyes and out of the way of a waiter who scrambled past, a loaded tray held at shoulder height. They stood just inside the door to the storeroom that held clean linens and cans of tomatoes.

'What's the architect's name?' Brunetti asked.

'Why do you want to know?' Marco demanded in the same sulky tone he'd used before.

Brunetti toyed with the idea of not explaining, but then he thought he would, if only to stop Marco from using that tone. 'Because I am going to go back to the Questura and see what I can find out about him, and if he has ever been in trouble or if there is any sort of case outstanding against him, I am going to endanger my job by threatening him with the abuse of my power until he agrees not to bring charges against you.' His voice had risen as he spoke, and he realized how similar his anger towards Marco was to that he sometimes felt towards the children. 'Does that answer your question? And now give me his name.'

'Piero Sbrissa,' Marco said. 'His studio is in San Marco.'

'Thanks,' Brunetti said, slipping around Marco and back into the restaurant, from where he called back, 'I'll call you. Don't talk to anyone,' and left.

At the Questura, Vianello spent an hour on the computer and Brunetti two on the phone, and by the end of that time, each had found sufficient indication that there might be some hope of persuading Architetto Sbrissa to see the wisdom of refraining from making any formal charge against his client, Marco Erizzo. The architect, it seemed, had more than once experienced unaccountably long delays in obtaining building permits, or so three of his former clients told Brunetti. In each case, they had agreed to Sbrissa's suggestion that they use a less than legal – though more than common – method of resolving their problems, though none of the men was willing to name the sum involved. Vianello, for his part, discovered that Sbrissa reported having earned only sixteen million lire from Marco Erizzo the previous year, though Marco's secretary, when the inspector called her, said that their records con-tained signed receipts for more than forty.

Brunetti called a friend of his at the *Carabinieri* station in San Zaccaria and learned that Sbrissa had called them that morning to report an attack and had agreed to go in later that day, after he'd seen a doctor, to make a formal *denuncia*. It was the work of a moment for Brunetti to pass on the information about Sbrissa's tax records and to ask his friend if Architetto Sbrissa might be persuaded to reconsider filing his complaint; the *carabiniere* said he'd discuss it with the architect himself but had no doubt whatsoever that Signor Sbrissa would see the path of greater wisdom.

Marco, when Brunetti phoned to tell him that the situation was being taken care of, at first refused to believe him. He wanted to know what Brunetti had done, and when Brunetti refused to tell him, Marco went silent, then blurted out that he had been *disonorato* by having had to ask the police for help.

With some effort, Brunetti restrained himself from com- menting and, instead, said only, 'You're my friend, Marco, and that's the end of it.'

'But you have to let me do something for you.'

'All right, you can,' Brunetti said immediately.

'Good. What? Anything.'

'The next time we eat at the restaurant, ask Signora Maria to give Paola the recipe for the filling she makes for the mussels.'

There was a long pause, but finally Marco said, as much in sorrow as in earnest, 'That's blackmail. She'd never do it.'

'It's too bad Signora Maria didn't hit Sbrissa, then.'

'No, you wouldn't get it, even then,' Marco said, resigned. 'She'd go to jail before she'd tell you about the mussels.'

'I was afraid of that,' Brunetti said, assured Marco that he'd think of some way he could pay his debt, and hung up.

Rewarding as this was at a personal level, it did little to advance Brunetti's understanding of what he had come to think of as the Leonardo, Guzzardi, Filipetto triangle. He went down to Signorina Elettra's office but found that she had left for the day: not surprising, really, as it was almost five, and she often complained of the tedium of the last two hours in the office. Just as he was turning to leave, the door to Vice-Questore Patta's office opened and the man himself emerged, his dove grey overcoat folded over one arm and a new briefcase Brunetti identified instantly as Bottega Veneta in his left hand.

'Ah, Brunetti,' Patta said at once, 'I've got a meeting with the Praetore in twenty minutes.' Brunetti, who cared nothing about whether Patta chose to come to work or not or how long he chose to remain there, thought it interesting that the man's response was always a kind of Pavlovian mendacity: he wondered if Patta planned a career in politics after retiring from the police.

'Then I won't keep you, sir,' Brunetti said and moved aside to allow his superior to pass.

'Has there been any progress on . . .' Patta began but, obviously unable to recall Claudia's surname, continued, 'the murder of that young girl?'

'I'm gathering information, sir,' Brunetti said.

Patta, with a hurried glance at his watch, gave him a distracted, 'Good, good,' said goodbye, and was gone.

Brunetti was curious as to whether Signorina Elettra had discovered anything, but he hesitated to approach her computer: if she had found anything important, she would surely have told him; and the information in her computer, given the suspicion with which she regarded some of the men who worked at the Questura, would surely be hedged round by moats and mazes more than sufficient to defeat any attempt he might make to penetrate them.

He went back upstairs to his own office and leafed through the file on Claudia's murder until he found the home phone number of her flatmate. He dialled the Milano prefix, then the number, and was soon talking to her mother, who agreed to call the girl to the phone; she warned Brunetti that her daughter was not to be upset, and said she'd be listening on the extension.

The call proved futile, however, for Lucia had no memory of hearing Claudia use Filipetto's name, nor did she remember hearing her speak of a notary. His sense of the mother's silent presence prevented Brunetti from asking the girl how she was, and when Lucia asked if there had been any progress, he could tell her nothing more than that they were investigating all possible leads and were optimistic that there would be progress soon. It distressed Brunetti to have to listen to himself coming out with such platitudes.

He was unable to set himself to anything after that, the echo of futility ringing clear in his ears, and so he left the Questura and headed back towards Rialto and home. At Piero's cheese stand, where he should have turned left, he continued straight on and allowed himself to head deeper into Santa Croce, toward Campo San Boldo. He didn't stop until he was in front of Signora Jacobs's home and ringing her doorbell.

He had to wait a long time before her deep voice asked who it was.

'Commissario Brunetti,' he answered.

'I told you I don't want to talk to you,' she said, sounding weary rather than angry.

'But I need to talk to you, Signora.'

'What about?'

'Notaio Filipetto.'

'Who?' she asked after a long time.

'Notaio Filipetto,' Brunetti repeated, offering no further clarification.

The door clicked open, surprising Brunetti. He went in and quickly up to her floor, where he found her propped against the door jamb as though drunk.

'Thank you, Signora,' he said, slipping his hand under her elbow and accompanying her back inside. He forced himself to pay no attention to the things in the room this time and took her slowly over to her chair, noting the lightness of her body. The instant she was seated, she reached beside her for a cigarette, but her hand was shaking so much that three of them jumped out of the packet and fell at her feet before she managed to get one lit. Just as he often wondered where all the food his children ate could possibly go, so too did he wonder, as he watched her inhale greedily, into what empty spaces in her lungs all of that smoke could possibly disappear.

He thought she would ask him something, but she remained silent until the cigarette was reduced to a tiny stub and dropped into a blue ceramic bowl already half filled with butts.

'Signora,' he began, 'the name of Dottor Filipetto has come up in our investigation.' He paused, waiting to see if she would question him or refer to the notary's name, but she did not. 'And so I've come to you,' he went on, 'to see if you can tell me why Claudia might have wanted to talk to him.'

'Claudia, is it, now?' she asked.

'I beg your pardon,' Brunetti said, genuinely taken aback.

'You speak of her as though she were a friend,' she said angrily. 'Claudia,' she repeated, and his thoughts fled to her.

Which was more intimate, Brunetti wondered, to startle a

person soon after sex or soon after death? Probably the latter, as they had been stripped of all pretence or opportunity to deceive. They lie there, exhausted and seeming painfully vulnerable, though they have been removed from all vulnerability and from all pain. To be helpless implies that help might be of some service: the dead were beyond that, beyond help and beyond hope.

'I wish that had been possible,' Brunetti said.

'Why?' she demanded, 'so you could ask her questions and pick at her secrets?'

'No, Signora, so that I could have talked to her about the books we both read.'

Signora Jacobs snorted in mingled disgust and disbelief.

Offended, though also intrigued by the idea that Claudia had secrets, Brunetti defended himself. 'She was one of my wife's students. We'd already talked about books.'

'Books,' she said, this time the disgust triumphant. Her anger caused her to catch her breath, and that in its turn provoked an explosion of coughing. It was a deep, humid smoker's cough, and she went on for so long that Brunetti finally went into the kitchen and brought her a glass of water. He held it out until she took it and waited as she forced it down in tiny sips and finally stopped coughing.

'Thank you,' she said quite naturally and handed him the glass.

'You're welcome,' he said, with equal ease, set the glass on the desk to her left and pulled his chair across so that he could sit facing her.

'Signora,' he began, 'I don't know what you think of the police, or what you think of me, but you must believe that all I want is to find the person who killed her. I don't want to know anything that she might have wanted to remain secret, not unless it will help me do that. If such a thing is possible, I want her to rest in peace.' He looked at her all the time he was speaking, willing her to believe him.

Signora Jacobs reached for another cigarette and lit it. Again she inhaled deeply and Brunetti felt himself grow tense, waiting for another explosion of coughing. But none came. When the butt was smouldering in the blue bowl she said, 'Her family hasn't the knack.'

Confused, he asked, 'Of what?'

'Resting in peace. Doing anything in peace.'

'I'm sorry, but I don't know anyone in her family, only Claudia.' He considered how to phrase the next question, then abandoned caution and asked simply, 'Would you tell me about them?'

She pulled her hands to her face and made a steeple of them, touching her mouth with her forefingers. It was an attitude usually associated with prayer, though Brunetti suspected it had been a long time since this woman had prayed for, or to, anything.

'You know who her grandfather was,' she said. Brunetti nodded. 'And her father?' This time he shook his head.

'He was born during the war, so of course his father named him Benito.' She looked at him and smiled, as though she had just told a joke, but Brunetti did not return her smile. He waited for her to continue.

'He was that kind of man, Luca.'

To Brunetti, Luca Guzzardi was a political opportunist who had died in a madhouse, so he thought it best to remain silent.

'He really believed in it all. The marching and the uniforms and the return to the glory of the Roman Empire.' She shook her head at this but did not smile. 'At least he believed it at the beginning.'

Brunetti had never known, nor had either of his parents ever told him, if his father believed in all this. He didn't know if it made a difference or, if it did, what kind. He bided his time silently, knowing that the old will always return to their subject.

'He was a beautiful man.' Signora Jacobs turned towards the sideboard that stood against the wall, gesturing with one hand to a ragged row of bleached photographs. Sensing that it was expected of him, Brunetti got to his feet and went over to examine the pictures. The first was a half-portrait of a young man, his head all but obscured by the plume-crested helmet of the *Bersaglieri*, an element of uniform the adult Brunetti had always found especially ludicrous. In another, the same young man held a rifle, in the one next to it, a sword, his body half draped in a long dark cloak. In each photo the pose was self-consciously belligerent, the chin thrust out, the gaze unyielding in response to the need to immortalize this moment of high patriotism. Brunetti found the poses as silly as the plumes and ribbons and epaulettes with which the young man's uniform was bedecked. So resistant was Brunetti to the lure of the military that he could rarely resist the temptation to superimpose upon men in uniform the template of New Guinean tribesmen with bones stuck through their noses, their naked bodies painted white, their penises safeguarded by metre-long bamboo sheaths. Official ceremonies and parades thus caused him a certain amount of difficulty.

He continued to look at the photographs until he judged the necessary period of time had passed, and then he returned to his seat opposite Signora Jacobs. 'Tell me more about him, Signora.'

Her glance was direct, its keenness touched by the faint clouding of age. 'What's to tell? We were young, I was in love, and the future was ours.'

Brunetti permitted himself to respond to the intimacy of her remark. 'Only you were in love?'

Her smile was that of an old person, one who had left almost everything behind. 'I told you: he was beautiful. Men like that, in the end, love only themselves.' Before he could comment, she added, 'I didn't know that then. Or didn't want to.' She reached for another cigarette and lit it. Blowing out a long trail of smoke, she said, 'It comes to the same thing, though, doesn't it?' She turned the burning tip of the cigarette towards herself, looked at it for a moment, then said, 'The strange thing is that, even knowing this about him, it doesn't change the way I loved him. And still do.' She glanced up at him, then down at her lap. Softly, she said, 'That's why I want to give him back his good name.'

Brunetti remained silent, not wanting to interrupt her. Sensing this, she went on, 'It was all so exciting, the sense or the hope that everything would be made new. Austria had been full of it for years, and so it never occurred to me to question it. And when I saw it again here, in men like Luca and his friends, I couldn't see what it really was or what they were really like or that all it would bring us, all of us, was death and suffering.' She sighed and then added, 'Neither could Luca.'

When it began to seem as if she would not speak again, Brunetti asked, 'How long did you know him?'

She considered this, then answered, 'Six years, all through the last years of the war and his trial and then . . .' her voice trailed off, leaving Brunetti curious as to how she would put it. 'And then what came after,' was all she said.

'Did you see him on San Servolo?'

She cleared her throat, a tearing, wet sound that set Brunetti's teeth on edge, so deeply did it speak of illness and dark liquids. 'Yes. I went out once a week until they wouldn't let me see him any more.'

'Why was that?'

'I think it was because they didn't want anyone to know how they were kept.'

'But why the change? If they'd let you go in the beginning, that is,' Brunetti explained.

'Because he got much worse after he was there. And after he realized he wasn't going to leave.'

'Should he have?' Brunetti asked, then clarified his question. 'That is, when he first went in, did he or did you think he was going to be able to leave?'

'That was the agreement,' she said.

'With whom?' Brunetti asked.

'Why are you asking all of this?' she asked him.

'Because I want to understand things. About him, and about the past.'

'Why?'

He thought that should be obvious to her. 'Because it might help.'

'About Claudia?' she asked. He wished there had been some trace of hope in her voice, but he knew she was too old to find hope in anything that followed death.

He decided to tell her the truth, rather than what he wanted to say. 'Perhaps.' Then he led her back to his original question. 'What was the agreement?'

She lit another cigarette and smoked half of it before she decided to answer. 'With the judges. That he would confess to everything and, when he had his collapse, they'd send him to San Servolo, where he could stay a year or two and when everyone had forgotten about him, he'd be released.' She finished the cigarette and stuffed it among the others in the ashtray. 'And come back to me,' she added. After a long pause, she said, 'That was all I wanted.'

'But what happened?'

She studied Brunetti's face, then answered, 'You're too young to know about San Servolo, about what really happened there.'

He nodded.

'I was never told. I went there one Saturday morning. I went out every week, even when all they did was tell me I couldn't see him and send me home. But that time they told me he had died.' Her voice ground to a halt, and she looked down at her lap, where her hands lay, inert. She turned them over and looked down at the smooth palms, rubbing at the left with the tips of the first three fingers of the right in what seemed to Brunetti an attempt to erase the lifeline. 'That's all they told me,' she went on. 'No explanation. But it could have been anything. One of the other patients could have killed him. That was always covered up, when it happened. Or it could have been one of the guards. Or it could have been typhus, for all I know. They were kept like animals, once people stopped coming to see them.' She drew her hands into tight fists and pressed them on her thighs.

'But what about the agreement with the judges?' Brunetti asked.

She smiled and laughed, almost as if she really found his question amusing. 'You, of all people, Commissario, should know better than to believe anything a judge promises you.' When Brunetti didn't argue the point, she continued. 'Two of the judges were Communists, so they wanted someone to be punished, and the third was the son of the Fascist Party chief in Mestre, so he had to prove that he was the purest of the pure and not at all influenced by his father's politics.'

'What about the Amnesty?' Brunetti asked, thinking of the general slate-cleaning Togliatti had orchestrated just after the end of the war, pardoning all crimes committed by either side during the Fascist era. He didn't understand how Guzzardi could have been convicted when thousands went free for having done the same things, or far worse.

'The judges declared that the crime took place on Swiss territory,' she said simply. 'No amnesty would cover that.'

'I don't understand,' Brunetti protested.

'The home of the Swiss Consul. They said it was Swiss territory.'

'But that's absurd,' Brunetti said.

'That's not what the judges said,' she insisted. 'And the appeal court confirmed it. Legally, I did everything I could.' Her voice was truculent and had taken on that hard edge voices acquire when they are used to defend a belief rather than a fact.

Brunetti had heard enough stories from his father's friends about what went on just after the end of the war to believe that Guzzardi had been convicted because of this invented technicality. Many grudges and injuries had been racked up during the war, and many of them were paid back after the German surrender. The judges could easily have persuaded Guzzardi, or his lawyer, to accept their offer, only to renege on it once the convicted man had been taken to San Servolo.

He glanced at the old woman and saw that she sat with one fist pressed against her lips. 'When Claudia came to me,' he said, 'she wanted to know if it were possible to reverse a judgment for someone who was convicted just after the war, and when I asked her about it, she said only that it was for her grandfather, but she didn't give me much information.' He paused to see if she would respond; when she did not, he went on. 'Now after what you've said, I have a clearer understanding. It's been a long time since I studied law, Signora, but I don't think the case is very complicated. I think it's likely that a formal request to reverse this decision would be granted, but I don't think that would lead to an official proclamation of innocence.'

She watched him as he said these last sentences, and he watched her making other calculations or recalling other words. A very long time passed before she spoke. 'Are you sure of this? That there would be no official declaration, some sort of ceremony that would restore his honour and his good name?'

From what Brunetti had heard of Guzzardi, it seemed unlikely that he had ever had much honour worth saving, but Signora Jacobs was too old and too frail to be told that. 'Signora, to the best of my knowledge, there is no legal mechanism or process for that. Whoever might have told you that the possibility of such a thing exists is either misinformed or is intentionally telling you something that isn't true.' Brunetti stopped here, not willing to consider, or mention, how long the reversal of a judgment made a half a century ago would be likely to take, as it would not be achieved in this woman's lifetime. If the redemption of her grandfather's good name had been something Claudia wanted to offer to her grandmother, then her trip to Brunetti's office had been a fool's errand, but the old woman hardly needed to hear this.

She turned her head and looked over at the line of photos, and for a long time she ignored Brunetti and stared at them. She pressed her thin lips together and closed her eyes, letting her head fall forward wearily. As they sat, Brunetti decided to ask her about the events that had precipitated Guzzardi's Luciferian fall from high estate to the dark horror of San Servolo. As she raised a hand from her lap, Brunetti asked, 'What happened to the drawings?'

She had been reaching for another cigarette when he spoke, and he saw her hand hesitate in mid-air. She gave him a surprised glance, then looked back at her hand, followed through on the gesture, and took a cigarette. 'What drawings?' she asked; her look had prepared Brunetti for her protestation of ignorance.

'Someone told me that the Swiss Consul had given some drawings to the Guzzardis.'

'Sold some, you mean,' she said with a heavy emphasis on the first word.

'As you like,' Brunetti conceded and left it at that.

'That was something else that happened after the war,' she said, sounding tired. 'People who had sold things tried to get them back by saying they'd been forced to sell them. Whole collections had to be given back by people who had bought them in good faith.' She managed to sound indignant.

Brunetti had no doubt that things like this had happened, but he had read enough to know that most of the injustice had been suffered by those who, from timidity or outright menace, had been led to sell or sign away their possession. He saw no point, however, in disputing this with Signora Jacobs.

'*Certo, certo,*' Brunetti mumbled.

Suddenly he felt his wrist imprisoned by her thin fingers. 'It's the truth,' she whispered, her voice tight and passionate. 'When he was on trial they all got in touch with the judges, saying he had cheated them out of this or that, demanding their things back.' She yanked savagely on his hand, pulling him closer until his face was a hand's breath from hers. 'It was all lies. Then and now. All of the things are his, legally his. No one can trick me.' Brunetti breathed in the raw stench of tobacco and bad teeth, saw something fierce flare up in her eyes. 'Luca could never have done something like that. He could never have done anything dishonourable.' Her voice had the measured cadence of one who had said the same thing many times, as if repetition would force it to be true.

There was nothing to be said here, so he waited, though he moved slowly back from her, waiting to hear what her next defence would be.

It seemed, however, that Signora Jacobs had said all she was going to, for she reached over for another cigarette, lit it, and puffed at it as though it were the only thing of interest in the room. At last, when the cigarette was finished and she had dropped it on top of the pile of butts, she said, without bothering to turn to him, 'You can go now.'

19

Walking home, Brunetti played back in his mind the conversation with Signora Jacobs. He was puzzled by the paradox between her bleak observation that Guzzardi was capable of loving only himself and the profundity of the love she still felt for him. Love rendered people foolish, he knew, sometimes more than that, but it usually provided them with the anaesthesia necessary to blind them to the contradictions in their own behaviour. Not so Signora Jacobs, who seemed utterly devoid of illusions about her former lover. How sad, to be as clear-eyed about your weakness as helpless to resist it. Guzzardi had been handsome, but it was a kind of slick-haired, matinée idol beauty that was today usually associated with pimps and hairdressers rather than with those men which current taste defined as handsome, most of whom looked to Brunetti like nonentities in suits or little blond boys bent on keeping puberty at bay.

But the signs of long-term love were there. She had been eager to speak to Guzzardi, had certainly wanted Brunetti to admire his photo, a strange thing to expect one man to do of another. She had spoken of his trial and of his time – it must have been a terrible time – in San Servolo with visible pain, and there was no disguising the effect it had upon her, even now, after so much time, to speak of his death.

She had said the Guzzardis had no knack of resting in peace. Recalling that remark, he remembered that she had made it in reference to Luca Guzzardi's son, Benito, but then the conversation had sheered away from him, and so Brunetti had never learned in what way he had failed to find peace. And if there had been a son, and there had been Claudia, then there was a mother. Claudia had said her mother's mother was German, and had referred to her own in the past tense; Lucia told him Claudia had said her father was dead; Signora Gallante said that, although Claudia spoke of her mother as gone, the old woman did not have the sense that this meant she was dead. She could, Claudia's mother, be anywhere from her late thirties to her fifties and anywhere in the world, but all he knew was that her name was Leonardo, hardly a German surname.

He allowed his mind to run over the available sources of information. With Claudia's date of birth, they could find out where in the city her mother had been resident when she was born. But Claudia had no Venetian accent, so she could have been born on the mainland, indeed, even in some other country. His thoughts keeping pace with his steps, he realized that all of this information would be easily available either at the university or in the Ufficio Anagrafe, where she would have to be registered. She was so young that all of the information would be computerized and thus readily available to Signorina Elettra. He glanced up and smiled to himself, pleased to have found something else with which to engage Signorina Elettra and thus remind her of how essential she was to the successful running of the Questura.

Claudia's grandmother had gone off with a British soldier after the war, taking Claudia's father with her. How, then, had the girl ended up in Venice, speaking Italian with no trace of accent, and how had it happened that she had come to think of Signora Jacobs as her adoptive grandmother? Much as he told himself that all speculation on these matters was futile, Brunetti could not keep his imagination from worrying at them.

These thoughts accompanied him home, but as he turned into the final flight of steps leading up to the apartment, he made a conscious effort to leave them on the stairway until the following morning took him back into the world of death.

This decision proved a wise one, for there would have been no room for the people who filled his thoughts at a table that already held not only his family but Sara Paganuzzi, Raffi's girlfriend, and Michela Fabris, a schoolfriend of Chiara's, come to spend the night.

Because Marco had caused him to miss his lunch, Brunetti felt justified in accepting a second portion of the spinach and ricotta crêpes that Paola had made as a first course. He was too busy sating his hunger to say much as he ate them, and so talk broke into two sections, like the chorus in a Scarlatti oratorio: Paola talked with Chiara and Michela about a movie actor whose name Brunetti didn't recognize but with whom his only daughter seemed to be hopelessly besotted; while Raffi and Sara conversed in the impenetrable code of young love. Brunetti remembered having once been able to speak it.

As his hunger diminished, he found himself better able to pay attention to what was going on around him, as though tuning in to a radio station. 'I think he's wonderful,' Michela sighed, encouraging Brunetti to change stations and tune in to Sara, but listening was no easier on that channel, save that the object of her adoration was his only son.

It was Paola who saved him by bringing to the table an enormous frying pan filled with stewed rabbit with what looked to him, as she set it down in the centre of the table, like olives. 'And walnuts?' he asked, pointing to some small tan chunks that lay on the top.

'Yes,' Paola said, reaching for Michela's plate.

The girl passed it to her but asked, sounding rather nervous, 'Is that rabbit, Signora Brunetti?'

'No, it's chicken, Michela,' she said with an easy smile, placing a thigh on the girl's plate.

Chiara started to say something, but Brunetti surprised her into silence by reaching over to pick up her plate, which he passed to Paola. 'And what else is in it?' Brunetti asked.

'Oh, some celery for taste, and the usual spices.'

Passing the plate to Chiara, Brunetti asked Michela, 'What movie were you and Chiara talking about?'

As she told him, not forgetting to extol the charms of the young actor who held her in thrall, Brunetti ate his rabbit, smiling and nodding at Michela as he tried to determine whether Paola had put a bay leaf in, as well as rosemary. Raffi and Sara ate quietly, and Paola came back to the table with a platter of small roasted potatoes and zucchini cooked with thin slices of almonds. Michela turned to the two previous films which had catapulted her actor to stardom, and Brunetti served himself another piece of rabbit.

As she spoke, Michela ate her way through everything, pausing only when Paola slipped another spoonful of meat and gravy on to her plate, at which point she said, 'The chicken is delicious, Signora.'

Paola smiled her thanks.

After dinner, when Chiara and Michela were back in her room, giggling at a volume achievable only by teenage girls, Brunetti kept Paola company as she did the dishes. He sipped at nothing more than a drop of plum liquor while Paola slipped the dishes into the drying rack above the sink.

'Why wouldn't she eat rabbit?' he finally asked.

'Kids are like that. They don't like to eat animals they can be sentimental about,' Paola explained with every indication of sympathy for the idea.

'It doesn't stop Chiara from eating veal,' Brunetti said.

'Or lamb, for that matter,' Paola agreed.

'Then why wouldn't Michela want to eat rabbit?' Brunetti asked doggedly.

'Because a rabbit is cuddly and something every city child can see or touch, even if it's only in a pet shop. To touch the other ones you have to go to a farm, so they aren't really real.'

'You think that's why we don't eat dogs and cats?' Brunetti asked. 'Because we have them around all the time and they become our friends?'

'We don't eat snake, either,' Paola said.

'Yes, but that's because of Adam and Eve. Lots of people have no trouble eating them. The Chinese, for example.'

'And we eat eel,' she agreed. She came and stood beside him, reached down for his glass, and took a sip.

'Why did you lie to her?' he finally asked.

'Because she's a nice girl, and I didn't want her to have to eat something she didn't want to eat or to embarrass herself by saying she didn't want to eat it.'

'But it was delicious,' he insisted.

'If that was a compliment, thank you,' Paola said, handing him back the glass. 'Besides, she'll get over it, or she'll forget about it as she gets older.'

'And eat rabbit?'

'Probably.'

'I don't think I have much of a feeling for young girls,' he finally said.

'For which I suppose I should be very grateful,' she answered.

The next morning he went directly to Signorina Elettra's office, where he found her engaged in conversation with Lieutenant Scarpa. As the lieutenant never failed to bring out the venom in his superior's secretary, Brunetti said a general good morning intended for both of them and moved over to stand by the window, waiting for them to finish their conversation.

'I'm not sure you're authorized to take files from the archives,' the lieutenant said.

'Would you like me to come and ask for your authorization each time I want to consult a file, Lieutenant?' she asked with her most dangerous smile.

'Of course not. But you have to follow procedures.'

'Which procedures would those be, Lieutenant?' she asked, picking up a pen and moving a notepad closer to her.

'You have to ask for authorization.'

'Yes, and from whom?'

'From the person who is authorized to give it,' he said, his voice no longer pleasant.

'Yes, but can you tell me who that person is?'

'It's whoever is listed on the personnel directive that details the chain of command and responsibility.'

'And where might I find a copy of the directive?' she asked, tapping the point of her pen on the pad, but lightly and only once.

'In the file of directives,' the lieutenant said, voice even closer to the edge of his control.

'Ah,' Signorina Elettra said with a happy smile. 'And who can authorize me to consult that file?'

Scarpa turned and walked from her office, pausing at the door as if eager to slam it but then, aware of Brunetti's bland presence, resisting the temptation.

Brunetti moved over to her desk. 'I've warned you about him, Signorina,' he said, managing to keep any hint of disapproval out of his voice.

'I know, I know,' she said, pursing her lips and letting out an exasperated sigh. 'But the temptation is too strong. Every time he comes in here telling me what I have to do, I can't resist the impulse to go right for his jugular.'

'It will only cause you trouble,' he admonished.

She shrugged this away. 'It's like having a second dessert, I suppose. You know you shouldn't, but it just tastes so good you can't resist.'

Brunetti, who had had his own fair share of trouble with the lieutenant, would hardly have chosen that simile, but his nature was not as combative as Signorina Elettra's and so he let it pass. Besides, any sign of aggressiveness on Signorina Elettra's part was to be welcomed as evidence of her general return to good spirits, however paradoxical that might seem to anyone who didn't know her, so Brunetti asked, 'What have you learned about Guzzardi?'

'I told you I was looking into his ownership of houses when he died, didn't I?'

He nodded.

'Only he didn't own them at the time of his death. Ownership was transferred to Hedi Jacobs when he was in jail, awaiting trial.'

'Interestinger and interestinger,' Brunetti said in English. 'Transferred how?'

'Sold to her. It was all perfectly legal; the papers are all in order.'

'What about his will?'

'I found a copy at the College of Notaries.'

'How did you know where to look?'

She gave her most seraphic smile. 'There's only one notary who's been named in all of this,' she said, but she said it modestly.

'Filipetto?' Brunetti asked.

The smile returned.

'He was Guzzardi's notary?'

'The will was recorded in his register soon after Guzzardi's death,' she said, no longer able to keep the glow of pride from her voice. 'And when Filipetto retired, all of his records were sent to the college, where I found it.' She opened her top drawer and drew out a photocopy of a document typed in the now archaic letters of a manual typewriter.

Brunetti took it from her and went over to the light of the window to read. Guzzardi declared that all of his possessions were to pass directly to his son, Benito and, in the event that his son should predecease him, to his son's heirs. It could not have been more simple. No mention was made of Hedi Jacobs, and no indication was given as to what his estate might consist of. 'His wife? Is there any sign she contested this?' he asked, holding up the document.

'There's no record in Filipetto's files that she did.' Before Brunetti could ask, she added, 'And that probably means that she divorced him before he died or didn't know or didn't care that he did die.'

Brunetti went back to her desk. 'The son?'

'The only mention of him is what you were told, sir, that his mother took him to England after the war.'

'Nothing more?' Brunetti couldn't disguise his irritation that a person could so easily disappear.

'I've sent a request to Rome, but all I have to give them is his name, not even an exact date of birth.' They shared a moment's despair at the likelihood of getting any sort of a response from Rome. 'I've also contacted a friend in London,' she went on, 'and asked him to check the records there. It seems the British have a system that works.'

'When can you expect an answer?' Brunetti asked.

'Long before I can expect anything from Rome, certainly.'

'I'd like you to contact the university and the Ufficio Anagrafe and see what information they have about Claudia Leonardo. Her parents' names should be listed, perhaps their dates of birth, which you might send to London to see if that will help.' He thought of the German grandmother, but before he asked Signorina Elettra to begin to investigate the possibilities that created, he would see what there was to find here in the city and in London.

As he went back upstairs he remembered a passage from an ancient poem Paola had insisted on reading to him years ago. The lines described, if he recalled correctly, a dragon that sat on top of what the poet described as treasure trove, breathing fire and destruction at all who came near. He wasn't sure why it came to him, but he had a strange vision of Signora Jacobs nesting upon her treasures, willing destruction upon anyone who tried to extract anything from her hoard.

Even before he got to his office, he changed his mind and went back downstairs and out of the Questura. It was rash, he knew, and he shouldn't go back to Signora Jacobs's so soon after being dismissed, but she was the only person who could answer his questions about the treasures that surrounded her. He should have left word where he was going; he should have sat at his desk and answered the phone and initialled papers; no doubt he should also have reprimanded Signorina Elettra for her lack of deference to Lieutenant Scarpa.

Given the hour and the crowds of tourists who flooded the boats, he decided to walk, sure that he could avoid the worst gaggles of them until he neared Rialto and equally certain that their numbers would decrease again once he got past the *pescheria*. So it proved, but the brief period he spent pushing and evading his way through the streets between San Lio and the fish market soured his humour and brought his ever-simmering dislike of tourists to the boil. Why were they so slow and fat and lethargic? Why did they all have to get in his way? Why couldn't they, for God's sake, learn to walk properly in a city and not moon about like people at a country fair asked to judge the fattest pig?

His mood lifted as soon as he was free of them and moving through empty streets toward Campo San Boldo. He rang the bell, but there was no answer. Remembering a technique Vianello had employed to awaken people who fell asleep with the television on too loud, he pressed his thumb against the bell and left it there while he counted to a hundred. He counted slowly. There was still no answer.

The man in the tobacco shop had said he took the cigarettes up to her, so Brunetti went back, showed his warrant card and asked if the man had a key to the apartment.

The man behind the counter seemed not at all interested that the police wanted to speak to Signora Jacobs. He reached into his cash drawer and pulled out a single key. 'All I have is the key to the *portone* downstairs. She always let me into the apartment.'

Brunetti thanked him and said he'd bring the key back. He used it to open the heavy ground floor door and went up the steps that led to her apartment. He rang the bell, but there was no answer. He knocked on the door, but still there was no sound from inside. He employed Vianello's technique again.

Later, he realized that he knew, in the silence that expanded across the landing when he took his thumb off the bell: knew that the door would be unlocked and would open when he turned the handle. And he supposed he also knew that he would find her dead, fallen or thrown from her chair, a thin thread of blood trailing from her nose. If anything surprised him, it was to discover that he had been right, and when he realized he felt nothing stronger than that, he tried to trace the cause. He accepted then that he hadn't liked this woman, though the habit of compassion for old people had been strong enough to disguise his dislike and convince him that what he felt was the usual pity and sympathy.

He pulled himself from these reflections and called the Questura, asking to speak to Vianello: he explained what had happened and asked him to organize a crew to come to the apartment.

When Vianello hung up, Brunetti clasped his hands behind his back, embarrassed at having got this idea from a television crime show, and began to walk through the apartment.

He moved towards the back and found that, aside from the room in which she had received him, there was only a bedroom, plus a kitchen and a bath. Both of these surprised him by being spotless, a fact which spoke of the existence of someone who came to clean.

The bedroom walls held what looked like celestial maps, scores of them of all sizes, framed in black and looking as if they came from the same collection or the hand of the same framer. Some were coloured in pastels, some in the original black and white. He flicked on the light to study them better. From knee height to a metre below the very tall ceiling, they hung in disorderly rows. He recognized what had to be a Cellarius, counted the ones above and below it and realized there were two complete sets. Only an expert could put a price on them, but Brunetti knew they would be worth hundreds of millions. There was a single, monk-like bed, a tall *armadio* against the wall, and a nightstand beside the bed that held a reading lamp, a few bottles of pills and a glass of water on a tray and, when Brunetti moved close enough to read the title, a German bible. A threadbare silk carpet stood beside the bed, a pair of slippers neatly tucked under the hem of the bedspread. There was no sign or scent that she smoked in this room. The wardrobe held only two long skirts and another woollen shawl.

Back in the living room he used a credit card to slide open the bottom drawer of the desk. Then, working up from the bottom, he slid them all open and looked at, but did not touch, the contents. One drawer held neat piles of bills, another what looked like photograph albums, stacked on one another in diminishing order of size; the top one held more bills and a few newspaper clippings.

Brunetti, staring around the room, didn't know whether to call it spartan or monastic.

He went back into the kitchen and opened the refrigerator. A litre of milk, a piece of butter inside a covered glass dish, the heel of a loaf of bread. The cabinets held just as little: a jar of honey, some salt, butter, tea bags and a tin of ground coffee. Either the woman didn't eat or her meals were brought to her in the same way as were her cigarettes.

In the bathroom there was a plastic container for false teeth, a flannel nightgown hanging on the back of the door, some toiletries, and four bottles of pills in the cabinet. Returning to the living room, he chose not to look at the dead woman, knowing he would have too much of that once the scene of crime team arrived.

He moved to the window and stood with his back against it and tried to make some sense out of what he saw. The room contained, he was sure, billions of lire in art works: the Cézanne that stood to the left of the door opposite him might be worth that just by itself. He studied the walls, looking for a paler rectangle that would speak of a newly empty space. No thief, no matter how ignorant a thief, could fail to see the value of the things in this room; yet there was no sign that anything had been removed, nor was there any indication that Signora Jacobs had died of anything other than a heart attack.

He knew, from long experience, the danger of imposing preconceived notions on to an investigation; it was one of the first things he warned new inspectors to guard against. Yet here he was, prepared to reject any evidence, no matter how persuasive, that suggested accidental or natural death. His bones, his radar, his very soul suspected that Signora Jacobs had been murdered, and though there was no sign of violence, he had little doubt that the killer was the same person who had murdered her adoptive granddaughter. He remembered Galileo and his response to the threats marshalled against him. '*Eppur si muove*,' he whispered and went to the door to meet Vianello and the other officers.

Logic dictates that a task should become easier, and its execution faster, the more often it is performed. Thus the examination of the locus of death should be performed with greater speed each time it is necessary, especially in a case such as this, where an old woman lies dead beside her easy chair, with no sign of violence and no sign of forced entry. Or perhaps, Brunetti reflected, the passing of time is a completely subjective experience, and the photographers and fingerprint technicians were moving with great alacrity. Certainly, as he asked them to photograph and dust, he was aware of their unspoken scepticism at his treating this as a crime scene. What could be easier and more self-explanatory: an old woman, sprawled on the floor, a bottle of pills rolled halfway across the room from her?

Rizzardi, when he showed up, appeared puzzled that he, and not the woman's doctor, had been called, but he was too good a friend of Brunetti's to question this. Instead, he pronounced her dead, examined her superficially, said it looked as though she had died the night before, and gave no further sign that he found Brunetti's request for an autopsy strange.

'If I'm asked to justify it?' the doctor asked, getting to his feet.

'I'll get a magistrate to order it, don't worry,' Brunetti answered.

'I'll let you know,' the doctor said, bending to brush ash off the knees of his trousers.

'Thanks,' Brunetti replied, glad to be spared even the doctor's passive curiosity. He knew he could not find the words with which to describe what he felt about Signora Jacobs's death, and he realized how weak any attempt to explain would be.

It could have been hours later that Brunetti found himself alone in the apartment with Vianello, but the light that came in from the windows was still late morning light. He looked at his watch, astonished to see that it was not yet one o'clock and that all of this interior time had passed, and all of these things had happened.

'Do you want to go for lunch?' Brunetti asked, conscious as he addressed Vianello in the more familiar 'tu' of how comfortable it felt. There were few people on the force with whom he would more like to make this grammatical declaration of equality.

'Well, we're not going to eat what's in the kitchen, are we?' Vianello asked with a smile then added, serious, 'Let's have a look around here first, if you like.'

Brunetti grunted his agreement but stayed where he was, studying the room and thinking.

'What are we looking for?' Vianello asked him.

'I've no idea. Something about the paintings and the other things,' he said, with a broad wave that took in all the objects in the room. 'A copy of her will or an indication of where it might be. Name of a notary or a receipt from one.'

'Papers, then?' Vianello asked, switching on the light in the corridor and placing himself with his back to one of the shelves of books. At Brunetti's muttered agreement, Vianello reached up to the first book on the top shelf and pulled it down. Holding it in his right hand, he flipped it open with the left and leafed through all of the pages from the back to the front, then switched it to the other hand and leafed through it the other way. Satisfied that nothing lurked between its pages, he stooped and placed it on the floor to the right of the bookcase and pulled down the next book.

Brunetti took the papers from the top drawer of the desk through to the kitchen and set them on the table. He pulled out a chair, sat, and drew the stack of papers towards him.

Some time later – Brunetti didn't even bother to look at his watch to see how long it had been – Vianello came into the kitchen, went to the sink and washed a film of dust from his hands, then ran the water until it was cold and drank two glasses.

Neither man spoke. Later, Brunetti heard Vianello go into the bathroom and use the toilet. Mechanically, he read through every receipt and piece of paper, placing them to one side after he had done so. When he was finished, he went back to the desk and took the papers from the bottom drawer and sat down to read. Arranged in precise chronological order, they told the story of the occasional sale of one of the apartments owned by Signora Jacobs, the first more than forty years ago. Every twelve years or so, she sold an apartment. There was no bank book, so Brunetti could assume only that payment had been made in cash and kept in the apartment. He took a letter from the gas company and turned it over. Assuming that the declared price of a house, as was usual, was something approximating half of the real price, Brunetti quickly calculated that the money from the sale of each house should have lasted from eight to ten years, given what he could see of her bills for utilities and rent. He found it strange that a woman who had once owned several apartments would live in a rented one, but he had the rent receipts to prove it.

He came upon a small stack of receipts, all from the Patmos Gallery in Lausanne, all initialled 'EL', and all written for the sale of what was described as 'objects of value'.

He got to his feet then and went back to the corridor, where he found Vianello almost finished with the second bookshelf. Hillocks of books drifted up the walls to both sides of each bookcase; in one place, an avalanche had fallen across the corridor.

Vianello saw him when he came in. 'Nothing,' he said. 'Not even a used vaporetto ticket or a matchbook cover.'

'I've found the source of Claudia's Leonardo's allowance,' Brunetti said.

Vianello's glance was sharp, curious.

'Receipts from the Patmos Gallery for "objects of value",' he explained.

'Are you sure?' Vianello asked, already familiar with the name of the gallery.

'The first receipt is dated one month before the first deposit in the girl's account.'

Vianello gave a nod of approval.

'Here, let me help,' Brunetti said, clambering over a low mound of books and reaching down to the bottom shelf. Side by side, they flicked through the remaining books until the bookcase was empty, but they found nothing in the books other than what had been placed there by the authors.

Brunetti closed the last one and set it down on its side on the shelf at his elbow. 'That's enough. Let's get something to eat.'

Vianello was not at all inclined to disagree. They left the apartment, Brunetti using the tobacconist's key to lock the door behind them.

20

After a disappointing lunch, the two men walked back to the Questura, occasionally suggesting to one another some connection that had yet to be explored or some question that remained unanswered. No matter how conscientiously Rizzardi might seek evidence that Signor Jacobs had been the victim of violence, in the absence of concrete evidence, no judge would authorize an investigation of her death; much less would Patta, who was reluctant to authorize anything unless the last words of the dying victim had been the name of the killer.

They separated when they entered the Questura, and Brunetti went up to Signorina Elettra's office. As he walked in, she looked up and said, 'I heard.'

'Rizzardi said it might have been a heart attack.'

'I don't believe it, either,' she said, not even bothering to ask his opinion. 'What now?'

'We wait to see the results of the autopsy, and then we wait to see who inherits the things in her apartment.'

'Are they really that wonderful?' she asked, having heard him talk of them.

'Not to be believed. If they're real, then it was one of the best collections in the city.'

'It doesn't make any sense, does it? To live like that, in the midst of all that wealth.'

'The place was clean, and someone brought her cigarettes and food,' Brunetti answered. 'It's not as if she was living in a pit.'

'No, I suppose not. But we tend to think that, well, we tend to think that people will live differently if they have the money.'

'Maybe that's how she wanted to live,' Brunetti said.

'Possibly,' Signorina Elettra conceded reluctantly.

'Perhaps it was enough for her to be able to look at those things,' he suggested.

'Would it be? For you?' she asked.

'I'm not eighty-three,' Brunetti said, then, changing the subject, he asked, 'What about London?'

She handed him a single sheet of paper. 'As I said, the British are much better at these things.'

Reading quickly, Brunetti learned that Benito Guzzardi, born in Venice in 1942, had died of lung cancer in Manchester in 1995. Claudia's birth had been registered in London twenty-one years ago, but only her mother's name, Petra Leonhard, was listed. There was no listing for her mother's marriage or death. 'That explains the last name, doesn't it?' he asked.

Signorina Elettra handed him a copy of Claudia's application to the university. 'It was easy enough. She simply presented documents with the name Leonhard and wrote it down as Leonardo.'

Before Brunetti could inquire, Signorina Elettra said, 'The name of her aunt was listed on her passport as the person to contact in case of accident.'

'The one in England?'

'Yes. I called her. She hadn't been notified of Claudia's death. No one here had thought to do it.'

'How did she take it?'

'Very badly. She said Claudia had spent summers with her since she was a little girl.'

'Is she the mother's sister or the father's?'

'No,' she said with a confused shake of her head at such things, 'it's like the grandmother. She's not really an aunt at all, but Claudia always called her that. She was the mother's best friend.'

'Was? Is she dead?'

'No. She's disappeared.' Before Brunetti could ask, she explained, 'But not in the sense we'd usually use. Nothing bad's happened to her. The woman said she's just one of those free spirits who come and go through life as they please.' She stopped there and then added her own editorial comment, 'Leaving other people to pick up behind them.' When Brunetti remained silent, she continued. 'The last this woman heard from her was a few months after the father's death, a postcard from Bhutan, asking her to keep an eye on Claudia.'

Suddenly protective of the dead girl and outraged that her mother could have discarded her like this, Brunetti demanded, 'Keep an eye on her? How old was she – fifteen, sixteen? What was she supposed to do while her mother was off finding inner harmony or whatever it is people do in Bhutan?'

As this is the sort of question to which there is no answer, Elettra waited for his anger to pass away a bit and then said, 'The aunt told me Claudia lived with her parents until her father's death but then chose to come back to Italy, to a private school in Rome. That's when she got in touch with Signora Jacobs, I think. In the summers she went back to England and lived with the aunt.'

Listening to her explain Claudia's story calmed him somewhat, and after a time he said, 'Claudia told me her parents never married but that the father accepted parentage.'

Signorina Elettra nodded. 'That's what the woman told me.'

'So Claudia was Guzzardi's heir,' Brunetti said.

'Heir to very little, it would seem,' Signorina Elettra said. Head tilted to one side, she looked up at him and added, 'Unless . . .'

'I don't know what the law is regarding someone who dies in possession of objects the ownership of which is unclear,' Brunetti said, reading her mind. 'Then again, it's not normal to question the ownership of the things that are in a person's home when they die.'

'Not normally, no,' Signorina Elettra agreed. 'But in this case . . .' She allowed her voice to trail off in an invocation of possibility.

'There was nothing in her papers, no bills of sale for any of it.' Brunetti said.

She followed the current of his thoughts. 'Her notary or lawyer might have them.'

Brunetti shook his head: there had been nothing from either a lawyer or a notary among her papers, and the search through the pages of the books had proven entirely fruitless. It was Signorina Elettra who gave voice to the consequence of this thought. 'If there's no will, then it goes to her family.'

'If she has a family.'

And in their absence, both realized, everything would go to the state. They were Italian and thus believed that nothing worse could happen to a person: everything they possessed, doomed to fall into the hands of faceless bureaucrats and plundered before being sent for storage, cataloguing and shifting, until what little survived the winnowing was eventually sold or forgotten in the cellar of some museum.

'Might as well just put it all out on to the street,' Signorina Elettra said.

Though in complete agreement, Brunetti did not think it

fitting to admit this, so he asked, instead, 'What about Claudia's phone calls to Filipetto?'

'I haven't printed them out yet, sir,' she said, 'but if you'll have a look, you can see.' She touched some keys and letters flicked across the screen of her computer. The screen rolled to black for an instant, then came back to life filled with short columns of numbers. Signorina Elettra tapped her finger against the heading of each and explained: 'Number called, date, time, and length of call. Those are her calls to Filipetto,' she said, then touched another key, and further columns inserted themselves below. 'And these are the ones from his house to hers.' She gave him a moment to study the numbers and then asked, 'Strange, isn't it, seven calls between people who didn't know one another?'

She punched more keys, and new numbers replaced the old ones.

'What are those?' Brunetti asked.

'The calls between her number and the Library. I haven't had time to separate them yet, so they're mixed in together in chronological order.'

He studied the column of figures. The first three were from her number to the Library. Then one from the Library. One from her. Then, after a gap of three weeks, a series of calls from the Library began. They were repeated at four- or five-day intervals and went on for six weeks. At first, Brunetti assumed they must be calls from Claudia to her flatmate, but then he saw that some of the calls were made after nine at night, a strange time for anyone to be in the Library. He studied the final column, which gave the length of each call, and found that, although the later calls in the series had lasted for five or ten minutes, the last one was very short, less than a minute.

Signorina Elettra had been studying the list along with him and said, 'I've had it happen to me, so I recognize the pattern.'

'Harassment?' Brunetti asked, forced to use the English

word and struck by its absence from Italian. Does that mean we lack the concept, as well as the word? he wondered.

'I'd say so.'

'Can you print me a copy of the first ones?' he asked, and at her nod, he explained, 'I think I'll go and speak to Dottor Filipetto again. See if the list refreshes his memory.'

The woman Filipetto called Eleonora let Brunetti in again and, without bothering to inquire as to the reason for his visit, led him into the study. Had Brunetti been asked, he would have sworn that the old man had not moved since they had spoken. As they had the last time, papers and magazines covered the surface in front of him.

'Ah, Commissario,' Filipetto said with every suggestion of pleasure, 'you've come back.' He waved Brunetti forward and held up a restraining hand to the woman, gesturing for her, however, not to leave the room. Brunetti was vaguely conscious of her presence behind him, somewhere near the door.

'Yes, sir, I've come to ask you a few more questions about that girl,' Brunetti said as he took the chair the old man indicated.

'Girl?' Filipetto asked, sounding befuddled; to Brunetti, it seemed intentionally so.

'Yes, sir, Claudia Leonardo.'

Filipetto stared up at Brunetti and blinked a few times. 'Leonardo?' he asked. 'Is this someone I know?'

'That's what I've come to ask about, sir. I came here a few days ago and you said you'd never heard of her.'

'That's true,' Filipetto said, a slight irritation audible in his voice. 'I've never heard the name.'

'Are you sure of that, sir?' Brunetti asked blandly.

'Of course I'm sure of that,' Filipetto insisted. 'Why do you question my word?'

'I'm not questioning your word, sir; I'm merely questioning the accuracy of your memory.'

'And what is that supposed to mean?' the old man demanded.

'Nothing at all, sir, just that we sometimes forget things, all of us.'

'I'm an old man . . . Filipetto began, but then stopped, and Brunetti watched as a transformation took place. Filipetto hunched down in his chair; his mouth fell open and one hand scrabbled over the surface of the desk to rest on the other one. 'I don't remember everything, you know,' Filipetto said in a voice that was suddenly high pitched, the voice of a querulous old man.

Brunetti felt like Odysseus' dog, the only one able to penetrate his master's deceit and disguise. Had he not watched Filipetto deliberately turn himself into a feeble old man, compassion would have prevented his asking further questions. Even so, guile stood upon his tongue and stopped him from mentioning the record of the calls to and from Claudia Leonardo.

With a smile he worked hard to make appear as warm as it was credulous, Brunetti asked, 'Then you might have known her, sir?'

Filipetto raised his right hand and waved it weakly in the air. 'Oh, perhaps, perhaps. I don't remember much any more.' He raised his head and called to the woman near the door, 'Eleonora, did I know anyone called . . .' He turned to Brunetti and asked, as if she had not been perfectly able to hear Claudia's name, 'What did you say her name was?'

'Claudia Leonardo,' Brunetti supplied neutrally.

The woman's response was a long time in coming. Finally she said, 'Yes, I think the name is familiar, but I can't remember why it is I know it.' She said no more and didn't ask Brunetti to tell her who Claudia was.

Though it angered him to have been outmanoeuvred, Brunetti felt a grudging admiration for the way in which Filipetto had capitalized on his age and apparent infirmity.

The phone records, now, could do no more than prompt his old man's memory into recalling that, yes, yes, now that Brunetti mentioned it, perhaps he had spoken to some young girl, but he couldn't remember what it was they'd talked about.

Defeat would be no less decisive, Brunetti realized, if he were to stay to ask more questions. He put his hands on his knees and pushed himself to his feet. Leaning across the desk, he shook Filipetto's hand and said, 'Thank you for your help, Notaio. I'm sorry to have bothered you with these questions.' Filipetto's grasp had actually grown weaker; his hand felt as insubstantial as a handful of dry spaghetti. The old man, speechless, could do no more than nod in Brunetti's direction.

Brunetti turned towards the door, and the woman stepped aside to let him pass. He stopped at the end of the hall, just at the door of the apartment. With no preparation, he said, 'May I ask what your relationship to Dottor Filipetto is?'

She gave him a long, steady look and answered, 'I'm his daughter.'

Brunetti thanked her, did not offer to shake her hand, and left.

21

Aware that any decision concerning what he thought of as Signora Jacobs's murder must wait upon Rizzardi's report, Brunetti found himself purposeless and without the will to do any specific thing. He did not want to go back to work, nor did he want to begin to question the people who lived near the old woman; least of all did he want to think about Claudia Leonardo and her death. He walked.

He set off from Filipetto's and cut back toward San Lorenzo, but when he reached the bridge in front of the Greek church his courage failed him and he ducked into the underpass rather than continue to the Questura. He passed through Campo Santa Maria Formosa and saw what looked like a tribe of Kurds camped in front of the abandoned *palazzo*, their meagre possessions spread in front of them as they squatted and stooped on bright-coloured carpets. The men wore sober suits and black skullcaps, but the women's long skirts and scarves flared out in orange, yellow, and red. Their uninterest in passers-by seemed total; all they lacked were campfires and donkeys; they could just as easily have been in the middle of the plains.

He crossed Santi Apostoli, continued past Standa, then turned to the right and back toward the waters of the *laguna*. He passed the Misericordia and the stone relief of the turbaned merchant leading his camel, and then cut right again, walking by instinct until he came out at the vaporetto stop at Madonna dell' Orto. A vaporetto was just pulling off to the right, but when the pilot saw him he threw the motor into idle, then reverse, and backed up to the *embarcadero*, engine throbbing a command to step abroad. The sailor slid the metal bars back and Brunetti jumped on, although he had had no intention of taking a boat.

As the vaporetto pulled into Fondamente Nuove he made a decision and switched to another one that was leaving for the cemetery. He got off there, the one man among a crowd of women, most of them old and all of them carrying flowers. As he had done since he started walking, he moved forward by instinct alone, as if his feet were entirely in charge of the rest of his body.

He turned right through the cloister, then went up and down low flights of steps until he stood in front of the marble plaque behind which rested his father's bones. He read the name and the dates. Brunetti was almost as old as his father had been when he died, and he had as many children. It had always been his mother's custom to come out here to discuss things with her husband after his death, though he had not, even when living, been much help to her in deciding anything. Once Brunetti had asked her about it, and she said only that it helped her to feel close to someone again. Years passed before he accepted the bleak criticism of her remark, but by then his mother had slipped through the hands of love and concern and drifted into the waters of the senile and the mad, and so he had never been able to ask her pardon or make it up to her.

The flowers resting in a small silver vase below the plaque were fresh, but Brunetti had no idea who might have left them: perhaps his brother or his sister-in-law? Most assuredly it had not been their children or his own: young people seemed to have no interest in the cult of the dead, and so the graves of his generation would probably be left flowerless and unvisited. Once Paola was gone, who would come to talk to him here? Had anyone questioned him or had Brunetti thought to question himself, he would have attributed his assumption that he would be the first to die to a wealth of statistics: men died first, and women lived on alone. But the real answer probably lay in some fundamental difference in their characters: Paola usually opted for light and the forward leap into life, while his spirit felt more comfortable one step back from the stage, where things were less well illuminated and he could study them and adjust his vision before deciding what to do.

He placed his right hand on the letters of his father's name. He stood for a moment, then glanced to his left, at the long row of tombs lined up in their orderly ranks, one on top of the other, each occupying the same amount of space. Soon enough, both Claudia Leonardo and Signora Jacobs would take their places here. In the neatly tended field behind him stood the marble tombs of the wealthy, enormous monuments in every shape and style. He thought of Ivan Ilych, advising his family to forgo, and he thought of Ozymandias, King of Kings, but he thought most of how little real emotion he felt standing here, at his father's tomb. He left the cemetery and took the boat back to Fondamente Nuove.

Brunetti had to search for a public phone with which to call Vianello and tell him he wouldn't be back in the office that afternoon. As was usual in an age when everyone was encouraged to have a *telefonino*, it proved impossible to find a public phone, so Brunetti ended up going into a bar and ordering a coffee he didn't want in order to justify using their phone. After he spoke to Vianello he called home, but there was no one there, just his own voice giving the phone number and asking him to leave a message.

In a state of complete inattention, Brunetti passed through the city and towards his home, almost dizzy with the desire to be there. So glad was he to arrive that he actually leaned against the front door after he closed it, though the action made him feel like the heroine of some cheap melodrama, relieved at having escaped the menaces of the slavering suitor who still lurked beyond the door.

Eyes closed, he said aloud, 'God, I'll be hiding under the bed next.'

From his left, he heard Paola say, 'If this is the first sign of madness, I'm not sure I'm ready for it.' He turned and saw her standing at the door to her study, a book in her hand, smiling.

'I doubt it's the first sign you've seen,' he said and pushed himself away from the door. 'Why are you home this afternoon? It's Tuesday, isn't it?'

'I put a note on my office door, saying I was sick,' she explained.

He studied her face: her eyes glistened with good humour, her skin with health. 'Sick?' he asked.

'Of sitting in my office.'

'But never of the books?' he asked.

'Never,' she asserted, then asked, 'Why are you home so early?'

'As you heard me saying, I want to hide under the bed.'

She turned back into her study, saying, 'Come and tell me about it.'

Twenty minutes later Brunetti had told her all there was to say about the death of Signora Jacobs and his belief that it had been neither natural nor accidental.

'Who would want to kill them both?' Paola asked, sharing his conclusion that the two deaths had to be related.

'If I knew why, it would be easy enough to find out who,' Brunetti answered.

'The why has got to be the paintings,' Paola pronounced, and Brunetti saw no reason to question her conclusion.

'Then all we've got to do is wait until a will is found or a notary presents one for probate?' he asked sceptically.

'That seems a bit simplistic to me,' Paola answered. She gazed at the wall of books opposite them for a long time and then said, 'It's all very much like *The Spoils of Poynton*.'

'Tell me,' he prodded, knowing that she would, even if he didn't ask.

'It's one of the Master's novellas. It's all about possession of a house full of beautiful objects and reveals what people are really like by the way they respond to the objects.'

'For example?' Brunetti asked, always finding it easier to have Paola tell him about the books of Henry James than actually to read them.

'Well, I think it would be easier if you read it yourself,' she said.

Brunetti said only, 'Give me one example.'

'The woman's son – that is, the son of the woman who owns all of the beautiful things – has no appreciation of the beauty of her possessions, is deaf or blind to them, just as he's blind and deaf to the young companion of his mother, who would be the ideal wife for him, instead of the young woman he gets engaged to. He can't appreciate their obvious beauty, and he can't appreciate her hidden beauty.' She thought about what she'd said for a moment, then added, in quick apology to the Master, 'The story tells this far better, but that's pretty much what it's about.'

'All right, I'll ask,' Brunetti said when he realized she had finished. 'How do you connect this with Signora Jacobs?'

He sat and watched her trying to formulate an answer he would understand. Finally she said, 'In the end, are things more important than people? Which do you pull from the burning building, the Rembrandt or the baby? And how, in this greedy age of ours, do you separate beauty from value?'

'Now tell me without the rhetorical questions,' he asked.

She laughed at his answer, not at all offended, and went on. 'I think it's a sign of some sort of spiritual illumination to respond to beauty,' she began, letting him know he was in for one of her convoluted explanations, though he did not doubt that it would lead somewhere interesting. 'But I think our age has so transformed art into a form of investment or specu-lation that many people can no longer see the beauty of an object or care much about it if they do: they see only the value, the convertibility of the object into a particular sum of money.'

'And is that bad?' he asked.

'I think so,' she said, glancing at him and then smiling again as she added, 'but you know what a terrible snob I am.' When he did not take advantage of the pause she left him to deny this, she went on, 'I think that once we convert beauty into financial value, we're willing to go to different lengths to acquire it. That is, I don't find it at all strange that a person should kill to obtain a painting that they viewed only in terms of how much money it's worth, but I can't imagine that anyone would kill in order to obtain one painted by his favourite artist simply because he admired it.' She laid her head back against the top of the sofa, closed her eyes, then opened them and went on. 'Different goals drive people to different lengths. Or perhaps different people are driven by different goals. At any rate, I think people will do more if they are after something they view as a manifestation of money than if they view it as a manifestation of beauty.'

'And in this case?' he asked.

'Murder's pretty far,' she said by way of an answer.

'And the mad art collector who wants to own everything?' Brunetti asked.

'There are probably some, but I suspect very few of them go about stabbing young girls or killing old women to get the things they want. Besides, no one knows yet where these pieces are going to end up, do they?'

Brunetti shook his head. That was the still unanswered question.

She broke into his silence by saying, 'I remember what you always say, Guido.'

'What's that?'

'That crime is always about money, sex or power.' And, indeed, he often did say that, simply because he had seen so little evidence of other motives. 'Well, if Claudia was a virgin and Signora Jacobs was over eighty, then I think we can exclude sex,' she went on. 'And I can't see how power could be an issue, can you?' He shook his head, and she concluded by asking, 'Well?'

He was still mulling over Paola's thoughts when he arrived at the Questura the following morning. He went directly to his office without bothering to tell anyone he was there. The first thing he did was call Lucia Mazzotti in Milano and was surprised when the girl answered the phone herself. She sounded like a different person, all timidity gone from her voice, and Brunetti marvelled at the ability of the young to recover from everything. He began with the usual platitudes but, aware that the girl's mother might be there, he quickly turned to the business of his call and asked if Claudia had ever said anything to her about someone who was too attentive to her or bothered her with his attentions. The line went silent. After a long time Lucia said, 'She got phone calls. A couple of times when I was there.'

'What sort of phone calls?' Brunetti asked.

'Oh, you know, from some guy who wants to go out with you or just talk to you. That you don't want to talk to or see.' She spoke with authority, her youth and her beauty ensuring that calls like this would be part of her normal experience. 'That's what I thought from the way she talked.'

'Do you have any idea who this man might be, Lucia?'

There was a long silence, and Brunetti wondered why Lucia should be reluctant to tell him, but at last she said, 'I don't think it was always a man.'

'Excuse me,' Brunetti said. 'Would you explain that to me, Lucia.'

Sounding a little impatient, Lucia said, 'I told you. It wasn't always a man. One time, about two weeks ago, Claudia got a call, and the person who called was a woman. But it was the same kind of call, from someone she didn't want to talk to.'

'Would you tell me about it?' Brunetti asked.

'I answered the phone, and she asked for Claudia.'

Brunetti wondered why she hadn't told him this while he was questioning her, but then he remembered that the girl's flatmate lay dead above them when they spoke, and so he kept his voice calm and asked, 'What did she say?'

'She asked to speak to Claudia,' Lucia repeated simply in a tone that suggested only an idiot wouldn't recall what she had just said.

'Do you remember if she asked for Claudia or Signorina Leonardo?' Brunetti asked.

After a long pause, the girl said, 'I don't remember, really, but it might have been Signorina Leonardo.' She thought again and then said, all impatience gone from her tone, 'I'm sorry, I really don't remember. I didn't pay much attention since it was a woman. I thought it would be work or something.'

'Do you remember what time it was?'

'Before dinner some time.'

'Could it have been the Austrian woman?'

'No, she had an accent, and this woman didn't.'

'Was she Italian?'

'Yes.'

'Venetian?'

'I didn't listen to her long enough to know. But I'm sure she was Italian. That's why I thought it was about work.'

'You said it was someone she didn't want to talk to. What made you think that?'

'Oh, from the way Claudia spoke to her. Well, mostly listened to her. I was in the kitchen, making dinner, but I could hear Claudia and she sounded, well, she sounded sort of angry.'

'What did she say?'

'I don't know, really. I could only tell from her voice that she didn't like talking to this woman. I was frying onions so I couldn't hear her words, only that she didn't like the call or the caller. Finally she hung up.'

'Did she say anything to you about it?'

'No, not really. She came into the kitchen and she said something about people being so stupid she couldn't believe it, but she didn't want to talk about it, so we talked about school.'

'And then?'

'And then we ate dinner. And then both of us had a lot of reading to do.'

'Did she ever mention this again?'

'No, not that I remember.'

'Did she get any more calls?'

'Not that I know about.'

'And the man?'

'I never answered the phone when he called, so I can't tell you anything about him. Anyway, it's more a feeling I had than anything I know for certain. Someone called her, and she'd listen for a while, saying "yes" or "no", and then she'd say a couple of words, and then she'd hang up.'

'You never asked her about it?'

'No. You see, we weren't really friends, Claudia and I. I mean, we were friends, but not the sort of friends who tell one another things.'

'I see,' Brunetti said, sure that even though he did not understand the distinction his daughter certainly would.

'And she never said anything about these calls?'

'Not really. Besides, I was only there a couple of times when she got them.'

'Did she get other calls, when you knew who the caller was?'

'Once in a while. I knew the Austrian woman's voice, and her aunt's.'

'The one in England?'

'Yes.'

Brunetti could think of nothing else to ask the girl, and so he thanked her for her help and said he might have to call her again but hoped he wouldn't have to disturb her any more about this.

'That's all right, Commissario. I'd like you to find the person who did it,' she said.

22

The next day when Brunetti got to the Questura, the guard at the door handed him an envelope as he came in. 'A man said to give this to you when you came in, Commissario.'

'What kind of man?' Brunetti asked, looking down at the manila envelope in the man's hand and thinking of letter bombs, terrorists, sudden death.

'It's all right, sir. He spoke Veneziano,' the guard said.

Brunetti accepted the envelope and started up the stairs. It was a bit larger than letter size and appeared to contain a package of some sort, perhaps a number of papers. He squeezed it, shook it, but waited until he got to his desk to open it. He flipped it over and looked at the front, where he saw his name written in block capital letters in purple ink.

Only one person he knew used ink that colour: Marco Erizzo had been the first one of their group to buy and use a Mont Blanc fountain pen, and to this day he carried two of them in the pocket of his jacket.

Brunetti's heart sank at the thought of what would be in the envelope: a package of papers could mean only one thing, and from his friend. He determined to say nothing, to give it to charity, never to speak to Marco again. The word *'disonorato'* came into his mind, and he felt his throat tighten at the death of friendship.

He slipped his thumbnail under the flap, ripped the envelope open roughly, and took out a thick sheet of beige foolscap and a small, sealed envelope. He folded the page open and saw the same slanted letters and the same ink.

'In the other envelope is some of the rosemary Maria's son sends her from Sardinia. She said to use only about a half-teaspoon for a kilo of mussels and half a kilo of tomatoes and not to use any other spice.'

Brunetti held the smaller envelope to his nose and breathed in the odour of love.

As the day continued, however, he found that his strange lack of will regarding the death of Signora Jacobs was not to be shaken off. Rizzardi's report arrived by fax at about eleven and stated that, though there were bruises on the dead woman's arms, they were not inconsistent with a fall. The actual cause of death was a heart attack, one so severe that the pills she took might not have been sufficient to save her.

Vianello came up just before lunch to report that he had spoken to her neighbours, but, in an unsettling echo of the answers his question had earned from Claudia Leonardo's neighbours, none of them had heard or seen anything out of the ordinary the day before. When Brunetti asked if he had spoken to the man in the tobacco shop Vianello had no idea what he was talking about, and when Brunetti explained about the key, Vianello said no one had thought to ask.

And there things stood. Patta called him into his office later that afternoon and asked what progress there had been in the murder of 'that girl', and Brunetti was forced to put on an earnest expression and tell him that they were investigating every possibility. More than one hundred Mafia bosses had been released from jail that week because the Ministry of Justice had not got around to bringing them to trial within the appointed time, so the press was baying at the Minister with sufficient savagery to distract them from one small murder in Venice, hence Patta seemed less disturbed than usual at the lack of progress. Not for an instant did it pass through Brunetti's mind to suggest that Claudia Leonardo's death might be linked to Signora Jacobs's.

The day passed and then another. Claudia's aunt in England besieged the Questura with questions, and then with demands for the release of Claudia's body, which she wanted sent to her for burial, but the bureaucracy could not be made to provide the necessary consent and so the body remained in Venice. On the third day Brunetti realized that he had been thinking of her as 'the body' and not 'the girl', and after that he no longer read the aunt's faxes. Signorina Elettra was sent to Milano on a training course in some new form of computer wizardry, and her absence added to the general spirit of lethargy that had fallen upon the Questura. Signora Jacobs was buried in the Protestant part of the cemetery, but Brunetti did not attend. He did, however, see that a team was sent into her apartment to photograph the art works in place and make a complete catalogue.

And so things continued to drift until, one morning, as Brunetti put on a jacket he had not worn for a week, he put his hand in the pocket and found the key to Signora Jacobs's apartment. There was no tag, no key holder, but he recognized it instantly and, as it was a bright morning and he remembered that there was a particularly good *pasticceria* down by San Boldo, he resolved to walk down that way, have a coffee and a brioche, give back the key and have a word with the *tabacchaio*, then take the vaporetto to work.

The brioche more than justified the trip: it was crisp and soft at the same time and filled with more jam than the average person would like, which meant just enough to satisfy Brunetti. With a sense of virtue at having resisted a second, Brunetti continued on past the door to Signora Jacobs's house and into the tobacco shop.

The man behind the counter seemed alarmed to see him and said, even before Brunetti could speak, 'I know, I know I should have called you. But I didn't want her to get into any trouble. She's a good woman.'

Though he was just as surprised as the other man, Brunetti had the presence of mind to respond calmly, 'I don't doubt that. But you still should have called us. It might have been important.' He kept his voice calm, suggesting he already knew everything the man could tell him but might perhaps like to hear it in his own words. He took out the key and held it up, as though this were the missing clue that had brought him back to hear the man's full story.

The man put his hands down at his sides, fingers tightened into fists as if to make it unthinkable that he would accept the key. 'No, I don't want it.' He shook his head to add emphasis to his assertion. 'You keep it. After all, that's the cause of all the trouble in the first place, isn't it?'

Brunetti nodded and slipped the key back into the pocket of his jacket. He wasn't sure how to play this, though he had no sense that the man felt anything more than embarrassment at not having done whatever it was he should have done about this woman, whoever she was. 'Why didn't you call? After all, how much trouble could she get into?' he asked, hoping that would sound sufficiently unthreatening to lead the man into further explanation.

'She's illegal. And she's working in black. She was terrified she'd be made to leave if anyone found out, that you'd send her back.'

Brunetti permitted himself a smile. 'There's little danger of that, unless she does something . . .' he was about to say that there would be no danger unless the woman, whoever she was, did something criminal, but he didn't want to present even this possibility to the man, and so he finished by saying, 'stupid'.

'I know, I know,' the man said, raising his hands and using them to gesticulate as he spoke. 'Just think of all the Albanians there are, doing whatever they like, robbing and killing whoever they please, and no one thinks of sending them back, the bastards.'

Brunetti allowed himself to relax and nodded to the man, as if in agreement with this opinion of the Albanians.

'God knows, poor devils, they live in hell, but at least let them come here and work, like the rest of us. Like Salima. She's not even a Christian, but she works like one. And the Signora, may she rest in peace, said you could trust her with anything, give her ten million lire and ask her to hold it for you for a week and she'd give it back and no need to count it.' The man considered this and then added, 'I wish I could get her to work here for me, but she's afraid of the authorities – God knows what happened to her in Africa – and won't do anything to get papers. Nothing I do or say can convince her even to try.'

'I suppose she's afraid she'll be arrested,' Brunetti suggested, making it sound as though the police were some alien force and he had nothing to do with them.

'Precisely. That's why I think she had trouble before, either where she came from or when she got here.'

Brunetti shook his head in sympathy; he still had no idea where this flow of information was carrying them.

'I suppose you'll have to speak to her, eh?' the man asked, 'because of the keys?'

'I'm afraid so,' Brunetti admitted, making himself sound very reluctant.

'That's why I should have called you, you see,' the man said. 'Because I knew that sooner or later you'd have to talk to her. But I couldn't do it to her, frighten her that way, either by telling her I was going to call or by calling you.'

'I understand,' Brunetti said, and at least in part this was true. He had never had much to do with illegal immigrants or their problems, but colleagues of his had told him stories of what many had experienced, not only at the hands of the police in their own countries, but at the hands of the police in this country to which they had fled in hopes of a better life. Extortion, violence and rape didn't disappear at the borders, so if this woman was afraid of the police, which meant afraid of Brunetti, then she probably had good cause to be so. Yet he still had to speak to her. About the keys and about Signora Jacobs.

'Maybe it would be easier if you took me to her,' Brunetti suggested. 'Does she live near here?'

'I've got the address somewhere,' the man said as he bent to open the bottom drawer in front of him. He pulled out a thin ledger and, first wetting a finger with his tongue, began to page through it slowly. On the seventh page he found what he sought. 'Here it is. San Polo 2365. It's over by Campo San Stin somewhere.' He glanced up at Brunetti and tilted his head in a silent question.

Uncertain whether this was meant to ask if Brunetti knew where the address was or if he still wanted the man to go with him or if he wanted them to go now, Brunetti nodded an affirmative to all three. Without the least resistance, perhaps even curious now to see how things would turn out, the man took a set of keys from his pocket and came around the counter. While Brunetti waited for him in the *calle*, the man shut and locked the door to his shop.

During the few minutes it took them to walk to Campo San Stin, the *tabacchaio*, whose name was Mario Mingardo, explained that it was his wife who had found Salima when the woman who cleaned both for her mother and for Signora Jacobs had moved to Treviso and she'd had to look for someone new. This had proven difficult, at least until a neighbour had suggested the woman who cleaned for her, a black woman from Africa but very clean and a good worker. That had been two years ago, and since then Salima had become a fixture in their lives.

'I don't know much about her,' Mingardo said, 'except what my mother-in-law says, and the Signora.'

'What about her family?'

'I think she has family back there, but she never talks about them.'

They crossed over the Rio di Sant' Agostin and were quickly out into the *campo*. 'It's got to be over here on the right somewhere,' Mingardo said, turning into the first *calle*. 'I'm just assuming she'll be at home,' he said. 'She hasn't been back since the Signora's death and I don't know if she'd have the courage to try to find a new job on her own.' Mingardo took the single step up to the building, looked at the names on the bells, and rang the bottom one. Brunetti could see that the name was 'Luisotti', which he did not think was an African name.

'*Sì?*' a woman's voice asked.

'It's me, Salima, Mario. I've come about the Signora.'

They had to wait a long time before they heard footsteps behind the door, and an even longer time elapsed before it began to open. Mingardo put out his hand and pushed it open, stepping over the threshold and holding the door for Brunetti to follow him.

When the woman inside saw a second man, she whipped around before Brunetti had a clear look at her and took one step towards the door that stood open halfway down the corridor, but Mingardo called out, 'He's a friend, Salima. It's all right.'

She froze in place, one arm still swung out in front of her to give extra momentum to help her flee towards safety. Slowly, she turned to look back at the two men, and when he saw her Brunetti took a short breath, struck both by her beauty and by the fact that Mingardo had said nothing about it.

She was in her late twenties, perhaps even younger. She had the narrow face and skull, the fine arching nose, and eyes of such almond perfection as to awaken his memory of the bust of Nefertiti he had seen in Berlin many years ago. The skin under her eyes was darker still than the mahogany of the rest of her face but served only to make her teeth and eyes seem all the whiter. My God, he caught himself thinking, what must we look like to these people: great potato lumps with little pudding eyes? Solid hunks of some badly cured meat? How can they stand to move around our great hulking paleness, and what must it be to gaze from such beauty at such pale ungainliness?

Mario said Brunetti's name and he stepped forward, offering her his hand, hoping it would be the hand of friendship and not betrayal. 'I'd like to talk to you, Signora,' Brunetti said.

Mingardo looked down at his watch, then up at the woman. 'You can trust him, Salima,' he said. 'I have to get back to work but you're all right with him. He's my friend.' He smiled at the woman, then at Brunetti, then turned and left quickly without offering his hand to either of them.

Still the woman had not said a word, and still she stood in place and studied Brunetti, assessing what danger there was to be had from this man, even though Mingardo had said he was a friend.

She unfroze and turned fully to walk towards her apartment, leaving Brunetti to follow. At the door she paused a moment and made a small bow, as if it were a ceremony too sacred to ignore, even with a man who brought she knew not what danger.

Brunetti asked permission and went in. He put his hand on the handle of the door and looked at the woman, who indicated that he should close it. He did so and turned into the room. A simple woven rush mat lay on the floor, and beyond it a divan covered with a piece of dark green embroidered cloth and a small pile of similarly embroidered pillows. There was a small wooden table and two chairs, and against one wall a chest with five drawers. In the centre of the table was an oval wooden bowl containing apples, and against the back wall there was a hot plate and a small sink, above which hung a double-doored cabinet. The single door to the left must lead to the bathroom. The room breathed the exotic scent of spices, among which he thought he could identify clove and cinnamon, but it was far richer than those. Brunetti estimated that the total area of the apartment was smaller than his daughter's bedroom.

He went to the table and pulled out one of the chairs, then stood away from it, smiled and gestured to her to sit. When she did, he took the other, careful to place it as far from her as possible, and sat.

'I'd like to speak to you, Signora.' When she said nothing, he continued, 'About Signora Jacobs.'

She nodded to acknowledge that she understood but still said nothing.

'How long did you work for her, Signora?'

'Two years,' she said, a phrase so simple as to give no indication of how well she spoke Italian.

'Did you enjoy working for the Signora?'

'She was a good woman,' Salima said. 'There was not a lot of work to do, and she was always as generous with me as she could be.'

'Was she a poor woman, do you think?'

She shrugged, as if any Western definition of poverty was bound to be absurd, if not insulting.

'In what way was she generous?'

'She would give me food and sometimes she gave me extra money.'

'I would imagine many employers are not generous,' Brunetti observed, hoping that this would somehow break through her formal reserve.

But the attempt was too obvious, and she ignored his words, sat quietly and waited for his next question.

'Did you have keys to her apartment?'

She looked up at him, and he saw her consider the risk of telling the truth. His impulse was to reassure her that there would be no danger in telling him the truth, but he knew that to be a lie and so he said nothing.

'Yes.'

'How often did you go?'

'I went to clean once a week. But sometimes I went in to bring her a meal. She didn't eat enough. And always smoking.' Her Italian was excellent, and he realized she must be from Somalia, a place where his father had fought, he with his machine-gun against men with spears.

'Did she ever talk about the things in her apartment?'

'They are *harram*,' she said, 'and she knew I didn't like to talk about them or look at them.'

'I'm sorry, Signora, but I don't know what that means,' Brunetti confessed.

'*Harram*, dirty. The Prophet tells us not to make pictures of people or animals. It is wrong, and they are unclean.'

'Thank you, I understand now,' he said, glad that she had explained, though he marvelled at the idea that anyone could think one of those delicate little dancing girls was unclean.

'But did she ever talk about them?'

'She told me that many people would value them, but I didn't want to look at them for fear of what it would do to me.'

'Did you ever meet the girl Signora Jacobs called her granddaughter?'

Salima smiled. 'Yes, I met her three or four times. She always called me "Signora" and spoke to me with respect. Once, when I was cleaning the bedroom, she made me a cup of tea and brought it to me. She remembered to put in a lot of sugar: I told her once that's how my people like to drink it. She was a good girl.'

'Did you know that she was killed?'

Salima closed her eyes at the thought of that good girl, dead, opened them and said, 'Yes.'

'Do you have any idea who might have wanted to harm her?'

'How could I know that and not go to the police?' she asked with real indignation, the first emotion she had shown since he began to talk to her.

'Signor Mario told me you were afraid of the police.' Brunetti said.

'I am,' she said shortly. 'But that doesn't matter, not if I knew something. Of course I'd tell them.'

'So you know nothing?'

'No. Nothing. But I think that's what killed the Signora.'

'Why do you say that?'

'She knew she was going to die. Some days after the girl died she told me that she was in danger.' Her voice had returned to calm neutrality.

'Danger?' Brunetti repeated.

'That's the word she used. I knew about her heart and she was using her pills much more, taking many more of them every day.'

'Did she say that was the danger?' Brunetti asked.

Salima considered his question for a long time, as if holding it up to the light at a different angle and seeing it in a different manner. 'No. She said only that she was in danger. She didn't say from what.'

'But you assumed it meant her heart?'

'Yes.'

'Could it have been something else?'

Her answer was long delayed. 'Yes.'

'Did she say anything else to you?'

She pulled her lips together, and then he saw her tongue

226

shoot out and moisten them. Her hands were folded primly on the edge of the table, and she looked down at them. She bowed her head and said something so softly that Brunetti couldn't hear.

'I'm sorry, Signora. I didn't hear.'

'She gave me something.'

'What was that, Signora?'

'I think it was papers.'

'You only think?'

'It was an envelope. She gave me an envelope and told me to keep it.'

'Until when?'

'She didn't say. She just told me to hold on to it.'

'When did she give it to you?'

He watched her count out the time. 'Two days after the girl died.'

'Did she say anything?'

'No, but I think she was afraid.'

'What makes you say that, Signora?'

She raised those perfect eyes to his and said, 'Because I am familiar with fear.'

Brunetti glanced away. 'Do you still have it?'

'Yes.'

'Would you get it for me, Signora?'

'You're police, aren't you?' she asked, head still bowed, her full beauty hidden from him, as if fearful of what it could provoke in a man with power over her.

'Yes. But you've done nothing wrong, Signora, and nothing will happen to you.'

Her sigh was as deep as the gulf between their cultures. 'What must I do for you?' she asked, her voice tired now, resigned.

'Nothing, Signora. Only give me the papers and then I'll go. No more police will come to bother you.'

She still hesitated, and he thought she must be trying to

think of something she could have him swear by, something that would be sacred to both of them. Whatever it was she sought in that silence, she failed to find it. Without looking at him, she got silently to her feet and went to the chest of drawers.

She pulled open the top drawer and from right on top pulled out a large manilla envelope that bulged with whatever was inside. Careful to hold it in both hands, she passed it to him.

Brunetti thanked her and took it. With no hesitation, he unhooked the two metal wings that held it closed. It was not taped or glued, and he would not insult her by asking if she had ever opened it.

He slipped his right hand inside and felt the soft crinkle of tissue paper extending from the top of what further exploration revealed were twin pieces of cardboard. At the bottom he felt another envelope, this one thick. He took his hand out and, using only the tips of his fingers, extracted whatever was held inside the sheets of cardboard. He slipped the tissue-clad paper from inside the cardboard and laid it on the table: it was a rectangle little larger than a book, perhaps the size of a small magazine. A small piece of paper was taped to the outside of the tissue paper, and on it a slanting hand, trained to write a script more angular than Italian, was written, 'This is for Salima Maffeki, a free gift of something that has long been in my personal possession.' It was signed 'Hedwig Jacobs' and bore a date three days before her death.

Brunetti peeled back the tissue paper and opened it, as he would the doors of an Advent calendar. 'Oddio,' he said, exclaiming as he identified the sketched figure which lay in his mother's arms. It could only be a Tiziano, but he did not have the expert's eye to be able to say more than that.

She had turned towards him, not in curiosity at the drawing but at his exclamation, and he looked up to see her turn away from that than which nothing could be more *harram*, an image of their false god, this god so false that he could die. She turned as from obscenity.

Brunetti folded the tissue paper carefully closed and slipped the drawing back inside the joined sheets of cardboard, saying nothing. He set it aside and pulled out the second envelope. It, too, was unsealed. He lifted the flap and took out a batch of what might have been letters, all neatly folded into three horizontal sections held together by an elastic.

He opened the first: 'I, Alberto Foa, sell the following paintings to Luca Guzzardi for the sum of four hundred thousand lire.' The paper was dated 11 January 1943 and contained a listing of nine paintings, all by famous artists. He opened two others and discovered that they, too, were bills of sale to Luca Guzzardi, both bearing dates before Mussolini's fall. One of them referred to drawings; the other listed paintings and statues.

Brunetti counted the remaining sheets of paper. Twenty-nine. With the three he had opened, a total of thirty-two bills of sale, no doubt all signed and dated and perfectly legitimate and, more importantly, legally binding proof that the objects in Signora Jacobs's possession had been the legitimate possessions of Luca Guzzardi, her lover, mad and dead this half-century.

More interestingly, that they were the inheritance of Claudia Leonardo, Guzzardi's granddaughter, stabbed to death and dead intestate.

He folded the three bills of sale and put them back on the pile, then caught them up in the elastic and slipped them back into their envelope.

He put that and, very carefully, the Tiziano sketch back into the larger envelope. 'Signora,' he said, looking across at her. 'I have to take this with me.'

She nodded.

'Signora, you must believe me when I tell you that you are

in no danger. If you like, I will bring my wife and my daughter here and you can ask them if I am an honest man. I think they'll tell you that I am, but I'll do that if you want me to.'

'I believe you,' she said, still not looking at him.

'Then believe this, Signora, because it's important. Signora Jacobs has given you a great deal of money. I don't know how much it is, and I won't know until I speak to a man who can tell me. But it is a great deal.'

'Is it five million lire?' she asked with such longing that she must have believed that with that sum she could buy joy or peace or a place in paradise.

'Why do you need that amount, Signora?'

'My husband. And my daughter. If I can send them that much, then they can get out and come here. That's why I'm here, to work and save and bring them.'

'It will be more than that,' he said, though he had no idea of the value of the drawing; at least that, probably inestimably more.

He turned his attention to the envelope and started to bend the metal flanges together to seal it again, so he didn't see her move. Her hands came up quickly and took one of his. Turning his hand palm down, she bowed over it and touched it with her forehead, pressing it there for long seconds. He felt her hands tremble.

She released his hand and got to her feet.

Brunetti stood and went to the door, the envelope dangling from one hand. At the door, he extended his hand to shake hers, but she shook her head and kept her hands at her sides, a modest woman who would not shake the hand of a strange man.

23

Brunetti walked away with knees he was surprised to find unsteady. He didn't know if it was the effect of the woman's strange gesture, one that had, he realized, created in him the obligation to see that she received the money that would bring her family to her, or whether his response was to the importance of the receipts she had given him.

From a bar he called Lele Bortoluzzi and arranged to meet him at his gallery in twenty minutes, which is what he estimated it would take him to get there if he took the 82 from Rialto. When he arrived, the artist was talking to a client, an American who insisted on looking at all of his paintings, asking about the technique, the kind of paint, the light, Lele's mood when he painted each picture and who, after almost a quarter of an hour, left the gallery without buying anything.

Lele came over to Brunetti, who stood in front of a seascape, and embraced him, then kissed him on both cheeks. The closest friend of Brunetti's late father, Lele had always displayed a paternal concern and affection for him, as if he could thus make up for Brunetti's father's inability to display whatever emotion he felt for his sons.

With a nod of his head towards the painting, Brunetti said, 'That's beautiful.'

'Yes, it is, isn't it?' the artist replied without the least awkwardness. 'Especially that cloud on the left, there, just above the horizon.' He placed the tip of his right forefinger just above the canvas, then tapped the end of his nail on the cloud once, twice. 'It's the most beautiful cloud I've ever painted, really wonderful.'

It was unusual for Lele to comment on his own work, so Brunetti took a closer look at the cloud, but all he saw was still a cloud.

He put the manila envelope on the table, opened it and took out the wrapped drawing, careful to pull it out straight and not bend the cardboard. He laid it on the table and said, 'Take a look.'

The painter slipped the tissue-covered drawing out from inside the cardboard, pulled back the paper, saw what it protected, and an involuntary, '*Mamma mia*' escaped his lips. He looked at Brunetti, but the beauty of the drawing drew his eyes back to it again. Still staring at it, moving his eyes to every corner, following every line of the dead Christ's body, he asked, 'Where did you get this?'

'I can't say.'

'Is it stolen?'

'I don't think so,' Brunetti answered, then, after thinking for a while, he said more authoritatively, 'No, it's not.'

'What do you want me to do with it?' Lele asked.

'Sell it.'

'You're sure it's not stolen?' the painter asked.

'Lele, it's not stolen, but I need you to sell it.'

'I won't,' the painter said but before Brunetti could protest or question him, he added, 'I'll buy it.'

Lele picked it up and walked nearer to the light that

232

filtered in through the door and windows. He held the drawing up closer to his eyes, then moved it away, then came back and set it down on the table. He brushed lightly across the bottom left hand corner of the drawing with the last finger of his right hand. 'The paper's right. It's Venetian, sixteenth century.' He picked it up again and studied it for what seemed like minutes to Brunetti. Finally he set it down again and said, 'At a guess, I'd say it's worth about two hundred million. But I have to check the prices on the last few auctions, and I know Pietro sold one about three years ago, so I can ask him what he got for it.'

'Palma?' Brunetti asked, naming a famous art dealer in the city.

'Yes. He'll lie, the bastard. He always does, but I can figure out what he really got from what he tells me. But it's going to be somewhere between one hundred and fifty and two hundred.' Very casually, too casually, Lele asked, 'Is it yours?'

'No, but I've been given it to sell.' This was, in a certain sense, true; no one had asked him to sell it, but it was certainly his to sell. Immediately he began to worry about the money, how to see that Salima got it, where to put it until she could find a way to use it. 'Can it be cash?' he asked.

'It's always cash in things like this, Guido. It leaves no footprints in the snow.'

Brunetti couldn't remember how many times he'd heard the painter say just this, and it was only now that he appreciated how true it was, and how very convenient. But then he wondered what he'd do with this much money. To put it in the bank could cause trouble: the Finanza would be interested in finding out how a senior police official suddenly came by so much cash. They had no safe in the house, and he could hardly imagine himself putting it in his sock drawer.

'How do you want me to pay you, and when?' the painter asked.

'I'll let you know. It's not for me, but this person doesn't have any way to keep it.' Brunetti quickly ran through various possibilities, and at the end said, 'Why don't you keep it until I have some idea of how to get it to her.'

Lele obviously had no interest in who the owner might be, not now that he considered himself the real owner of the drawing. 'Do you want some now?' he asked, and Brunetti realized the painter was eager to have some formal acknowledgement that he had bought the drawing.

'It's yours, Lele,' Brunetti said. 'I'll talk to you next week about what to do about the money.'

'Fine, fine,' Lele muttered, eyes drawn down again by the dead Christ.

While he had the painter there, Brunetti decided to take advantage of his knowledge. He took out the other envelope and removed the various bills of sale. Choosing one at random, he handed it to Lele and asked, 'Tell me about this.'

Lele took it, read it quickly, then went back and read through the declaration of sale and, even more slowly, the list of paintings and drawings it named. '*Caspita*,' he said, placing it flat on the table and taking more. He read two or three, laying each one flat on the table in front of him after he'd read it. When he placed the fourth one down, he said, 'So that's where they went.'

'You recognize things?'

'Some of them, yes. At least I think I do from the descriptions. Things like "Iznik carnation tile" are too general, and I don't know much about Turkish ceramics, anyway, but something described as, "Guardi View of the Arsenale" I do recognize, especially when I see that it came from the Orvieto family.'

Pointing down at the opened sheets of paper, Lele asked, 'Are these the things in the old woman's apartment?'

'Yes.' Brunetti wasn't completely sure, but there seemed no other explanation.

234

'I hope it's guarded,' Lele said, causing Brunetti immediately to recall the thickness of the door that guarded Signora Jacobs's apartment and then Salima and the keys he had not thought of asking her to return to him.

'I ordered an inventory,' Brunetti said.

'And lead us not into temptation.'

'I know, I know, but now that we have these,' Brunetti said, holding up the bills of sale, 'we know what's in there.'

'Or was,' Lele added drily.

Though it was, he realized, a poor defence of the police, Brunetti explained, 'The two who were sent to do it, Riverre and Alvise, are idiots. They wouldn't know the difference between a Manet and the cover of *Gente*.' After a pause he added, 'Though they'd probably prefer the second.'

The aesthetic sensibilities of law enforcement professionals not being of vital interest to the painter, he asked, 'What will happen to it all?'

Brunetti shrugged, a gesture that conveyed his uncertainty and his unwillingness to speculate with someone not involved with the investigation, even a friend as close as Lele. 'For the time being it will stay there, in her apartment.'

'Until what?' Lele asked.

The best Brunetti could think of to answer was, 'Until whatever happens.'

At lunch that day, an unusually silent Brunetti listened as family talk swirled around him: Raffi said he needed a *telefonino*, which prompted Chiara to say that she needed one as well. When Paola demanded what either of them needed it for, both said it was to keep in touch with their friends or to use in case they were in danger.

When she heard this, Paola cupped her hands at the corners of her mouth, creating a megaphone, and called across the table to her daughter, 'Earth to Chiara. Earth to Chiara. Can you hear me? Come in, Chiara. Can you read me?'

'What's that mean, *Mamma*?' Chiara demanded, making no attempt to disguise her annoyance.

'It's to remind you that you live in Venice, which is probably the safest place in the world to live.' As Chiara started to object, Paola ran right over her: 'Which means that it is unlikely that you are going to be in danger here, aside from *acqua alta*, that is, and a *telefonino* isn't going to be much help against that.' And again, as Chiara opened her mouth, Paola concluded, 'Which means no.'

Raffi attempted to render himself as invisible as it was possible to be while eating a second piece of pear cake buried in whipped cream. He kept his eyes on his plate and moved slowly, like a gazelle attempting to drink from a pool it knew to be infested with crocodiles.

Paola did not strike, but she did float to the surface and peer at him with reptilian eyes. 'If you want to buy yourself one, Raffi, go ahead. But you pay for it.' He nodded.

Silence fell. Brunetti had been somewhere else during all of this or at least he had not been paying much attention to the scuffle, though Paola's disapproval of what she considered their children's profligacy had caught his attention. With no preparation, he asked out loud, addressing them all equally, 'Aren't you ashamed that you pay all of your attention to acquiring as much money as you can, without giving any thought to truth and understanding and the perfection of your soul?'

Surprised, Paola asked, 'Where'd all that come from?'

'Plato,' Brunetti said and began to eat his cake.

The rest of the meal passed in silence, Chiara and Raffi exchanging inquisitive looks and shrugs, Paola trying to figure out the reason for Brunetti's remark or, more accurately, to understand which particular circumstances or actions had led him to recall the quotation, which she thought she recognized from the *Apology*.

After lunch he disappeared into the bedroom, where he

took off his shoes and lay down on the bed, staring out the window at the clouds which, he realized, were not to be blamed for looking so happy. After a time, Paola came in and sat beside him on the edge of the bed.

'You talked about retiring a while ago. Is this a relapse?'

He turned his head towards her and reached out with his left hand to take hers. 'No. I suppose it was nothing more than a sudden attack of moral tiredness.'

'Understandable, given your job,' she agreed.

'Maybe it's because we have so much, or I'm becoming allergic to wealth, but I just can't understand how people can do some of the things they do in order to get money.'

'Like kill, do you mean?'

'No, not only that. Even lesser things, like lie and steal and spend their lives doing things they don't like doing. Or, if you'll let me say this, how some women can stay married to horrible men simply because they have money.'

She sensed the deadly earnestness in his voice and so resisted the impulse to joke and ask if he were talking about her. Instead, she asked, 'Do you like what you do?'

He pulled her hand closer and idly began to turn her wedding band around and around on her finger. 'I think I must. I know I complain about it a lot, but, in the end, it does do some good.'

'Is that why you do it?'

'No, not entirely. I think part of it is that I'm nosy by nature, and I always want to know how the story will end or how or why it got started. I want to know why people do things.'

'It will never make any sense to me, that you don't like Henry James,' she said seriously.

24

It wasn't until a week later that anything other than the routine shuffling of papers occurred in the investigation of the deaths of the two women, and then it came via that most Venetian of methods: the exchange of information resulting from friendship and a sense of mutual obligation. A functionary of the Office of the Registry of Public Documents, recalling that Signorina Elettra, who was the sister of his wife's doctor, had once displayed an interest in Claudia Leonardo and Hedwig Jacobs, called her one morning to tell her that the will of the second woman had been registered in their office two days previously.

Signorina Elettra asked him if it would be possible for him to fax her a copy of the will, and at his response, that it would be 'highly irregular but equally possible', she laughed and thanked him, thus providing him with the unspoken assurance that a certain latitude might be extended to him were he ever to come to the attention of the police. She broke the connection and immediately called Brunetti, suggesting he come down to her office.

He had no idea why she wanted to speak to him, and when he entered her office he heard the noise of the fax machine. Saying nothing, she stood and walked over to the fax, and as a sheet of paper stuck its tongue out, she made a deep bow and waved one hand toward the emerging paper, inviting Brunetti to look. Curious, he bent over it, starting to read even as the machine was giving birth. 'I, Hedwig Jacobs, Austrian citizen but resident in Venice, Santa Croce 3456, declare that I have no living relatives who can make a claim on my estate.' He read the first sentence, glanced across to Signorina Elettra, who watched him, her self-satisfaction evident only in a small grin. The paper jolted forward and he bent over it again. 'I desire, therefore, that all of my possessions, in the event of my death, be given to Claudia Leonardo, also resident in this city, granddaughter of Luca Guzzardi. If for any reason this bequest does not pass to her, I will that it pass irrevocably to her heirs. I further declare that six Tiepolo drawings in my possession, so marked on the back of the frames, be given to the Director of the Biblioteca della Patria in memory of Luca Guzzardi and to be used as he decides in pursuit of the goals of the Biblioteca.' It was signed and dated about ten days before Claudia Leonardo's death. Seeing only whiteness under her signature, he looked back at Signorina Elettra, but then the machine pushed out another few centimetres of paper, and as he watched there emerged the name and signature of the notary with whom the will had been registered. 'Massimo Sanpaolo.' The signatures of the two witnesses were illegible.

Brunetti took the paper from the machine and handed it to Signorina Elettra. She read it through and, like him, looked up in surprise at the name of the notary. 'Oh, my,' she said in English, then switched to Italian and added, 'What a coincidence.'

'Of all things,' said Brunetti. 'The Filipetto family seems to be turning up everywhere.'

Even before he could suggest it, she volunteered, moving back to her desk, 'Shall we have a look?'

No family could have been easier to trace through the archives of the various offices and institutions of the city. Gianpaolo, whom Brunetti had come to think of as *his* Filipetto, was the only son of a notary, and had himself produced only one son, who had died of cancer. One of his daughters had married into the Sanpaolo family, another famous family of notaries, and it was their son, Massimo, who had taken over the Filipetto studio upon the death of his uncle. Massimo was married, already the father of two sons, whom Brunetti had no doubt were already, at six and seven, being schooled in the arcana of notary lore, raised to become transmitters of the family wealth and position. The younger daughter had married a foreigner, but not until she was well into her forties, so there were no children.

The studio of Notaio Sanpaolo was on a small *calle* near the Teatro Goldoni. Brunetti preferred to show up unannounced, which he did about twenty minutes later. He gave his name to one of the two secretaries in the outer office but was told that the Notary had just begun *un rogito*, the transfer of title of a house. Brunetti knew that there was likely to be a pause very shortly as buyer and seller exchanged the money paid for the house. The Notary would excuse himself, saying he was going to check on some technicality, and in his absence the buyers would hand over to the sellers the real price of the house, always about twice the declared, and therefore taxed, price. As payment was in cash and as hundreds of millions of lire had usually to be counted, a notary could always depend on a long break before going back to witness the signing of the papers. More importantly, because he was the officer of the state who served as legal witness to this proceeding, his absence from his office during the counting allowed him honestly to say that he had seen no exchange of cash.

As Brunetti had anticipated, Sanpaolo came out of his

office about ten minutes later, recognized Brunetti, pretended that he did not, and went over to talk to one of the secretaries. She pointed him back towards Brunetti, saying that this gentleman wanted to speak to him.

Sanpaolo was a tall man with a broad frame, heavily bearded and in need of a haircut. He had probably been very handsome in his youth, but good living had thickened his features and his body and so he looked more like an athlete run to fat than he did a notary. Brunetti thought that the younger man would probably be a bad liar: men with children often were, though Brunetti didn't know why this was so. Perhaps giving hostages to fortune made men nervous.

'Yes?' he asked as he came toward Brunetti, his hands at his sides, making no attempt at civility.

'I've come about the will of Signora Hedwig Jacobs,' Brunetti said, keeping his voice level and not bothering to identify himself.

'What about it?' Sanpaolo asked, not asking Brunetti to repeat the name.

'I'd like to know how it came into your possession.'

'My possession?' Sanpaolo demanded with singular lack of grace.

'How it is that you came to prepare it for her and submit it for probate,' Brunetti clarified.

'Signora Jacobs was a client of mine, and I prepared the will for her and witnessed her signature and the signatures of the two witnesses.'

'And who are they?'

'What right do you have to ask these questions?' Sanpaolo's nervousness was turning into anger and he began to bluster. This was more than enough to push Brunetti to new heights of calm dispassion.

'I'm investigating a murder, and Signora Jacobs's will is of importance in that investigation.'

'How can that be?'

'I'm not at liberty to tell you that, sir, but I assure you that I have every right to inquire about her will.'

'We'll see about that,' Sanpaolo said and wheeled away, heading back to the counter. He said something to one of the women and went through a door that stood to the left of the one to his office. The woman opened a large black address book, checked a number, and then dialled the phone. She listened for a moment, said a few words, pushed a button on the phone, then set it back in the receiver. At no time in any of this did either secretary glance in Brunetti's direction. Very casually, looking as bored and impatient as he could, Brunetti glanced at his watch and made a note of the time: it would make it that much easier when he asked Signorina Elettra to check Sanpaolo's outgoing phone calls.

A few minutes later the door to Sanpaolo's office opened slowly and a man stuck his head out, saying that the Notary could come back into his office now. The secretary who had made the call said the Notary had just received a call from South America and would be with him in a minute. The man went back into the office and closed the door.

Minutes passed, then a few more. The man in the office opened the door again and asked what was going on; the secretary asked if she could bring them something to drink. Saying nothing to her offer, the man went back into the office and closed the door, this time loudly.

Finally, after more than ten minutes, Sanpaolo came out of the second office, looking less tall than when he went inside. The secretary said something, but he waved at her with the back of his hand, as at a bothersome insect.

He approached Brunetti. 'I went to her home on the day the will was signed. I took the will and my two secretaries with me, and they witnessed her signature.' He spoke loud enough for the women to hear him, and both of them, looking first at Sanpaolo and then at Brunetti, nodded.

'And how was it that you were asked to go to her home?' Brunetti asked.

'She called and asked me,' Sanpaolo said, his face flushing as he answered.

'Had you worked for Signora Jacobs before?' Brunetti asked, and at that moment the door to Sanpaolo's office opened again, and this time a different man put his head out.

'Well?' he demanded of Sanpaolo.

'Two minutes, Carlo,' Sanpaolo said with a broad smile that didn't reach his eyes.

This time the door slammed.

Sanpaolo turned back to Brunetti, who calmly repeated the question, quite as if there had been no interruption, 'Had you worked for Signora Jacobs before?'

The answer was a long time in coming. Brunetti watched the Notary consider the possibility of falsifying notes or entries in an appointment book, then abandon the idea. 'No.'

'Then how was it that she selected you of all of the notaries in the city, Dottor Sanpaolo?'

'I don't know.'

'Could it have been that someone recommended you?'

'Perhaps.'

'Your grandfather?'

Sanpaolo's eyes closed. 'Perhaps.'

'Perhaps or yes, Dottore?' Brunetti demanded.

'Yes.'

Brunetti fought down the contempt he felt for Sanpaolo for so easily having given in. Nothing, he realized, could be more perverse than to wish for better opponents. This was not a game, some sort of male competition for territory, but an attempt to find out who had driven that knife into Claudia Leonardo's chest and left her to bleed to death.

'You said you took the will with you.'

Sanpaolo nodded.

'Whose words are used in it?'

'I don't understand what you mean,' he said and Brunetti believed him, suspected the man was so terrified of the consequence of his original evasions that he could no longer accurately process what he heard.

'Who gave you the words to use in the will?'

Again, he watched Sanpaolo chase through the maze of consequences, should he lie. The Notary slid a sideways glance at the two women, both of them now conspicuously busy at their computers, and Brunetti watched him weigh how much he could trust them to cover him should he lie and what they'd have to do in order to do so. And Brunetti watched him abandon the idea.

'My grandfather.'

'How?'

'He called me the day before and told me when she'd be expecting me, and then he dictated it to Cinzia on the phone, and she prepared a copy. That's what I took when I went to see her.'

'Did you know anything about this before your grandfather called you?'

'No.'

'Did she sign it of her free will?' Brunetti asked.

Sanpaolo was indignant that his original behaviour could have suggested to Brunetti that he would violate the rules of his profession. 'Of course,' he insisted. He turned and indicated the two women, both of them still busy with heads bowed over their computers. 'You can ask them.'

Brunetti did, surprising them both and surprising Sanpaolo, perhaps because his word had never been so obviously called into question. 'Is that true, ladies?' Brunetti called across the room.

They looked up from their keyboards, one of them pretending to be shocked.

'Yes, sir.'

'Yes, sir.'

Brunetti turned his attention back to Sanpaolo. 'Did your grandfather give you any explanation of this?'

Sanpaolo shook his head. 'No, he just called and dictated the will and told me to take it to her the next day, have it witnessed, and enter it in my register.'

'No explanation at all?'

Again Sanpaolo shook his head.

'Didn't you ask for one?'

This time Sanpaolo couldn't disguise his surprise. 'No one questions my grandfather,' he said, as though this were catechism class and he called upon to recite one of the Commandments. The childlike simplicity of his next words turned any remaining contempt Brunetti might have had for him into pity. 'We're not allowed to question Nonno.'

Brunetti left him then and started back to the Questura, leaving it to his feet to navigate for him as he mused on Filipetto's guile and legendary rapacity. He would hardly risk having his grandson name himself as heir in a will he prepared, but why the Biblioteca della Patria? As he approached San Marco, he found his thoughts flailing about for the point where the lines converged. Too many of the lines crossed: Claudia and Signora Jacobs; Filipetto and Signora Jacobs; the politics that Claudia loathed and her grandfather loved. And then there was the line that was hacked off with a knife.

Standing in front of the guards at the offices of the Justice of Peace, Brunetti pulled out his *telefonino* and dialled Signorina Elettra's direct number. When she answered, he said, 'I'm interested in anything you can find about Filipetto, professional or personal, and about La Biblioteca della Patria.'

'Officially?'

'Yes, but also what people say.'

'When will you be here, sir?'

'Twenty minutes at the most.'

'I'll make some calls now, sir,' she said and broke the connection.

He didn't hasten his steps but strolled along the *bacino*, taking the opportunity offered by a day cast in silver to look across to San Giorgio, then turned completely around and looked at the cupolas of the churches that lined the water on the other side of the canal. The Madonna had once saved the city from plague, and now there was a church. The Americans had saved the country from the Germans, and now there was McDonald's.

When he got to the Questura, Brunetti went directly to her office. 'Any luck?' he asked when he went in.

'Yes. I called around a little.' He was curious to discover what this might mean.

'And?'

'A couple of years ago, his younger daughter married a foreigner who was working here in the city,' she said, holding up a page from her notepad. 'She has a considerable fortune from her mother, and she used it to create a job for him, a very well-paid job. He's much younger than she and is said not to allow his marriage vows to interfere with his personal life. In fact, someone told me that they were asked to leave a restaurant a few months ago.'

Though he wasn't particularly interested in any of this, Brunetti still asked, 'Why?'

'The person who told me about it said that the Filipetto woman didn't like the way her husband was looking at a girl at the next table. Apparently she became quite abusive.'

'To her husband?' Brunetti asked, surprised that Eleonora Filipetto would be capable of any emotion at all.

'No, to the girl.'

'What happened?'

'The owners had to ask them to leave.'

'But what about Filipetto, and the Biblioteca?' he asked, suddenly irritated at her very Venetian interest in gossip.

He heard her sigh. 'It might be more useful if you pursued the last subject, sir,' she said.

'What subject?'

'Her husband.'

Suddenly angry with games, he snapped, 'I don't care about gossip. I want to know about Filipetto.'

She made no attempt to disguise how much his response offended her. Instead of answering, she handed him the sheet of paper. 'You might be interested in this, sir,' she said with painful courtesy and turned to her computer.

He stepped forward, took the paper, but before he looked at it he said, 'I'm sorry, Elettra. I shouldn't speak to you like that.'

Her smile mingled relief and childlike eagerness. 'Look at her name,' she said, pointing to the paper.

He did. '*Gesù Bambino*,' he exclaimed, though that was not the name written on the paper. 'She married Maxwell Ford.' He said it aloud and listened to the racket in his mind as various pieces began to slide, then fall, then thunder into place.

'What was he doing when they got married?'

'He was a stringer for one of the English papers. The Biblioteca was set up soon after they married.'

'With the father's approval?'

'Dottor Filipetto is not known to be an approving sort of man, and this removed from his home the woman who had taken care of him since his wife died twenty-five years ago.'

'But she's still there.'

'Only two afternoons a week, when the usual woman is out.'

'Why doesn't he get someone else to come in on those days?'

'I've no idea, sir, but the Filipettos have never been known for spending money easily. And this way, he can keep an eye on her and see she doesn't slip entirely out from his control.'

'What does she do the rest of the time?'

'She works in the Biblioteca.'

It suddenly occurred to Brunetti and he asked, 'How do you know all this?'

'I asked around,' she said evasively.

'Who?'

'My Aunt Ippolita, for one. The woman who works for Filipetto goes in to iron for her two afternoons every week.'

'And who else?' Brunetti asked, familiar with her delaying tactics.

'Your father-in-law,' she said neutrally.

Brunetti stared at her. 'You asked him?'

'Well, I know he's a patient of my sister's, and I know he knows I work here, and my father once told me that they had been together in the Resistance. So I took the liberty of calling him and explaining what you'd asked me to do.' She paused to allow him time, perhaps to snap at her again, but when he made no comment she went on, 'He seemed very happy to tell me what he knew. I don't think he has any great affection for the Filipettos.'

'What sort of things did he tell you?'

'She was engaged about twenty years ago, the daughter, but the man changed his mind or left Venice. The Count wasn't sure, but he thought the father had something to do with it, perhaps paid him to leave or to leave her alone.'

'I thought you said they don't like to spend money.'

'This was probably a special case because it interfered with his power and his convenience. If she'd married he would have had to hire a servant, and some of them have been known to talk back to their employers, you know, and insist on being paid.'

'But why would she finally disobey him?' he asked, thinking of Sanpaolo's abject submissiveness.

'Love, Commissario. Love.' She said this in a tone that suggested she might be speaking not only about Eleonora Filipetto.

Brunetti chose not to inquire further about this and said, 'He told me his wife is the other director of the Library.'

'Which is where Claudia worked,' she said, leaving both the sentence and the thought open to speculation.

'Those phone calls,' he said. 'Let me look at them again.'

She busied herself over her computer and less than a minute later the list of all of Claudia's calls was there. Responding to Brunetti's unspoken request, she pressed a few keys and the information about all of the calls other than those between Claudia Leonardo and La Biblioteca della Patria disappeared. Together they read it, the early short calls, then the longer and longer ones, and then the thunderbolt of that final call, twenty-two seconds long.

'You think she's capable of it?' Signorina Elettra asked.

'I think I'll go and ask her husband if she is,' Brunetti said.

25

Signorina Elettra printed out a copy of the phone details, and when he had them he went downstairs and asked Vianello to come with him. On the way to the Biblioteca, Brunetti explained about Eleonora Filipetto's marriage and about the timing and duration of the phone calls, and then the conclusions he had drawn from them.

'There could be some other explanation, I suppose,' Vianello asked.

'Of course,' Brunetti conceded, not believing it, either.

'And you say Filipetto's daughter is one of the directors of this Biblioteca?' Vianello asked.

'That's what her husband said, yes. Why?'

Vianello slowed his pace and glanced aside at Brunetti, waiting to see if he'd drawn the same conclusions. When Brunetti failed to speak, Vianello asked, 'Don't you see?'

'No. What?'

'A name like that – "Biblioteca della Patria" – means they'll get money from both sides. No matter who these old men fought for in the war, they'll give their contributions to the

Biblioteca, sure that it represents their ideals.' The inspector went silent and Brunetti could sense him following his idea to its various conclusions. Finally Vianello said, 'And they're probably listed as a charity, so no one will ask questions about where the money goes.' He made a spitting sound.

'You can't be sure of that,' Brunetti said.

'Of course I can. She's a Filipetto.'

Lapsing into silence after that, Vianello matched his steps to Brunetti's as they walked along the narrow canals of Castello, back toward San Pietro di Castello and the Biblioteca. When they got there, Brunetti saw what he had not noticed the last time, a plaque to the side of the door that gave the opening hours. He rang the bell and a few seconds later the *portone* snapped open and they went in.

The door at the top of the stairs was not locked and they let themselves into the library. There was no sign of Ford, and the door to his office was closed. An old man, bent and looking faintly musty, sat at one of the long tables, a book open in the pool of light from the lamp. Another old man stood by the display cabinet, looking at the notebooks it held. Even at a distance of some metres Brunetti caught the characteristic odour of old men: dry, sour clothing and skin that had gone too long without washing. It was impossible to tell from which one of them the smell came, perhaps from both.

Neither man looked at them when they came in. Brunetti walked over to the man standing in front of the display case. The man looked up then. Careful to speak in Veneziano, Brunetti said, with no introduction, 'It's good to see that someone has respect for the old things,' and waved a hand above them at what looked like a regimental flag.

The old man smiled and nodded but said nothing.

'My father went to Africa and Russia,' Brunetti offered.

'Did he come back?' the old man asked. His dialect was purest Castello, and what he said would probably have been incomprehensible to a non-Venetian.

'Yes.'

'Good. My brother didn't. Betrayed by the Allies. All of us. They tricked the King into surrendering. If he hadn't, if we'd fought on, we would have won.' Then looking round, he added, 'At least they know that here.'

'Absolutely,' Brunetti agreed, thinking of Vianello's convictions about how the Biblioteca was being used. 'And we'd be living in a better place if we had.' He put all the force of conviction into his voice.

'We'd have discipline,' the old man said.

'And order,' came the antiphon from the man at the table, he too speaking in dialect.

'That stupid girl didn't understand these things,' Brunetti said, voice rich with contempt. 'Always saying bad things about the past and the Duce and how we should take in these immigrants who come flooding in from everywhere to steal our jobs. First thing you know, there won't be anywhere for us any more.' He didn't bother to strive for coherence: cliché and prejudice would suffice.

The man standing next to him snorted in approval.

'I don't know why he let her work here,' Brunetti said, nodding in the direction of Ford's office door. 'She was the wrong . . .' he started to say, but the one at the table cut him off.

'You know what he's like,' the old man said, leering across at the two of them. 'All he had to do was see her tits and he lost his head. Couldn't keep his eyes off her, just like the last one. He certainly spent enough time looking at *her* tits until his wife chased her out.'

'God knows what they got up to in his office,' the one at the display case said, voice tight with secret hopes.

'It's a good thing his wife found out about this one, too,' Brunetti said, relief palpable in his voice, the sanctity of the family saved from the temptation offered by immoral young women.

'Did she?' the one at the table asked, curious.

'Of course. You should have seen the way she looked at her, with her tight jeans and her ass all over the place,' the other one explained.

'I know what I would have done with that ass,' the one at the table said, putting his hands under the table and moving them up and down in what Brunetti thought was meant to be a comic gesture but which seemed to him obscene. He thought of Claudia's ghost and hoped she'd forgive him, and these sad old fools, for spitting on her grave.

'Is he here, the Director?' Brunetti asked, as if he'd been called from this fascinating conversation to the reason he had come.

Both nodded. The one at the table pulled his hands back into sight and used them to prop up his head. Seeing that he'd somehow lost the attention of his audience, he bent his attention back to the pages of his book.

Brunetti made a quick gesture, signalling Vianello to remain in the reading room, and went over to the door to Ford's office. He knocked, and a voice from inside called out, '*Avanti.*'

He opened the door and went in.

'Ah, Commissario,' Ford said, getting to his feet. 'How pleasant to see you again.' He came closer and held out his hand. Brunetti took it and smiled. 'Are you any closer to finding the person responsible for Claudia's death?' Ford asked as he shook Brunetti's hand.

'I think I have a good idea of who's responsible for her death, but that's not the same as knowing as who it was that killed her,' Brunetti said with an Olympian calm that startled even himself.

Ford took his hand from Brunetti's and said, 'What do you mean by that?'

'Exactly what I said, Signore: the reason for her death is not far to seek, nor, I suspect, is the person who killed her. It's just that I haven't managed to satisfy myself how one led to the other; not just yet, that is.'

'I have no idea what you're talking about,' Ford said, backing away from Brunetti and standing at the side of his desk, as though its wooden solidity would bolster his words.

'Perhaps your wife will. Is she here, Signore?'

'What do you want to speak to my wife about?'

'The same thing, Signor Ford: Claudia Leonardo's death.'

'That's ridiculous. How can my wife know anything about that?'

'How, indeed?' Brunetti asked, then added, 'Your wife is the other director of the Biblioteca, isn't she?'

'Yes, of course.'

'You didn't mention that the last time I was here,' Brunetti said.

'Of course I did. I told you she was co-director.'

'But you didn't tell me who your wife is, Signor Ford.'

'She's my wife. What more do you need to know about her than that?' Ford insisted. For a moment, Brunetti entertained the thought of what Paola's response would be if she were to hear him say the same thing about her. He did not give voice to this speculation and instead asked again, 'Is she here?'

'That's none of your business.'

'Anything that has to do with Claudia Leonardo's death is my business.'

'You can't talk to her,' Ford said, almost shouting.

Brunetti stepped back from him, saying nothing, turned and started for the door.

'Where are you going?'

'Back to the Questura to get an order from a magistrate that your wife be brought there for questioning.'

'You can't do that,' Ford said, voice even louder.

Brunetti wheeled around and took one step towards him, his anger so palpable that the other man moved back. 'What I can and cannot do is determined by the law, Signor Ford, not by what you might or might not want. And I will talk to your wife.' He turned away from the Englishman, making it clear that he had nothing else to say. He thought Ford would call him back and give in, but he did not, and so Brunetti went out into the reading room, where Vianello had propped himself against one of the tables, a book open in his hands. Neither acknowledged the other, and Vianello looked immediately back at the book.

Brunetti was halfway through the door to the stairway when Ford came out of his office. 'Wait,' he called after Brunetti's retreating back. Brunetti stopped, half turned, but made no move to come back to the reading room.

'Commissario,' Ford said, his voice calm but his face still suffused with the memory of anger. 'Perhaps we can talk about this.' Ford glanced at the two old men, but they looked quickly back at whatever it was they'd been reading when Ford came in. Vianello ignored them all.

The Englishman extended a conciliatory hand. 'Commissario. Come into my office and we can talk.'

Brunetti was very careful to demonstrate his reluctance and moved with willed slowness. As he passed Vianello, he shot his finger out and pointed at the two men, and Vianello nodded. Brunetti followed the Englishman back into his office, waited while he closed the door, then went back to the chair he had sat in last time. This time Ford retreated behind his desk.

It was not difficult for Brunetti to remain silent: long experience had shown him how effective a technique it was in forcing others to talk.

Finally Ford said, 'I think I can explain.' In the face of Brunetti's continuing silence, Ford went on. 'The girl was a terrible flirt.' He watched to see how Brunetti responded to this and when he seemed interested, Ford went on, 'Of course, I had no idea of this when she first came here and asked to use the library. She seemed like a serious enough girl. And she stayed that way until she had the job, and then she started.'

'Started what?' Brunetti asked in a tone that suggested he was both intrigued and willing to believe.

'Oh, finding excuses to come in here to ask me about certain documents or to help her find a book she said someone had asked about.' He gave Brunetti a small smile that was probably meant to be boyish and embarrassed but which Brunetti thought merely looked sly. 'I suppose, at first I found it flattering. You know, that she'd want my help or my advice. It wasn't long before I realized how simple many of the questions were and how, well, how disproportionate her thanks were.' He stopped there, as if puzzled how to progress, a gentleman trapped in the dilemma of telling the truth at the cost of a young woman's reputation.

As Brunetti watched, he seemed to overcome the obstacle of false chivalry and opt to tell the truth. 'She really became quite shameless. Finally, I had no choice but to let her go.'

'Meaning?'

'I had to ask her to leave the Biblioteca.'

'You mean fire her?'

Ford smiled. 'Not exactly. She didn't work here officially. I mean, not as a regular employee. She was a volunteer, and because she was working that way, it was easier to ask her to leave.' He bowed his head but continued to speak. 'It was still very difficult to ask her to leave, very embarrassing.' When Brunetti seemed puzzled by this, Ford went on, 'I didn't want to hurt her feelings.'

Brunetti had no doubt that Claudia's departure from the Biblioteca had been embarrassing, but he wasn't certain that the explanation he had just given accurately described its cause. He took his bottom lip between his thumb and first two fingers and fell into what he did his best to make look like a contemplative pose. 'Did your wife know about this?'

Ford hesitated a moment before he answered; to Brunetti the fact of the hesitation, not its length, mattered.

'I never said anything to her, if that's what you mean,' Ford said, not without suggesting that it was indiscreet of Brunetti to ask. Rather than point out that he had not answered the question, Brunetti simply waited and at last the Englishman said, 'I'm afraid she may have noticed. Eleonora is very observant.' With a man like this, Brunetti reflected, she'd have every reason to be.

'Did you ever discuss the girl with your wife?' Brunetti asked.

'No, of course not,' he protested, the injured gentleman. 'Early on, I may have said something about her, that she was a good worker, but as I took no real interest in the girl I probably did nothing more than that.'

'Did Claudia work for your wife or when your wife was here in the Biblioteca?'

'Ah,' Ford said with an easy smile, 'I'm afraid I haven't explained. My wife's directorship is purely administrative. That is, she deals with the bureaucracy and the red tape from the city and regional offices who take an interest in our work.' He tried a small smile. 'Because she's Italian, and more specifically because she's Venetian, she knows how to manoeuvre her way around. I'm afraid I, as a foreigner, would be quite helpless.'

Brunetti smiled in return, thinking that, if there were any adjective that might be attributed to Mr Ford, 'helpless' most decidedly was not it.

'Then what do you do, Signore?'

'I attend to the daily running of the Biblioteca,' Ford said.

'I see,' Brunetti answered, finally accepting Vianello's conclusions about the real purpose of the Library.

Ford remained silent, a ghost of a smile on his lips. When it was evident that he had nothing further to say, Brunetti got to his feet, saying, 'I'm afraid I still have to speak to your wife.'

'She'll be very upset by that.'

'Why?'

The answer was some time in coming. 'She was very fond of Claudia and I think it would upset her to talk about her death.'

Brunetti didn't ask how she could have been so fond of a girl with whom her husband had suggested she had had almost no contact. 'I'm afraid there's nothing I can do about that, Signore. I have to speak to her.'

He watched Ford weigh the possible cost of opposing this demand. The man said he was not familiar with Italian bureaucracy, but anyone who had lived here for even a few years would know that, sooner or later, she would have to speak to the police. Brunetti waited patiently and allowed Ford more than enough time to decide. Finally he looked up at Brunetti and said, 'All right. But I'd like to speak to her first.'

'I'm afraid that's impossible,' Brunetti said quite equitably.

'Only to assure her there's nothing to be afraid of,' Ford added.

'I'll be very careful to do that,' Brunetti said, the firmness of his tone at odds with the pleasantness of what he said.

'All right,' Ford said, getting up and going towards the door to his office.

Again, Brunetti passed through the reading room. Both of the old men were gone and Vianello was now seated at one of the tables, the book open in front of him, seemingly so absorbed in it that he didn't look up when the two men came out of Ford's office. He did, however, tap the point of his pen on a sheet of paper which lay next to the book, a sheet that appeared to contain two names and addresses.

On the landing Ford waited for Brunetti, then led the way up the stairs. At the top he opened the single door without needing to unlock it. They could be in the middle of the countryside, with attentive neighbours careful to protect one another, not in the middle of a city besieged by thieves and burglars.

Inside, the simplicity of the rooms below was banished. On the floor of the entrance hall lay a Sarouk so thick and yet so richly coloured that Brunetti felt uncomfortably daring to walk on it while wearing shoes. Ford led him into a large sitting room that looked out to the *campo* on the other side of the canal. A celadon bowl in that extraterrestrial green that Brunetti had never liked sat on a low table in front of a beige satin-covered sofa.

Paintings, many of them portraits, hung from three walls; the fourth was lined with bookshelves. The centre of the room was covered with an enormous Nain, its pale arabesques in perfect harmony with the sofa.

'I'll just go and get her,' Ford said, starting for the back of the apartment.

Brunetti held up a monitory hand. 'I think it would be better if you called her, Signor Ford.'

Managing to look both confused and offended, Ford asked, 'Why?'

'Because I'd like to talk to her and without your saying anything to her first.'

'I don't see how that could possibly make a difference,' Ford said, this time not confused but certainly offended.

'I do,' Brunetti said shortly, standing in place just to the left of the door of the room and only a short step from being able to block it with his body. 'Please call her.'

Ford made a business of standing just inside the door and calling towards the back of the apartment, 'Eleonora.' There was no response, and he called again, 'Eleonora.'

Brunetti heard a voice say something from the back, but it was impossible to distinguish what it said.

'Could you come here a moment, Eleonora,' Ford called.

Brunetti thought the man might add something, but he did not. A minute passed, another, and then both of them could hear a door closing at the back of the apartment. While he waited, Brunetti studied one of the portraits, an unhappy-looking woman in a wide starched ruff, her hair pulled severely back in a tight bun, looking out at the world in sharp disapproval of all she saw. He wondered who could have been so blind, or so cruel, to have such a portrait hanging in the house where Eleonora Filipetto lived.

Though he tried to stop himself, he found himself thinking the same thing when Eleonora Filipetto came into the room. Like the woman in the portrait, her hair was streaked with grey, but unlike hers, it hung limp and close to her head. Both women had the same tight, colourless lips that could so easily be pulled together in dissatisfaction, as the living woman's were as she entered.

She recognized Brunetti, saw her husband, and chose to speak to Brunetti, 'Yes? What is it?' Her voice aimed at briskness but succeeded in seeming only nervous.

'I've come to ask you some questions about Claudia Leonardo, Signora,' he said.

She waited, looking at him, not asking why.

'The last time we met, Signora, when I was asking about Claudia, you didn't tell me you knew her.'

'You didn't ask me,' she said, voice as flat as her bosom.

'In such circumstances, you might have said more than that you recognized the name,' he suggested.

'You didn't ask me,' she repeated as though he had not just commented on that same answer.

'What did you think of Claudia?' Brunetti asked. He noticed that Ford made no attempt to catch her attention. In fact, he gradually moved over to the front of the room and stood by the window. When Brunetti glanced in his direction he saw that Ford was standing with his back to them, looking across at the façade of the church.

She looked across the room at her husband, as if she hoped to find the answer written on his back. 'I didn't think of her,' she finally said.

'And why is that, Signora?' Brunetti inquired politely.

'She was a young girl who worked in the Biblioteca. I saw her once or twice. Why should I think of her?' Though the words were defiant, her tone had become more hesitant and uncertain, and she asked it as a real question, not a sarcastic one.

Brunetti decided he was tired of games. 'Because she was a young woman, Signora, and because your husband has a history of finding young women attractive.'

'What are you talking about?' she demanded too quickly, glancing quickly at her husband.

'It seems simple enough to me, Signora. I'm talking about what everyone seems to know: your husband's tendency to betray you with younger women, more attractive women.'

Her face contorted, but not in pain or in any of the emotions he might have expected as a result of the remarks he had made sound as offhand and insulting as he could. If she looked anything, she looked startled, even shocked.

'What do you mean, that people know? How can they know about it?'

Keeping his voice entirely conversational, he said, 'In the reading room, when I was waiting, even the old men talked about it, about the way he was always grabbing at tits.' He looked pointedly at her chest and slipped from the precisely articulated Italian he had been speaking into the most heavily accented and vulgar Veneziano, 'I can see why he told me he likes to get his hands on a real pair of tits.'

She gasped so loud that Ford, who had understood nothing of what Brunetti had said in dialect, turned from the window. He saw his wife, hands clutched to her breast, staring open-mouthed at a calm and self-possessed Brunetti, who was leaning forward and saying politely, in precise Italian, 'Excuse me, Signora. Is something wrong?'

She stood, mouth still open, drawing immense gulps of air

into her lungs. 'He said that? He said that to you?' she gasped.

Ford moved quickly away from the window. He had no idea what was happening as he came towards his wife, his arms raised as if to embrace her protectively.

'Get away from me,' she said, voice tight, struggling to speak. 'You said that to him?' she hissed. 'You said that after what I did for you? First you betray me with that little whore and then you say that about me?' Her voice rose with every question, her face growing darker and more congested.

'Eleonora, be quiet,' Ford said as he drew even nearer. She raised a hand to push him away, and he put out one of his own to grab her arm. But she moved suddenly to the side, and his open hand came down, not on her wrist or her arm but on her breast.

She froze, and instinct or longing drove her forward, leaning into his hand, but then she pulled sharply back and raised a clenched fist. 'Don't touch me. Don't touch me there, the way you touched that little whore.' Her voice went up an octave. 'You won't touch her again, will you? Not with a knife in her chest where your hand was, will you?' Ford stood, frozen with horror. 'Will you?' she screamed, 'Will you?' Suddenly she pulled her fist back and brought it crashing down once, twice, three times, into his chest as the two men stood there paralysed in the face of her rage. After the third blow, she moved away from him. As suddenly as it had started, her rage evaporated and she started to cry, great tearing sobs. 'I did all of that for you, and you can still say that to him.'

'Shut up!' Ford shouted at her. 'Shut up, you fool.'

Tears streaming from her eyes, she looked up at him and asked, voice choking with sobs, 'Why do you always have to have pretty things? Both of you, Daddy and you, all you've ever wanted is pretty things. Neither of you ever wanted . . .' Sobbing overcame her and choked off her last word, but Brunetti had no doubt that it was going to be 'me'.

26

Though Ford tried to stop Brunetti with loud bluster, insisting that he had no right to arrest his wife, the woman offered no resistance and said that she would go along with him. Ford in their wake, hurling threats and the names of important people at their backs, Brunetti led her to the front door. Behind it they found Vianello, lounging up against the wall, his jacket unbuttoned and, to Brunetti's experienced eye, his pistol evident in its holster.

Brunetti was in some uncertainty as to what to say to Vianello, as he wasn't at all sure that what he had just heard Signora Ford say could be construed as a confession of murder. There had been no witness, save for Ford, and he could be counted upon to deny hearing what she had said or insist she'd said something else entirely. It depended, then, on his getting her to repeat her confession in Vianello's hearing or, even better, on getting her to the Questura, where she could record it or speak it while being videotaped. He knew that a future case based on his word alone would be laughed at by any prosecuting magistrate with experience in the courtroom; indeed, it would be laughed at by anyone with experience of the law.

'I've called for a boat, sir,' Vianello said quite calmly when he saw them. 'It should be here soon.'

Brunetti nodded, as though this were the most normal thing in the word for Vianello to have done.

'Where?' he asked.

'At the end of the *calle*,' Vianello said.

'You can't do this,' Ford again insisted, putting himself at the top of the steps and blocking Brunetti's path. 'My father-in-law knows the Praetore. You'll be fired for this.'

Brunetti didn't have to say a word. Vianello went over to Ford, said, '*Permesso*,' and moved him bodily to one side, freeing the stairway for his wife and Brunetti to start down. Brunetti didn't look behind him, but he could hear the Englishman arguing, then shouting, then making grunting noises that must have resulted from a futile attempt to shift Vianello from the top of the steps so that he could follow his wife.

The sun gleamed down, even though it was November and meant to be much colder. As they emerged from the building, Brunetti heard the motor of a boat from their right, and he led the silent woman down towards it. A police launch swept up to the steps at the end of the *calle* and stopped; at their approach, a uniformed officer set a wide piece of planking between the gunwales and the embankment, then helped the woman and Brunetti on board.

Brunetti led her down to the cabin, uncertain whether to speak to her or wait for her to begin to speak on her own. His curiosity made silence more difficult, but he opted for that and, sitting across from one another, they rode silently back to the Questura.

Inside, he took her to one of the small rooms used for questioning and advised her that everything they said would be recorded. He led her to a chair on one side of the table, sat opposite her, gave their names and the date and asked if she would like to have a lawyer with her as she talked. She waved a hand at him in dismissal, but he repeated the question until she said, 'No. No lawyer.'

She sat silent, looking down at the surface of the table in which people had, over the course of the years, carved initials and words and pictures. Her face was splotched with red, her eyes still swollen from crying. She traced some initials with the forefinger of her right hand then finally looked up at Brunetti.

'Is it true that Claudia Leonardo worked at the library where you are one of the directors?' He thought it best to avoid any reference to her husband until the interview had taken on its own momentum.

She nodded.

'I'm sorry, Signora,' he said with a softening of his face that was not quite a smile, 'but you must say something. Because of the recording.'

She looked around, searching for the microphones, but as they were set into two wall sockets that looked like light switches, she failed to identify them.

'Did Claudia Leonardo work at the Biblioteca della Patria?' he asked again.

'Yes.'

'How long after she began to work there did you meet her?'

'Not very long.'

'Could you tell me how you first met her? The circum-stances, I mean.'

She folded the fingers of her right hand into the palm and, using the nail of her thumb, began to dig idly at one of the letters on the table, freeing it of the greasy material that had accumulated over the years. As Brunetti watched, her nail pried free a tiny sliver of what looked like black wax. She brushed it to the floor. She looked at him. 'I had to go down to the library to look for a book, and when I came in she asked me how she could help me. She didn't know who I was.'

'What was your first impression of her, Signora?'

She shrugged the question away, but before Brunetti could remind her of the microphones, she said, 'I didn't have much of an impres . . .' Then, perhaps recalling where they were and why she was here, she sat up straighter in her chair, looked over at Brunetti and said, voice a bit firmer, 'She seemed like a nice girl.' She emphasized 'seemed'. 'She was very polite, and when I told her who I was she was very respectful.'

'Do you think that was an accurate assessment of the girl's character?' Brunetti asked.

She paused not an instant over this question and said, 'It can't be, not after what she did to my husband.'

'But what did you think at the beginning, when you first met her?' he asked.

It was evident to Brunetti that she had to overcome her reluctance to answer this question, but when she did she said, 'I was wrong. I saw the truth, but it took time.'

Abandoning the attempt to get her to describe her first impression of the girl, Brunetti asked, 'What did you come to believe?'

'I saw that she was, that she was, that she was . . .' Stuck on that phrase, her voice died away. She looked down at the initial on the table, dug a bit more material out of it, and finally said, 'That she was interested in my husband.'

'Interested in an improper way?' Brunetti suggested.

'Yes.'

'Was this something that had happened before, that women became interested in your husband?' He thought it might be better to phrase it this way, placing the guilt on the women, at least for the moment, until she was more adjusted to accepting the so-obvious truth.

She nodded, then quickly said, voice too loud and nervous, 'Yes.'

'Did this happen often?'

'I don't know.'

'Had it happened before with the employees of the Biblioteca?'

'Yes. The last one.'

'What happened?'

'I found out. About them. He told me what happened, that she was . . . well, that she was immoral. I sent her away, back to Geneva, where she came from.'

'And did you find out about Claudia, as well?'

'Yes.'

'Could you tell me how that happened?'

'I heard him talking on the phone to her.'

'Did you hear what he was saying?' When she nodded, he asked, 'Did you listen to the conversation or only to his part of it?'

'Only his part. He was in his office, but the door wasn't closed. So I could hear him talking.'

'What did he say?'

'That if she wanted to continued to work in the Biblioteca, nothing else would happen.' He watched her going back in time and listening to her husband's part of that conversation. 'He told her that if she would just forget about it and not tell anyone, he promised not to do anything else.'

'And you took that to mean that it was Claudia Leonardo who was bothering your husband?' Brunetti asked, not voicing his scepticism but curious that she could have interpreted his words this way.

'Of course.'

'Do you still think that now?'

Her voice suddenly grew fierce, the linked initials on the table below her forgotten. 'It had to be that way,' she said with tight conviction. 'She was his lover.'

'Who told you that she was his lover?' As he waited for her answer he studied this woman, the restrained frenzy in her hands, recalling the way she had hungrily leaned her breast into the accidental touch of her husband's hand, and an entirely new possibility came to him. 'Did your husband confess that they were lovers, Signora?' he asked in a softer voice.

First came the tears, which surprised him by coming without any emotion registering on her face. 'Yes,' she said, turning her attention back to the table.

Hunting dogs, Brunetti knew, were divided into two general classes: sight hounds and scent hounds. Like one of the second, he was off, racing through the thick, wet grass of an autumn day, leaping over obstacles that had been placed in his path, catching traces of his prey that had previously been obscured by heavier scents. His mind circling, leaping, lurching after its prey, he found himself back again at the starting point, and he asked, 'Whose idea was it to talk to the old woman, Signora, and offer her the chance to clear Guzzardi's name? Was it your husband's?'

She should have been surprised. She should have looked up at him, startled, and asked him what he was talking about. Had she done that, he would not have believed her, but he would have realized how far he still had to go before he hunted her to ground.

Instead, she surprised him by asking, 'How did you know about that?'

'It doesn't matter. But I know. Which of them had the idea?'

'Maxwell,' she said. 'One of the people who wrote a letter of recommendation for Claudia was Signora Jacobs. She'd been a patron of the Biblioteca for some time, always asking about Guzzardi and whether we had ever received any papers that would prove he didn't take those drawings.' She paused and Brunetti resisted the urge to prompt her. 'My father knew him and he said there never would be any proof because he did take them. They'd be worth a fortune now, my father said, but no one knew where they were.'

'No one knew that Signora Jacobs had them?'

'No, of course not. No one ever went to her house, and everyone knew how poor she was.' She paused, then corrected this, 'Or thought she was.'

'How did he find out?' he asked, still careful not to refer directly to her husband.

'Claudia. One day, talking about Signora Jacobs, she said something about the things that were in her house and what a pity it was that no one got to see them except her and the old woman. I think she was the only one who went there.' And the cleaning woman, Brunetti wanted to tell her. And the Somali cleaning woman so honest she was trusted with the keys while the rest of the city was kept away, untrusted and ignorant.

'How do you know about this, Signora?'

'I heard them talking, my father and Maxwell. They were both so used to ignoring me,' she began, and Brunetti marvelled that she could seem so casually accepting of this, 'that they talked about everything in front of me.'

'Was the idea of clearing Guzzardi's name a way to get the drawings from her?' Brunetti asked.

'I think so. Maxwell told Claudia that someone had come to the Biblioteca with papers that showed that Guzzardi was innocent.' He watched as she tried to recall what had been said in front of her.

'Did he suggest that Signora Jacobs give the drawings in exchange?'

'No, all he did was tell Claudia that there was proof that he was innocent and suggest she ask Signora Jacobs what she wanted to do.'

'And?'

'I don't know what happened. I think Claudia talked to her about it, and I think my father had someone go and talk to the old woman.' She sounded vague and uninterested in this, but then she glanced at him sharply and said, 'Then I heard him talking to Claudia on the phone.'

'And is that when he told you that they were lovers?' Brunetti asked.

'Yes. But he told me that it was over, that he'd ended it. In fact, he slammed the phone down on her that time, told her to be very careful what she told people about him. And he sounded so upset that I made a noise.' She stopped again.

Brunetti waited.

'He came out of his office and saw me, and he asked me what I'd heard. I told him, I told him that I couldn't stand it any more, him and those girls, that I was afraid of what I'd do if he didn't stop.' She nodded her head, no doubt hearing the words again, replaying the jealous scene between her and her husband.

After some time, she went on, 'That's when he told me about the way she had tempted him and how he hadn't wanted to do anything. But she'd thrown herself at him. Touched him.' She pronounced the words, 'tempted' and 'thrown' with disgust, but when she said 'touched' she spoke with shock that approached horror. 'And he told me then that he was afraid of what would happen if she came back, that he was a man, and he was weak. That it was me he loved but he didn't know what would happen if this wicked girl tempted him again.'

Seeing how agitated she was becoming, Brunetti decided it would be best to lead her away from these memories for a moment. 'Let me go back to one thing, Signora, to the conversation you heard when you came in. Your husband was telling her that, if she came back to the Biblioteca and didn't tell anyone, he wouldn't do anything else? Is that correct?'

She nodded.

'I'm sorry to have to remind you, Signora, but you have to speak.'

'Yes.'

'That's what he said?'

'Yes.'

'Is it possible that he might have been talking about something else? Have you thought about this?' he asked.

Her look was utterly candid, and she said, 'But that's what he told me he meant. That he would allow her to come back, and if she behaved he wouldn't do anything.'

'Why would he want her to come back?'

She smiled here, having been quicker than he to ask this question and understand the reason. 'He said he didn't want there to be any talk, that he didn't want me to be hurt by what people might say.' She smiled at this proof of her husband's consideration and, ineluctably, love.

'I see,' Brunetti said. 'But then, when he told you how frightened he was of his weakness, that she could tempt him again, how did you react?'

'I was proud of him, that he would be so honest with me and that I was worth so much to him. That he would confess to me.'

'Of course,' Brunetti muttered, understanding just what her husband's confession really had meant to achieve and how successful he had been. 'And did he ask you anything?' Brunetti asked. When she seemed reluctant to answer, he changed the words a bit, 'Did he ask for your help?'

That brought a smile. 'Yes. He wanted me to go and talk to her and try to make her agree to stay away from him.'

'Yes, I can see that that would be wise,' Brunetti said, seeing only too well her husband's wisdom in making the request. 'And did you go?'

'Not for a few more nights. I told him I trusted him to be strong. But then, a few days later, he came and told me that she had started again, had . . . had touched him again, and he didn't know how long he would be strong.' Again, her voice broke in horror at the girl's behaviour.

'And did he ask you again to go and talk to her?'

'No,' she said. 'He didn't have to. I knew it was what I

had to do, to go and tell her to leave him alone and not tempt him.'

'And?'

'And I went that night,' she said, folding her hands in front of her on the table, interlacing her fingers.

'And?' Brunetti asked.

'You know what happened,' she said with dismissive contempt for this charade.

'I'm afraid I do, Signora, but you have to say it.'

'I killed her,' she said, voice tight. 'She let me in and I started to talk to her. I have my pride, so I didn't say that Maxwell had asked me. I told her she'd have to stay away from him.'

'And what happened?'

'She told me that I was wrong, that she had no interest in him, that I had it all backwards and it was Maxwell who was bothering her.' She smiled confidently here. 'But he'd warned me that she'd lie and tell me that, so I was ready for it.'

'Then?'

'Then she said things about him, terrible things that I couldn't listen to.'

'What things?'

'That she knew that the idea of those papers about Guzzardi was just a way for Maxwell and my father to get money, that she'd told Maxwell she was going to tell Signora Jacobs about it.' She stopped, and Brunetti heard a distinct hardening in her voice as she said, 'And she made up lies about other girls and what people in the Biblioteca said about him.'

'And then?'

'And then she said the idea of sex with him made her sick.' Her tone struck out, even to the edge of doom, and he knew, without her having to tell him, that it was this that had driven her over the edge to violence.

'The weapon, Signora?'

272

'She was eating an apple. The knife was on the table.' Just like in *Tosca*, Brunetti thought. He shivered.

'She didn't scream?' he asked.

'No. I think she was too surprised. She had turned away for something, I don't know what, and when she turned around, I did it.'

'I see,' Brunetti said. He decided not to ask for details: it was more important that the typist outside be given the tape as soon as possible so that a written statement could be prepared for her to sign. But his curiosity got the better of him, and he asked, 'And Signora Jacobs?'

'What about her?' she asked, honestly puzzled.

Instantly Brunetti abandoned the question he was about to ask as well as his suspicion that Signora Jacobs had been murdered.

'I'm afraid it was too much for her,' the woman said and then surprised Brunetti by adding, 'I'm sorry that she died.'

'Are you sorry you killed the girl, Signora?'

She shook her head a number of times in calm, determined denial. 'No, not at all. I'm glad I did it.'

Obviously she had forgotten, or forgiven, her husband's supposed betrayal, just that afternoon, a false betrayal that had catapulted her into her own true self-betrayal.

Suddenly Brunetti's spirit was overcome with the weight of human folly and misery, and he stood, gave the time, said the interview was terminated, and left the room to go and have her confession typed out.

27

Brunetti succeeded in having Signora Ford sign her confession. He stood in the room with the secretary who
transcribed it and then took it back to the interview room
and to the waiting woman, who signed and dated it. No
sooner had she done so than her husband arrived with a
lawyer who protested that he had not been present while
his client was being questioned. Ford had obviously
thought to pull out all of the stops with the professional
classes and had brought along a doctor as well; he
demanded to see his patient and, after giving her a cursory
glance, said that it was necessary that she be hospitalized
immediately. The two of them struck Brunetti as looking
like a pair of salt and pepper shakers: both tall men and
very thin, the doctor had white hair and pale skin, while the
lawyer, Filippo Boscaro, had dark hair and a thick black
moustache.

Brunetti asked the reason for the hospitalization, and the
doctor, who stood in the interview room with a protective
hand on Signora Ford's shoulder, said that his patient was

obviously suffering from shock and was hardly in a position to answer any questions.

At this, Signora Ford glanced up at him, then at her husband, who knelt beside her, his hands wrapped protectively around hers. 'Don't worry, Eleonora,' he said, 'I'll take care of you.'

The woman leaned towards him, whispered something Brunetti could not hear. Ford kissed her softly on the cheek and she looked up at Brunetti, her face aglow with vindicated love. Brunetti said nothing, waiting to see what Ford would suggest.

The Library Director got awkwardly to his feet, unable to use his hands, which were still as much the captives as the captors of his wife's. When he was standing, he helped her to her feet and then put a supporting arm around her. Turning to the doctor he said, 'Giulio, will you take her?'

Before the doctor could answer, Brunetti interrupted, 'I'm afraid she can't leave unless a policewoman goes along with her.' The doctor, the librarian and the lawyer competed in displaying their umbrage at this, but Brunetti opened the door to the corridor and told the officer standing there to see that a woman officer be sent up immediately.

The lawyer, whom Brunetti recognized but about whom he knew little more than he was a criminal lawyer, said, 'I hope you realize, Commissario, that anything my client might have said during the time she was here is hardly to be admitted as evidence.'

'Evidence of what?' Brunetti asked.

'I beg your pardon?' the lawyer said.

'Evidence of what?' Brunetti repeated.

At a loss, all the lawyer could think of to say was, 'Of anything.'

'Could it be used as evidence that she had been here, do you think, *avvocato*?' Brunetti asked politely. 'Or perhaps as evidence that she knew what her name was?' Brunetti knew that nothing could come of baiting the lawyer, but still he could not stop himself from offending him.

'I don't know what you're talking about, Commissario,' Boscaro said, 'but I do think you are deliberately trying to provoke me.'

Brunetti, who was forced to agree with him, turned to the doctor. 'Could you tell me your name, Dottore?' he asked.

'Giulio Rampazzo,' the white-haired man said.

'And you are Signora Ford's regular doctor?'

'I'm a psychiatrist,' Dr Rampazzo said.

'I see,' Brunetti answered. 'And has Signora Ford been a patient of yours for some time?'

Her husband lost his patience here. Tightening his arm around his wife he led her towards the door. 'I don't see the sense of any of this. I'm taking my wife out of here.'

Brunetti knew better than to oppose him, especially when the man had both a doctor and a lawyer in tow. He was glad, however, to see a uniformed woman officer appear just outside the door. 'Officer, you're to accompany this woman.'

She saluted and said, 'Yes, sir,' without bothering to ask where she was to go with the woman or what she was meant to do in her company.

'Which hospital are you taking her to, Dottore?' Brunetti asked. Rampazzo hunted for an answer, trying not to look at Ford for a clue. Seeing this, Brunetti said, 'I'll have a launch take you to the Ospedale Civile, then.' Nodding to the officer who was still there, he sent him off to call for the launch.

As he walked in front of them down the steps towards the entrance of the Questura, Brunetti thought of the best way to handle this. With a doctor there, insisting that the woman was in shock, Ford would get her out of the Questura; Brunetti knew it was useless to oppose that. But the more normal and peaceful her departure was made to seem, the more weight would be given to the validity of her confession, during which she had certainly remained perfectly calm and coherent.

In front of the building, the police launch was waiting, motor throbbing idly. Brunetti stopped at the door and did not follow them from the building. The same uniformed policeman helped the two women and then the three men on board, then stepped on deck after them. When the launch moved off, Brunetti went back inside to make the phone calls he hoped would ensure that Signora Ford did not escape the bureaucratic labyrinth into which her confession had placed her.

Intermittently during the next months the attention of Venice was focused on that labyrinth and the slothlike progress – if that is not too wildly energetic a word – through it of the cases of Claudia Leonardo's murder and Hedwig Jacobs's possessions. Both had burst upon the public attention like comets, lighting up the front pages of local and national newspapers. All talk of other crimes or complexities was driven to the bottom of the front page by the sensational confession to murder by the daughter of one of the best known notaries in the city and the discovery of a patrimony in paintings and other art pieces in the modest home of a poor old woman.

Speculation ran rife about the first case: jealousy, passion, adultery; as to the second, the purported emotions were more muted: loyalty, love, devotion. Both stories soon shifted with their principals: Signora Ford was returned to her home, and her story moved to the inner pages; Signora Jacobs's story was buried, as she had been buried in the Protestant cemetery, but not before Brunetti had come to regret his error in believing her to have been murdered. Claudia's death had killed her, not Claudia's killer.

The case, sometimes called the Leonardo case and sometimes the Ford case, chugged on. The confession was called into question, accused of being yet another example of the stormtrooper mentality of the authorities, but finally, after six months of legal wrangling, was admitted as valid. But by then Doctor Rampazzo and his colleagues had argued that this was a woman driven beyond herself by jealousy. Not only beyond herself, but beyond all possibility of responsibility. Boscaro proved to be a man worthy of his reputation, and no doubt of his fee, by presenting this argument to a board of judges, who declared that Signora Ford was indeed in a position of diminished responsibility when she went to speak to Claudia Leonardo. What had happened then . . . As Signor Ford had told his wife: human flesh was weak and people did things they did not want to do.

Brunetti, caught up in another case, this time of even more corruption at the Casinò, followed Claudia's murder in the papers and by means of his friends in the magistracy, knowing himself helpless to effect any change in the way things would play themselves out.

The objects in the Jacobs case were inventoried again, this time by representatives of the Ministry of the Treasury and the Sovrintendenza delle Belle Arti. Claudia's mother was declared Claudia's legal heir, and that in turn made her heir to Frau Jacobs's possessions. Her continued absence, however, led to the opening of a waiting period of seven years, at the end of which she would be declared legally dead and possession would pass to the state. The paintings and ceramics, and the famous drawings that had, or had not, once belonged to the Swiss Consul and which now did or did not belong to Claudia's mother, all were taken to Rome. There, they were placed in storage and the seven years of the waiting period began to count themselves out.

One night, as they sat in the living room, Paola looked up from her book and said, surprising him, 'Jarndyce vs. Jarndyce.'

'What?' Brunetti asked.

She met his glance, her eyes slightly magnified by the

lenses of her reading glasses. 'Nothing, really,' she said. 'It's something in a book.'

Six months after that, Gianpaolo Filipetto died quietly in his sleep and, having been a parishoner of the church of San Giovanni in Bragora, he was buried there with all the pomp and ceremony due to his advanced years and his stature in the city.

Brunetti arrived late and missed the Requiem Mass, but he was on time to mingle with the people who emerged from the church and stood, respectful and silent, waiting for the coffin and the mourners to appear. Six men carried the dark mahogany coffin, its lid buried under an enormous blanket of red and white roses. The first to emerge from the dimness of the church was the pastor, a man bent under the weight of years almost as heavy as those of Filipetto. Behind him came Filipetto's daughter, released from house arrest to attend the funeral, her right arm held tightly by her husband. Ford had gained weight in the last few months and all but glowed with health and well-being, but she had grown even more angular and stick-like.

Ford kept his eyes on his wife's face as they walked; she kept hers on the ground. The crowd parted in advance of the pallbearers as they made their slow way out into the *campo*. A man walked quickly into the *campo* from the direction of the *bacino*, where the boat that would take the coffin to the cemetery was moored. The man saw the coffin, approached the pastor and had a word with him, and the old priest turned and pointed to Ford. The man signalled to Ford, who left his wife with a soft word and went to talk to him.

Brunetti took this opportunity to approach the woman.

'Signora,' he said as he came up to her.

She looked up, recognized him instantly, but said nothing. Brunetti saw that she had aged more years than months had passed; her cheeks were gaunt hollows on either side of a withered mouth. It was as though she had become a stranger to sleep.

She looked down and spoke so softly he had to bend to hear what she said, 'Tell me what you have to tell me before he comes back.' She spoke hurriedly, glancing to the left, where her husband stood talking to the other man.

'Have you read all of the papers in your case, Signora?' he asked.

She nodded.

'Have you read the autopsy report?'

Her eyes widened at this, and then she closed them for an instant. He took that as a yes, but he wanted to hear her say it.

'Have you read it?'

'Yes,' she said.

'Then you know she was a virgin.'

Her mouth opened, and he saw then that she had lost her two bottom front teeth and not bothered to replace them. 'He told me . . .' she began to say but then stopped, looking anxiously off towards her husband.

'I'm sure he did, Signora,' Brunetti said, and turned away, leaving her to the men in her life.

Read on for an extract from *A Sea of Troubles*,
now available in Arrow paperback.

1

Pellestrina is a long, narrow peninsula of sand that has, over the course of the centuries, been turned into habitable ground. Running north and south from San Pietro in Volta to Ca' Roman, Pellestrina is about ten kilometres long, but never more than a couple of hundred metres wide. To the east, it faces the Adriatic, a sea not known for the sweetness of its temper, but the west side rests in the Lagoon of Venice and is thus protected from wind, storm and wave. The earth is sandy and infertile, so the people of Pellestrina, though they sow, are able to reap little. This makes small difference to them; indeed, most of them would no doubt scoff at the very idea of earning a living, however rich, from the earth, for the people of Pellestrina have always taken theirs from the sea.

Many stories are told about the men of Pellestrina, the endurance and strength that have been forced upon them in their attempt to wrest a living from the sea. Old people in Venice remember a time when the men of Pellestrina were said to spend the nights, winter or summer, sleeping on the dirt floors of their cottages instead of in their beds so as to more easily push themselves out into the early morning and make the tide that would carry them into the Adriatic and thus to the fish. Like most stories that are told about how much tougher people were in the olden days, this is probably apocryphal. What is true, however, is the fact that most people who hear it, if they are Venetian, believe it, just as they would believe any tale that spoke of the toughness of the men of Pellestrina or of their indifference to pain or suffering, their own or that of others.

During the summer Pellestrina comes alive, as tourists arrive from Venice and its Lido or across from Chioggia on the mainland to eat fresh seafood and drink the crisp white wine, just short of sparkling, that is served in the bars and restaurants. Instead of bread, they are served *bussolai*, hard oval pretzels whose name, perhaps, comes from the *bussola*, or compass, that has the same shape. Along with the *bussolai* there is fish, often so fresh it was still alive when the tourists set out to make the long and inconvenient trip to Pellestrina. As the tourists pulled themselves from their hotel beds, the gills of the *orate* still fought against the alien element, the air; as the tourists filed on to an early morning vaporetto at Rialto, the *sardelle* still thrashed in the nets; as they climbed down from the vaporetto and crossed Piazzale Santa Maria Elisabetta, looking for the bus that would take them to Malamocco and the Alberoni, the *cefalo* was just being hauled out of the sea. The tourists often leave the bus for a while at Malamocco or the Alberoni, have a coffee, then walk on the sandy beach for a while and look at the enormous jetties that stretch out into the waters of the Adriatic in an attempt to prevent the waters from sweeping into the *laguna*.

The fish are all dead by then, though the tourists could not be expected to know that, or much care, so they get back on the bus, sit in it for the short ferry ride across the narrow canal, then continue by bus or on foot down toward Pellestrina and their lunch.

In winter things are vastly different. Too often the wind tears across the Adriatic from the former Yugoslavia, carrying before it rain or light snow, biting into the bones of anyone who tries to stay out in it for any length of time. The crowded restaurants of the summer are closed and will remain that way until late spring, leaving the tourists to fend for and feed themselves.

What remain unchanged, lined up in long rows on the inner side of the thin peninsula, are scores of *vongolari*, the clam-fishing boats that work all year, regardless of tourists, rain, cold and heat, regardless too of all the legends told about the noble, hard-working men of Pellestrina and their constant battle to win a living for their wives and children from the merciless sea. Their names sing out: *Concordia*, *Serena*, *Assunta*. They sit there, fat and high-nosed, looking very much like the boats painted in picture books for children. One longs, walking past in the bright summer sun, to reach up and pat them, stroke their noses, as it were, just as one would with a particularly winsome pony or an especially endearing Labrador.

To the unschooled eye the boats all look much the same, with their iron masts and the metal scoop at the prow that protrudes up into the air when the boat is docked. Rectangular and framed, these scoops all have the same grade of what looks like chicken wire strung across them, though it is far stronger than any chicken wire ever made, as it has to resist the pressure of rocks dug up on the seabed or chance encounters with the heavy and unforeseen obstacles that litter the bottom of the *laguna*. They also have, of course, to resist the seabed itself as they ram into and then under the nesting clams, dragging along the sea bottom and then to the surface kilos of shells, large and small, trapped within the rectangular tray, water and sand cascading out and back into the *laguna*.

The observable differences between the boats are insignificant: a clam scoop smaller or larger than that on the next boat; life buoys in need of paint or shining bright and smooth; decks so clean they gleam in the sunlight or stained with rust in the corners, where they touch the sides of the boat. The Pellestrina boats, during the day, ride in pleasant promiscuity one beside the next; their owners live in similar propinquity in the low houses that stretch from one side of the village to the other, from the *laguna* to the sea.

At about 3.30 on a morning in early May, a small fire broke out in the cabin of one of these boats, the *Squallus*, owned and captained by Giulio Bottin, resident at number 242 Via Santa Giustina. The men of Pellestrina are no longer solely dependent upon the power of the tides and winds and thus are no longer obliged to sail only when they are favourable, but the habits of centuries die hard, and so most fishermen rise and sail at dawn, as if the early morning breezes still made some difference to their speed. There remained two hours before the fishermen of Pellestrina – who now sleep in their homes and in their beds – had to get up, so they were at their deepest point of sleep when the fire broke out on the *Squallus*. The flames moved, at quite a leisurely pace, along the floor of the boat's cabin to the wooden sides and the teak control panel at the front. Teak, a hard wood, burns slowly, but it also burns at a higher temperature than softer woods, and so the fire that spread up the control panel and from it to the roof of the cabin and out on to the deck moved with frightening speed once it reached those softer woods. The fire burned a hole in the deck of the cabin, and burning pieces of wood fell below into the engine room where one fell on to a pile of oil-damp rags, which flared instantly into life and passed the fire gracefully towards the fuel line.

Slowly, the fire worked at the area around the narrow tube; slowly it burned away the surrounding wood and then, as the wood turned to ash and fell away, a small piece of solder melted, opening a gap that allowed the flame to enter the pipe and move with blinding speed down towards the engines and to the dual fuel tanks which supplied them.

None of the people sleeping in Pellestrina that night had any idea of the motion of the flames, but all of them were rocked awake when the fuel tanks on the *Squallus* exploded, filling the night air with a glaring burst of light and, seconds later, with a thud so loud that, the next day, people as far away as Chioggia claimed they heard it.

Fire is terrifying anywhere, but for some reason it seems more so at sea or, at least, on the water. The first people who looked out of their bedroom windows said later that they saw the boat shrouded in heavy, oily smoke that rose up as the fire was extinguished by the water. But by then the flames had had time to slip through the *Squallus* to the boats moored on either side of it and set them smouldering, and the exploding fuel had splashed in deadly arcs, not only to the decks of the boats moored beside it, but out on to the levee in front, where it set three wooden benches ablaze.

After the blast from the *Squallus*'s fuel tanks, there followed a moment of stunned silence, then Pellestrina exploded into noise and action. Doors flew open and men ran out into the night; some of them wore trousers pulled on over pyjamas, some wore only pyjamas, some had taken the time to dress, two were entirely naked, though no one paid any attention to that fact, so urgent was the need to save the boats. The owners of the boats moored alongside the *Squallus* jumped from the dock on to the decks at almost the same instant, though one had had to pull himself from the bed of his cousin's wife and had come twice as far as the other. Both of them yanked fire extinguishers from their stanchions on the deck and began to spray at the flames that had followed the burning oil.

The owners of boats moored further from the now empty space where the *Squallus* had once floated churned their engines to life and began frantically backing away from the burning boats. One of them, in his panic, forgot to cast off the mooring rope and yanked a metre-long strip of wood from the railing of his boat. But even as he looked back and saw the splintered wood floating where he had been moored, he didn't stop until his boat was a hundred metres from land and safe from the flames.

As he watched, those flames gradually lessened on the decks of the other boats. Two more men, each carrying a fire extinguisher, arrived from the nearby houses. Jumping on to the deck of one of the boats, they began spraying the flames, which were quickly controlled and then finally quelled. At about the same time the owner of the other boat, which had not been as heavily sprayed with fuel, managed to get the flames under control and then extinguished them with the thick white froth. Long after there was no more sign of fire, he continued spraying back and forth, back and forth, until the froth was gone and he lowered the empty fire extinguisher to the deck.

By then, more than a hundred people were clustered along the levee, shouting to the men on the boats that had managed to back out into the harbour, to one another, and to the men who had conquered the flames on their boats. Expressions of shock and concern flew from every lip, anxious questions about what had been seen, what could have started the fire.

The first to ask the question that was to silence them all, the silence slowly rippling out from her like infection from an uncleaned wound, was Chiara Petulli, the next-door neighbour of Giulio Bottin. She was standing at the front of the crowd, not more than two metres from the large metal stanchion from which dangled the scorched cable that had once held the *Squallus* safely in place. She turned to the woman next to her, the widow of a fisherman who had died in an accident only the year before, and asked, 'Where's Giulio?'

The widow looked around. She repeated the question. The person next to her picked it up and passed it on until, in a matter of moments the question had been passed through the entire crowd, asked but not answered.

'And Marco?' Chiara Petulli added. This time everyone heard her question. Though his boat lay in the shallow waters, its scorched masts just breaking the surface, Giulio Bottin was not there, nor was his son Marco, eighteen years old and already part owner of the *Squallus*, which lay burnt and dead at the bottom of the harbour of Pellestrina on this suddenly chill springtime morning.

2

The whispers started then, as people tried to remember when they had last seen Giulio or Marco. Giulio usually played cards in the bar after dinner; had anyone seen him last night? Marco had a girlfriend down in S. Pietro in Volta, but the girl's brother was in the crowd and said she'd gone to the movies on the Lido with her sisters. No one could think of a woman who would be with Giulio Bottin. Someone thought to look in the courtyard beside the Bottin house; both their cars were there, though the house was dark.

A curious reluctance, a kind of delicacy in the face of possibility, kept the people in the crowd from speculating where they might be. Renzo Marolo, who had lived next door for more than thirty years, found the courage to do what no one else was willing to do and took the spare key from where everyone in the village knew it to be, under the pot of pink geraniums on the windowsill to the right of the front door. Calling ahead of him, he opened the door and stepped into the familiar house. He switched on the lights in the small living room and, seeing no one there, went and looked in the kitchen, though he couldn't have explained why he did so, as the room was dark, and he didn't bother to turn the light on. Then, still calling out the names of the two men in a kind of unmusical voluntary, he went up the single flight of steps to the upper floor and down the hall to the larger of the two bedrooms.

'Giulio, it's me, Renzo,' he called, paused a moment, then stepped into the bedroom and switched on the light. The bed was empty and unslept in. Unsettled by this, he went across the hall and turned on the light in Marco's room. Here, too, though a pair of jeans and a light sweater lay folded on a chair, both bed and room were empty.

Marolo went back downstairs and outside, closing the door quietly behind him and replacing the key. To the waiting people, he said, 'They aren't here.'

As a group, somehow comforted by the fact that there were a number of them, they moved back towards the water, where most of the inhabitants of Pellestrina were gathered on the edge of the pier. Some of the boats that had found safety in the deeper water pulled slowly back, taking their accustomed places. When all of them were again moored to the *riva*, the single empty space left by the sunken *Squallus* seemed larger than it had when there had been only the two damaged boats on either side. From the middle of the empty slot, the masts of the *Squallus* poked through the water at a crazy angle.

Marolo's son, sixteen-year-old Luciano, came and stood beside his father. Off in the distance, a waterfowl cried out. 'Well, *Papà*?' the boy asked.

Renzo had watched his son grow up in the shadow or, to use a more nautical metaphor, in the wake of Marco Bottin, who had always been two years ahead of him at school and was thus to be admired and emulated.

Luciano had thrown on a pair of cut-off jeans when his father's shouts woke him but had had no time to put on a shirt. He stepped closer to the water, turned and signalled to his cousin Franco, who stood at the front of the crowd, an enormous flashlight in his left hand. Franco stepped forward reluctantly, shy about putting himself so conspicuously under the scrutiny of the assembled Pellestrinotti.

Luciano kicked off his sandals and knifed into the water just to the left of the sunken prow of the *Squallus*. Franco stepped forward and played the light into the water below, where his cousin's body moved with fishlike ease. A woman stepped forward, then another, and then the entire first rank of people moved to the edge of the pier and stared down. Two men holding flashlights pushed their way through and added their beams to Franco's.

After what was little more than a minute but seemed an eternity, Luciano's head broke the surface of the water. Shaking his hair back out of his eyes, he shouted up to his cousin, 'Shine it back towards the cabin,' and was gone, ducking under the water as quickly as a seal.

All three lights moved along the hulk of the *Squallus*. Occasionally they caught a flash of white from one of the soles of Luciano's feet, the only part of his body that was not tanned to near-blackness. They lost him for an instant, then his head and shoulders burst from the water, and he was gone again. Twice more he shot up and filled his lungs, diving back towards the wreck. At last he surfaced and lay on his back for a moment, pulling in great, rasping lungfuls of air. When they saw this, the people holding the flashlights moved the beams away from him, letting him float there illuminated only by the curiosity of the onlookers and the faint paling of the sky.

Luciano suddenly slipped over on to his stomach and paddled like a dog, a motion strangely awkward in such a powerful swimmer, to the edge of the embankment. He reached the ladder nailed to the wooden embankment wall, and started to pull himself up the rungs.

The crowd parted in front of the ladder and at just that instant the sun emerged from the waters of the Adriatic. Its first rays, rising above the sea wall and cutting across the narrow peninsula, caught Luciano as he paused at the top of the ladder, transforming this fisherman's son into a godlike presence that had arisen gleaming from the waters. There was a collective intake of breath, as in the presence of the numinous.

Luciano shook his head, and water spattered to both sides. Then, looking at his father, he said, 'They're both in the cabin.'